Also by Victoria Heckman

K.O.'d in Hawai'i Series:
K.O.'d in Honolulu
K.O.'d in the Volcano
K.O.'d in the Rift

Burn Out

Kapu

Pearl Harbor Blues

For Ainahou Young

And

Everyone Who Was *There*

Pearl Harbor Blues

Victoria Heckman

2014 Revenge Publishing

Published in the United States by Revenge Publishing.
ISBN 978-0-9846098-6-4

Cover by Liam Heckman
Author Photo Blue Moon Photography

Acknowledgements

This book took years of research and organization before I could write it. Many have helped along the way. Gratitude to Luci Zahray, "The Poison Lady;" Charles Donahue a Pearl Harbor veteran who answered a lot of questions, Jennifer Locke of the Smithsonian's Armed Forces History, John Esaki of the Japanese-American National Museum-Media Department, and Keith Leber who also answered a lot of questions, mostly botanical. Also, thank you to my fantastic editors, Margaret Searles and Sue McGinty who kept me honest. And, as always, love to my family and friends for supporting my writing and understanding that it's not a choice.

Chapter 1

Honolulu Star-Bulletin **Sunday, September 17, 1995**
Prominent Businessman and Philanthropist Found Dead
By Mick Kau'ula

    Local businessman and philanthropist, James "Kimo" Lemon, 75, was found dead in his Kahala home of an apparent heart attack last night at 10:07pm. His wife of 57 years, Mabel White Lemon, discovered his body slumped over the desk in his home office. He was rushed to Diamond Head Hospital, where he was pronounced dead.

    Kimo Lemon was the founder and CEO of O'ahu Cane and Pine, the islands' second largest sugar cane and pineapple grower and processer. Tomorrow would have been the fiftieth anniversary of the start of his first company. Festivities scheduled to celebrate this anniversary had been planned for months. It was unknown at press time whether or not the celebration will be cancelled or postponed. Lemon's son, Roger Lemon, is acting CEO, and it is presumed he will be named permanently to that post. He will share the helm with his mother who retains a position on the board. The

Board of Trustees is expected to meet shortly to insure a smooth transition. It is unknown if Kimo Lemon's daughter, Abigail Lemon, acclaimed surgeon at Royal Hospital, will take an active role in the company. Further details of the estate have not been released. Tomorrow *The Honolulu Star-Bulletin* begins a four part series on Kimo Lemon, his philanthropic efforts and his impact on our islands' economy, plus an update on the anniversary celebration.

*   *   *   *

Honolulu Star-Bulletin, 1st Extra

Honolulu, Territory of Hawaii, U.S.A.   Sunday, December 7, 1941
              PRICE FIVE CENTS

WAR!

OAHU BOMBED BY JAPANESE PLANES

(Associated Press by Transpacific Telephone)
San Francisco, Dec. 7
President Roosevelt announced this
morning that Japanese planes had attacked Manila
and Pearl Harbor.

10

Pearl Harbor, Hawaii, December 7, 1941

The sun was newly risen when the toddler wandered out of his house and down to the beach to play. No matter that his mother had repeatedly told him never to go to the beach alone; he was drawn by the sparkling waters of Pearl Harbor, and he continued down the shore, picking up glistening pebbles and playing in the sand.

A roaring sound came from the north and the little boy looked back toward the split between the two magnificent mountain ranges. He was astonished to see many airplanes screaming down the gap between the mountains right toward him as he stood on the edge of the water. As he watched, the planes dropped things from their bellies and popping sounds surrounded him while he cowered in the sand. The first of many huge explosions rocked the harbor, and ships upended and split. Across the water, he heard whistles, alarms and the shouts of men, and he lay frozen, hands over his ears. He did not hear his mother call him and he screamed when she jerked him into her arms and stumbled back to the bungalow.

"I found him," his mother gasped. The little house shook from the blasts. His father pulled on the splotched green/brown pants and shirt he wore to work.

"Why didn't you watch him better, you stupid bitch? All hell's breaking loose and I gotta stop to find my kid?"

"He's safe. It's okay." His mother collapsed onto the small sofa and held him tightly. The boy trembled.

"It's not okay. Does it sound like it's okay? Jeez. Where are your brains?" His father wrestled into his black boots and turned to face them.

"What the hell's the matter with you? Your mother told

you not to leave the house."

"I'm sorry, Daddy."

His father glared at him a moment longer. "I hope so, you little idiot." He finished lacing the boots and stood up. He bent toward his son, silver dog tags bouncing in the eastern light. The boy lifted his arms. The man slapped him across the face, and the boy's head bounced back against his mother's arm.

"He's only three years old! He won't do it again!" She twisted to shield her son.

"Well he's not gonna make it to four if he keeps going like this." The man grabbed his green/brown jacket.

"I gotta go. I don't know when I'll be back. I may not get back. I'm not going to wait for them to call me; I'm going to Fort Shafter to report in. Shit. Sounds like the whole fuckin' world's ending." His father slammed the door and the boy heard more popping sounds and the roar of planes directly overhead. Smoke and the pungent smell of burning wafted into the house. Through his tears, the boy watched the blue-gray tendrils dance lazily toward him. His mother dragged him off the sofa and into the narrow hallway. Over their crying he heard the sounds of his world coming to an end.

*   *   *   *

That afternoon, a family above the harbor in Red Hill sat huddled in their living room listening to the radio.

"I repeat, the Japanese have attacked Pearl Harbor. All citizens must remain in their homes. Martial law has been declared. Citizens found outside without authorization will be arrested. Blackout conditions will be in effect at sunset." The announcer droned on, further terrifying the little family.

"Husband! What is wrong? What is happening?" she asked

in Japanese.

He had understood the news. He explained it to his wife. "America will enter the war now, I think."

"What has happened in the harbor?" She rocked back and forth on her knees.

"Japan has bombed the ships." His seamed face grew older.

"Do you mean, we will be at war with our cousins?"

"Yes, we are at war with our family, now."

"I knew this day would come." Tears stained her kimono.

"Wife, we must be strong. This is our country now. Our home. We have done well here, and we will protect our children and our friends."

"As you say, husband. But Japan, we have family there also. My heart is there, too."

"As is mine."

"Where is Yoshi? He should have come home by now." The man asked.

"I don't know." His wife grasped his hand. "He's probably still at the Fujita's. He spent the night with Benny, remember?"

"I know, I know. But now with the restrictions, he may not be able to come home. What if he was caught outside in all the gunfire?"

A twelve year old girl sat at her parents' feet. "I will go to the Fujita's and see."

"No!" Both parents said at once.

"I will go." The father said.

"No! What if you are stopped?" His wife held more tightly to his work-worn hand.

"I will not be stopped. He is only a boy. He is my only son." He struggled out of the chair and turned to face his wife. "It will be all right. Stay in the house."

"Don't go." She whispered. Their daughter remained unmoving on the floor.

"Daughter?"

"Yes, Papa?"

"Take care of your mother 'til I get back." He gave her a long look, opened the door, and was gone.

His little house, not much better than a shack, sat on a rise above Pearl Harbor. He stepped out cautiously into the street. Plumes of smoke rose all over the island and filled the bright blue sky.

He made a living for his small family by doing odd jobs: cut and burned cane in season, acted as interpreter for the many Japanese who did not speak English. His wife took care of the house and the children. They scraped by.

When they were teenagers, he and his wife had come separately from Japan to work on the plantations. While working in the pineapple fields, they had met and married. Then he had hurt his back and could only work part-time. She lost their first child early in the pregnancy due to the strenuous work--stooping, bending, cutting. Bandanas they wore over their noses and mouths, protection from pervasive red dust, quickly became saturated with dirt, and breathing was difficult. Coarse clothing, worn head to toe to help protect against the pineapple's sharp spines, did not stop the spikes biting through.

Working so heavily clad in the hot Hawai'ian sun made the sweat run freely under their head wraps and hats, turning dust to mud. One day she became dizzy and cut herself with the sharp pineapple knife. To keep her job, she wrapped it in a filthy rag and continued. The wound became septic, and she fainted in a far field. She was taken to Royal Hospital where they managed to save her hand and her life, but not the baby.

"You must not go back to the fields when you are well again."

"But, husband, I must. Your back. How will we live?"

"I will find a way, but you will not work in the fields!"

She eventually took in bits of sewing and laundry, and several barren years later, when their next child was born, a daughter, she was named Michiko, meaning child of beauty and wisdom.

Many nights they ate only rice. She painstakingly built a business of laundering and seamstressing. He took any work offered; painting houses, cutting cane, hosing urine off the sidewalks outside the bars in the early morning, scrubbing toilets after the sailors had been sick in them. Long days, even nights, he worked, tired to death, but never ready to give up.

Their bond never wavered; their family grew ever tighter.

Yoshihiko was born on a terrible night. Storm surge raged in the harbor, mud raced like water down Red Hill. Mango trees wrenched from the earth, their fruit, missiles in the dark. In the early hours as the storm waned, he held his wife while she slept, drained. Four year old Michiko cradled her infant brother and drank in his smell, his newness, his innocence. Michiko loved him fiercely from that moment, and vowed no one would ever harm him.

Yoshi's father stepped from tree to tree, shadow to shadow. As he reached the Fujita's block, he heard the rumble of an approaching jeep. He looked for a place to hide. Finding none, he turned up the walk to the nearest house and faced the door, hoping not to be seen, or to be taken for the owner of the house. He gently touched the knob, but it was locked.

"Hey, you. Don't you know you're not supposed to be out now?"

He nodded his head without turning around.

"Turn around and talk to me, buddy." He slowly turned to face a young American soldier in fatigues at the wheel of an army jeep. "A Jap! I should shoot you right here for what you did to our country!" The soldier had drawn his gun and aimed it at him.

The man put his arms up. "No, I am an American; I have lived here for over twenty years. Please, I am looking for my son. He is only eight and I am afraid for him. He did not come home."

"You are not an American! Don't you ever say those words, you yellow piece of shit. I could care less about your lost dog of a kid." The soldier waved the gun and the man twitched.

"Ha. You're not so brave now there's not a couple hundred of you. Get in the jeep. You're under arrest."

"But I have done nothing wrong. Please! I am just looking for my son. Let me at least tell my family I could not find him."

"You did wrong when you came to this country. Now get in the jeep before I shoot you right here for spying." Slowly the man came down the walk and got in the jeep. The soldier drove to a nearby cane field.

"Are you arresting me? This is a dead end. I know the way to the base. Would you like directions?"

"Get out. Start walking. If you can make it to the cane field, you can live. Go!"

The man began an arthritic, desperate run toward the cane field, fifty feet away.

The soldier took careful aim from the comfort of his front seat. Just as the man reached the first stand of cane, the soldier fired, striking the man squarely in the back, and piercing his heart. He was dead before he hit the ground.

The soldier got out of the jeep and strolled to the body. He turned it with his boot, spit on it, and shot again. He carefully aimed the gun at his left thigh. He held his breath and fired. He staggered and dragged the corpse back to the jeep and heaved it into the back. A trail of blood led back to the jeep. He drove to Tripler, the military hospital, a loose collection of buildings near Fort Shafter where he was based, nearly hitting several cars on the way.

That afternoon, a soldier was found passed out in a jeep in front of Tripler Hospital, bleeding heavily from a gunshot wound to the thigh. The dead body of an older Japanese man lay crumpled next to him in the jeep. He was rushed to surgery.

"Hey, soldier, you're awake." He looked up and found a pretty nurse taking his pulse.

"Where am I?"

"You're at Tripler." At his blank look she added, "The hospital. You've been wounded."

"What happened?"

"It looks like you were shot in the leg, but you'll be okay. You'll probably be on desk duty for a while."

"Oh." He gazed into her eyes and saw compassion and warmth. "What's your name?"

"Elizabeth."

"Are you married, Elizabeth?"

She laughed. "Aren't you the charmer? Still in recovery, conscious five minutes and practically asking me out!"

"So, do you want to have coffee some time?"

"Tell you what. I'll come back and visit after I'm off. How's that?"

He sighed elaborately. "I guess that'll have to do."

"Boy, you tall, dark and handsome types are amazing. Good looking and sweet talkers. I'll see you later."

A military investigation of sorts followed his waking in the hospital. The bullet wound came from his own weapon, but he told a convincing story, and he was praised for doing his duty in a time of war.

"Soldier, explain in your own words what happened when you arrested the spy and were wounded."

"Well, sir, I was on regular patrol, right after the bombing. I was patrolling Red Hill, and you know sir, they were finding downed Japanese pilots and spies everywhere."

"It sure seemed like it, son. Go on."

"Yessir. Sorry, sir, but these stitches are paining me some."

"It's alright son, I understand."

"Anyway, I saw this man acting suspiciously and I told him to stop and state his business. He turned and ran. I chased him with the jeep, and then on foot. He almost escaped into a cane field, too. I caught up with him and interrogated him. He started spoutin' off all these Jap words. When I tried to arrest him, he grabbed for my weapon and fired it, hittin' me in the leg. I was still able to control my weapon and shoot him before he could shoot me again."

"What next?"

"I put him in the jeep and drove myself to Tripler before I passed out."

"You want ironic? The staff rushed out there and tried to save *him*!"

"Yes, that is a good one, sir."

"Do you want to add anything? No? Well, I can only say I wish we had more like you, son."

"Thank you, sir. I'm proud to serve my country the best way I can."

During the next two weeks he was recovering in the hospital, he and the nurse Elizabeth spent a great deal of time together. Although his wife visited with their young son, the two women never met. The day of his release, he stopped by the nurses' desk.

"How's about we go out for dinner to celebrate tonight? I gotta go back to the base and check in now. Let's meet in Waikiki." She readily agreed and they made plans.

Since a curfew was still in effect, they decided to eat early. After a nice dinner, he offered to take her for a drive. They wound up at a deserted lookout at the top of Tantalus, parked with a spectacular view of the city. He put his arm around her as she rested her head on his shoulder.

"This is so special Elizabeth. You're so special. I wish I wasn't in the service so we could go away together right now."

"Oh, I feel that way too." She turned her face up to him, and he kissed her. The kiss became more passionate and she pulled back.

"What's the matter, Lizzie? Don't you like it?"

"Call me Elizabeth. Yes, I like it. It's just that, well, you being in the service and all, I might never see you again." Her eyes were bright.

"You know, my hitch is over in a year, and we could get married then."

"Married! I hardly know you!" She laughed and kissed him again.

"I promise, it'll be great, okay? Now come here." He pulled her forcefully to him and slid on top of her. He grabbed her breast and pulled at the fabric of her blouse.

"Wait!" she protested. "I don't know about this. I like you and all, but this is too much." She tried to squirm out from under him.

"Don't be such a tease. You know you want to, and what were all those special visits in the hospital about? I really like you. Besides, I told you we'll get married. You'll like that, won't you?" He pushed up her skirt and dragged her panties down as he kissed

19

her roughly. She tried to roll and push but she had no leverage. He was extremely strong and determined. She felt pain as he entered her; fear escalated. She couldn't breathe. He grunted and strained and suddenly relaxed. She felt hot liquid dripping down her thigh, his weight crushed her. She turned her head away and took a shuddering breath.

"There, doll. That's how it's done. I didn't know you'd never done it before. But you liked it, didn't you? Aw, for Christ's sake, what are you crying for? Jeez. Let's go."

He started the engine. She began buttoning her blouse and found two buttons had been ripped off, leaving a gap that exposed her bra. Her panties' elastic was torn and would no longer stay up. Her new, expensive, real silk stockings were shredded; her garter belt had sprung a metal clasp. She slowly tucked in her blouse and straightened herself as best she could as the jeep made fast, jerky turns around the many curves of Round Top Road. She did not look for the buttons.

The next night in a poker game, he shared his conquest with his buddies.

"You know how it is, she wants it then she says she doesn't. Yeah, she sure did. She was a hot one, all right. Full house," he said laying down his hand.

"What's with you tonight, man? You're winning all over the place. You cheating or something?"

"Yeah, I'm cheating. How? I'm just a superior player is all. He pulled the pot to him. "Does that about clean everybody out? I thought so." He got up to leave to a chorus of, "Give us a chance to win it back. Aw, man, that's my whole pay."

He stepped out of the barracks for a smoke. One of the young poker players approached him.

"Can I get my money back?" He looked down and shuffled

his feet.

"What are you, nuts? I won all this. I'm not gonna *give* it back."

"But it's my whole pay. I got a wife and kid back home, and I got nothing to send."

"Well, you shoulda thoughta that before you pissed it all away. But, because I'm really a family man at heart, I'll tell you what."

"What?"

"I'll lend it to you."

"What do you mean?"

"Let's see. I'll lend you your pay for fifty percent interest, 'til next payday. How's that sound?"

"Fifty percent? I can't do that! I'll be behind forever."

"Okay, just tell the little woman you lost it all in a poker game."

"Oh, god. Okay. Okay! Just give it back."

"Here ya go." He turned and went back inside to his bunk. When he was sure no one was looking, he took his spare cards out of his belt and his socks, and threw them in his footlocker.

Approximately nine months after that, when the man had long been shipped back to active duty, a baby was born at Tripler to a lovely, young, unmarried nurse.

Chapter 2

Honolulu Star-Bulletin Monday, September 18, 1995
Life Was Sweet for Lemon
Part One of a Series
By Mick Kau'ula

Philanthropist and humanitarian Kimo Lemon, found dead of a heart attack in his Kahala home September 16, will be mourned by many. We will explore his impact on our community. The first and largest of his projects is the Lemon Foundation, an organization dedicated to lending money to Issei (Japanese immigrants) and Nisei (the first generation of Americans of Japanese descent) after the war. The Japanese in our community, as well as in the rest of the country, were not well-treated after the war. Kimo Lemon took it upon himself to lend various businessmen enough money to get back on their feet. As many readers know, most of the Japanese Americans' property was seized at the beginning of the war when they were sent to internment camps. Kimo Lemon approached those he felt he could help. With the interest from initial loans, he granted more loans, including families as well as businesses, so they could buy their homes back.

His wife, Mabel White Lemon, said in an earlier article (*Honolulu Star-Bulletin* June 30, 1992), "We didn't have much in those days, we lived pretty frugally on a soldier's pay. We had a little house near the harbor, and I kept to a tight budget. He was always giving. He also helped out his buddies by lending them money during the war, and that helped build up our nest egg. Of course, at first it made things even tighter, but it all worked out fine."

Today, the Lemon Foundation is best known for offering financial aid for college students of Japanese ancestry, single mothers, and others who might not ordinarily be able to afford college. The foundation also supports a job training division called "Lemon Tree" because, as Kimo Lemon once said, "I like branching out, and this is just part of the same big ol' tree." Graduates of Lemon Tree are highly qualified and pick their own jobs in the business world, but they often decided to work for Lemon Enterprises, including the megacorporation, O'ahu Cane and Pine. The company's fiftieth anniversary celebration has been postponed for at least a week until arrangements can be re-organized, according to Gerald Breem, Executive Vice President of OCP. Part Two tomorrow, on OCP.

*   *   *   *

"Mabel, dear, have you seen my glasses?" asked the woman in the nurse's smock as she came out of the huge foyer and into the living room. "Mabel?"

"Here, dear, out on the lanai. I can't find mine either, and I've looked." Mabel Lemon sat on the tiled deck facing the ocean, a throw rug on her lap to ward off the breeze. "Betty? What's going to happen now? What will I do?"

Betty, Mabel's private nurse for many years, sat in the wicker chair next to the wheelchair. Not a lot younger, but in much better physical shape than her patient, Betty took care of more than just Mabel's health. They had become friends. "Roger will take over Lemon Enterprises now, of course. And I know Abigail will help you if you need it."

"I know all that. I've lived all my life with him, and I feel lost. I didn't expect that."

"I know dear." The two old women sat together holding hands, looking out to sea.

At Lemon Enterprises, Roger James Lemon sat at the head of a long teak conference table and watched as the Board of Trustees continued to squabble.

"Roger doesn't know diddly about running this company," said one.

"That's not the point," said someone else.

"Then what is the point?"

"That Kimo wrote it this way for a reason, and Roger's the CEO now." The first one thumped his fist on the table.

"Well, he was out of his mind when he wrote it. Kimo's kept his son out of everything for years, and now Roger's just supposed to step in? That's preposterous!" said one with a stomach the size of a beach ball.

"He didn't plan on dying," said another.

"Yes, well, none of us do. Let's get back to the issue, please gentlemen."

The room became quiet. "What are we to do with Roger?"

"I have a suggestion," said a calm voice from the head of the table.

24

"Roger?   What could you possibly have to say at this juncture?"

"I have been aware of my father's wishes for the company for some time, and have been preparing for this."

"Oh. I see. And just how have you been preparing for this? And why?"

"The why, is easy. My father had not been in good health for the last several months and although he wouldn't speak of it, I could see it, and my mother expressed concern over it."

"What did your sister say?   Isn't she the doctor in the family?"

"Yes, well, as you know, their relationship had been strained for years. She only came to the house for mother's sake, and may not have been aware of my father's failing health."

"So, what is this preparation you say you've been doing?"

"I have been staying late at work, sometimes all night, going over documents and records. I have reviewed data and statistics, and I have some ideas for streamlining. I look forward to having your advice and support, but be aware I may not listen to you if I feel it is not in the best interests of Lemon Enterprises." Stunned silence.

"But Kimo never let you do anything!   How do you know all this?"

"I am my father's son. We are alike in some ways. While he was alive, there was no point in butting heads with him, so I did not waste my energy. But now that Lemon Enterprises is in my hands, I intend to make changes."

"But you were practically still the mail boy!"

"Not anymore."   Roger Lemon stood, and the boyish, compliant, indecisive facade fell away to reveal a sharp-jawed, cunning, perhaps even ruthless, leader of a Fortune 500 company.

In the executive offices of O'ahu Cane and Pine, Yoshi Onizuki, junior executive, was being downsized.

"Well, you're actually at the age our company encourages retirement, Yosh," Gerald Breem, Executive VP said.

"I have checked the records," Yoshi said, "and it is only the minimum age for basic retirement benefits. If I continue to work for three more years until I am sixty-five, I get maximum benefits. I would like to continue to work."

"Well, you see, Yosh, it's not gonna work out like that. You're slated for retirement this year, so that's what's going to happen."

"You can't force me to retire if I can work three more years!"

"Well, no, we can't, but if you don't, but we can fire you. I understand your wife's medical coverage for her physical therapy would be cut."

"You can't do that!" Yoshi paced the room. "I have rights! Mr. Lemon never would have done this!"

"Actually it was one of the things Mr. Lemon insisted on. You in particular. We're simply carrying out his wishes posthumously." Breem fiddled with the papers in front of him and smiled. "So," he stood, "if there's nothing else, I think we're done here. I'll have your retirement agreement on your desk by five o'clock. I suggest you sign it." Breem held the door open and waited for the other man to exit. Onizuki moved toward the door with a helpless gesture.

"How could Mr. Lemon do this to me? I've worked here for forty years! He gave me a chance in this company. How do I know you're telling the truth?"

Breem shuffled through the stack of papers and handed one to Onizuki. "We thought you might feel this way, so here. If you tell anyone, your wife's benefits will be cut and, although we may not be able to stop them forever, we can certainly delay them long enough to severely hamper her improvement. It's a shame about her stroke. Oh, and your company-paid caregiver will be a memory. Good day."

Onizuki left the offices a much older man than when he entered. He went back to his own desk, sat heavily and unfolded the paper Breem had given him. It was a copy of a typewritten note with a font he knew well; the typewriter in Kimo Lemon's office, used to write memos many years ago, retired now and left as a memento of the company's early days.

Onizuki:

I've just hired you, you pathetic scrap of Jap. I think you're smart, too smart, and I want you close to me. You're never going to get far in my company, but you'll get farther than you would somewhere else. Everybody hates you Japs after what you did to our country, and no one's going to hire you. But I'm smart too. I know there's way too many of you, and by hiring a bunch of you, I'll stay on your good side. Besides, who knows, in the future you slant eyes may be of some use. In the event of my death, or at our minimum retirement age, you're out of a job. You're never going to see this memo until that day.

The memo was unsigned, but something about the tone, the voice in the memo told Yoshi it was real.

*   *   *   *

At Royal Hospital in downtown Honolulu, surgeon Abigail Lemon reviewed the chart of a patient she had operated on the night before.

A nurse paused and looked over her shoulder as she stood by the nurses' station. "That guy was a piece of work. He doing okay now?"

"Yeah. I don't know what's holding all the sutures together. After his introduction to the world of the bar fight, he didn't have much to stitch."

"Somebody pull a knife?"

"Knife, broken bottle, and I detected some vees that I think were a bottle opener, if you can believe that. You've got to be smashed out of your mind to stab somebody with a bottle opener." She mimed jabbing a small opener at the nurse and they laughed.

The nurse sobered. "I also wanted to say I'm sorry about your dad. It will be a great loss to the community."

Abigail frowned. "Thanks. A great loss."

"When are the services? What are they doing? Something big, I bet."

"I don't know about the services. Depends when the Medical Examiner's office releases the body. And my mother."

"What do you mean?"

"Routine. Because he wasn't under the care of a physician when he died, a death investigator has to clear it."

"Does that bother you?"

"Not really. And there's nothing I can do about it anyway. Mother doesn't want an autopsy and is making a stink. We'll see what happens. It's not a very exciting case, they're just backlogged."

"Not exciting?"

"Okay, he was prominent, famous even. But it's not news. To me, anyway. They will have that stupid anniversary of the company thing anyway, I bet."

"A seventy-five year old man with more money than God wasn't under the care of a doctor?"

"Didn't believe in them. At least not women doctors," Abigail added under her breath. "Yeah, go figure. I've got rounds. See you later." Abigail pushed the chart into the slot on the desk and walked to the first door, hands clenched into fists inside her lab coat pockets.

*   *   *   *

In downtown Honolulu, a woman slumped in an alley near Chinatown. She dozed off and on, occasionally picking herself up to beg behind the restaurants and businesses.

She awoke unusually early. Chilled from the nearby harbor air, she scrabbled unsteadily to her feet. She picked her way to the diner, where sometimes they gave her coffee and toast. As she passed the newspaper dispenser, she glanced at the headline that proclaimed the death of Kimo Lemon. She headed into the diner, but instead of going to the counter, she went to the register. She was greeted familiarly by the matronly waitress in the too-short pink uniform.

"Hi, Peg. You're up early this morning. Coffee?"

"No. Can I use the phone?" Peg shuffled uncomfortably in the nearly empty diner. She cocooned farther into the piece of ragged quilt as the waitress studied her. Peg had never said more than two words before, much less asked to use the phone.

"Sure Peg. Here's a quarter, use the pay phone by the ladies' room. You'll have more privacy there." Peg grunted and took the coin. She dialed a familiar, but seldom used number.

"Lemon residence," said a Tagalog-accented female voice.

"Is Betty there?" Peg's voice was hoarse.

"Who is calling? Do you know what time it is?" The voice went up a notch with indignation.

"I don't know what time it is," Peg said laboriously. "Tell her. . .tell her, her daughter is calling."

29

Chapter 3

Honolulu Star-Bulletin **Tuesday, September 19, 1995**
Famous Family Fighting Autopsy
By Mick Kau'ula

The influential family of James "Kimo" Lemon, dead of a heart attack earlier this week, is protesting the retention of his body by officials. Mabel White Lemon, widow of the O'ahu Cane and Pine baron, says it's unnecessary and affecting her family's mourning.

The M.E.'s office claims a backlog, and will release the body as soon as possible.

Mrs. Lemon is petitioning everyone from the Governor on down to rush the release.

In a phone interview via her nurse, Betty D'Angelo, Mrs. Lemon said, "I don't understand what the fuss is. My Kimo is dead. Let's honor him, give him his due, and let him rest in peace."

The Governor's office issued this statement: "Mrs. Lemon is a grieving widow. Of course she wants to see her dear husband's memory honored, and his body put to rest. She has that right. We will do all we can to see that her wishes are met."

The Medical Examiner's office had no estimate on a release date.

Kimo Lemon died on September 16 of a presumed heart attack. He was found at his desk in his Kahala estate by his wife, Mabel White Lemon, and rushed to Diamond Head Hospital where he was pronounced dead.

Kimo Lemon is best known as the founder and CEO of O'ahu Cane and Pine, but also for other philanthropic roles. See A-2 for follow up on O'ahu Cane and Pine, and later stories this week for details of his contributions to the community.

***Honolulu Star-Bulletin* Tuesday, September 19, 1995**
Where It All Began - The Story Behind Kimo Lemon
By Mick Kau'ula

Kimo Lemon was born James Carter Lemon of Black Bluff, Texas on July 20, 1920, to a shoe salesman, George Lemon and his wife, Suzette Brady Lemon. He had an unremarkable childhood and school life, until he signed up for the army at age sixteen. Much to the surprise of his parents, he enlisted and was shipped off to basic training in 1936. After an uneventful duty rotation, he was later assigned to Fort Shafter on O'ahu, where he served during the bombing of Pearl Harbor. He fell in love with the islands and stayed after service to his country. He met Mabel Anne White, daughter of Texas businessman, Joseph White (of the still operational, national chain of "White's Whitewalls") while on leave in Black Bluff, and they married on March 17, 1938, returning to Hawai'i to live.

Their first child, Roger, was born in December of that year. In later years, Lemon had said, "that (Roger's birth) was his best Christmas present."

Lemon re-upped in 1940, saying he would have enough money saved to start his own business after that. The war came to the United States via the attack on Pearl Harbor. He served valiantly as a Military Police officer during the blackouts in those perilous times just after the attack. He was awarded a Purple Heart after he nearly died from a gunshot wound received when he intercepted a Japanese spy.

In 1944, an explosion resulted in a severe facial injury and prevented his return to duty. He received an honorable discharge in 1945, and immediately began to research what business would benefit the community. O'ahu Cane and Pine was founded by Kimo Lemon in January of 1946. He took his hard earned savings and invested in the first of several plots of land that eventually became the O'ahu Cane and Pine company we know today.

Lemon planted pineapple and sugar cane and hired local people. He tried to help them get back on their feet after the war.

He cultivated a reputation for favoring the Japanese; a reputation that earned him scorn in the local community, but kudos and gratitude from the returning post-war Japanese, most of whose possessions the government had removed when they were incarcerated after the attack at Pearl Harbor. Lemon went out of his way to bankroll Japanese businesses, and later, lent families money to purchase homes. It was many years before the Honolulu community saw Lemon for what he was: a generous man viewing the world beyond the bounds of race.

OC&P grew throughout the years and became a subsidiary of Lemon Enterprises, a megacorporation that stretches internationally including, not surprisingly, to Japan. OC&P expanded from growing and selling, to processing and marketing sugar cane and pineapple, as well as currently calling fifty percent of the cultivatable land on O'ahu its own.

Lemon boasted that for every dollar he's earned, he's put

half back into the community that made it happen. Mathematically, that is probably not accurate, but no one can deny the impact OC&P and Kimo Lemon had on this community.

He created Lemon Tree, Lemon Enterprises, and OC&P for a start. He has also bankrolled smaller groups such as the University Warriors baseball team, saying in an earlier interview, "Since I never got to play myself, I might as well make it nice for the other folks." He contributed heavily to the new stadium, and single handedly sponsored the team to play in Yokohama in 1990 for the international playoffs. He also has helped individuals for no discernible reason. He supported local singing groups, and counted among his successes are 'Sheila and the Shells,' and 'Kamuela Breeze.' No one could predict to whom Lemon would reach out.

He once responded to that question with, "If I could say why or what made me do it, I wouldn't be me."

Although he made his home here so many years ago, he never lost his Texas drawl, though it was peppered with pidgin phrases, and he could sound "local" with the best of them.

OCP Executive Vice President Gerald Breem said, "If he (Kimo) didn't want you to know it was him on the phone, he'd lay on the pidgin so thick, you'd think you were talking to a Kalihi boy." Kimo Lemon will be remembered for many things and by many people. Part three in our series will be interviews with people who knew him, then and now.

Chapter 4

Dr. Abigail Lemon pulled into her parents' semi-circular driveway. She had always loved the plantation style house with its wrap around front porch, white columns and white crushed-shell paths trailing off behind the house. The banana trees rose taller than the house and plumeria swayed in the light breeze; sweet blossoms drifted down to cover the shells and perfume the air.

She parked under a spreading banyan tree, already many years old when her father had bought the property, skirted puddles left from the morning's brief shower and climbed the steps. Bentwood rockers, slightly damp, rocked eerily. Her father had insisted there be more rockers than people, so guests would always have a place to sit and feel welcome. Except the family almost never sat in the front. The back lanai, with its marvelous view, was where everyone gathered.

She used her key, something she hadn't done for a long time. The age-dark hardwood hallway was long and straight, a seldom used parlor directly on the right. On the left, a formal dining room, and down the hall were stairs to the second and third floors. She headed down the hall toward the light and emerged in the addition her father had built in the seventies: a huge atrium with white ceramic tile, potted plants and a small pond, floor to ceiling glass and louvered doors the width of the room, opening to a covered, tiled lanai with a hundred and eighty degree view of the coast to Hawaii Kai and Koko Head crater. There she found her mother, her mother's nurse, and Roger.

"Hi, Mom, Betty, Roger." Abigail nodded to each. She stood in the entrance way of the lanai, unsure.

"Abigail!" Her mother held her hands out to her daughter. Abigail went to her and they hugged. "I'm so glad to see you. Welcome home."

"Yes, well, it's true I haven't felt very welcome here lately," she said.

Roger stood. "Here, sit down, and what can I get you?" He patted the back of the white wicker chair he had vacated, then waved vaguely in the direction of the wet bar.

"Diet Pepsi, thanks Roger." Abigail sat and took her mother's hand.

"Hello, Abigail." Betty said from Mabel's other side.

"How are you, Betty? How is Mother doing?"

"I'm well thank you, and you can ask your mother how she's doing."

"Well, Mother, how are you? Is the press leaving you alone? Thanks, Roger." Abigail took the glass and watched her mother. Roger pulled up another wicker chair and adjusted the floral cushion before he sat.

Mabel sighed. "I'm alright, I guess. I just don't know what to do without your father. Betty's been such a help, but I can't lean on her forever."

Betty patted her hand. "It's only been a few days. You lean all you want."

Roger cleared his throat. "I came here to talk to Mother about the estate." He turned to Mabel. "I know this is tough Mother, but we've got to discuss certain details. You and I are running Lemon Enterprises now, and we need to make a few decisions."

"Oh, Roger. I don't know. I don't know anything about this. Your father did everything. I'm only on the board because it looks good. I never went to any meetings. I have no idea what's going on, and I don't want to. I want you to take over."

"Are you sure Mom?" Abigail asked. "Roger can tell you what you need to know, but don't give up." Roger shot Abigail a warning look.

"I thought you'd say that Mother, so I brought along something for you to sign, and since Abigail and Betty are here, they can witness it."

"What is it?" all three women asked.

"It's a document relieving you of all responsibility at LE. You still benefit and receive an income, but all the decision making is left to me."

Abigail snorted. "To you? What about the board? And me? Aren't I involved?"

Roger shifted uncomfortably. "Actually, no. The board has the same rights as before, but I would just absorb Mother's role. She would still retain her shares and income, etcetera. As for you, after the medical school thing, father cut all your decision-making ability related to the company. You have an income now that he's gone, and later," he glanced at his mother, "you'll have a full share of the estate, but he changed a few things."

"I guess he did. You mean when I wanted to go to medical school, and he said no, and I did it anyway, he cut me out of Lemon Enterprises?"

"He didn't tell you?" Roger swirled the ice in his glass,

36

then rose to refill it.

"No, he didn't."

Mabel took her daughter's hand. "He was very angry dear, about you going to medical school. He assumed when he said no, and cut off your funds, that you would listen to him. You're an awful lot like him, but he didn't see that. Stubborn." She stroked Abigail's hand. "He was hurt and lashed out. He just didn't feel that women should have men's jobs."

"Men's jobs? You sound as bad as he did!"

"Those are his words, not mine, dear."

"He wanted to control me, that's what. Well, he found out that's not so easy. What a hypocrite. He puts all these strangers through college, but his own daughter, he just tosses away." Abigail took a gulp of her soda. Her eyes welled up and she rummaged angrily in her bag for a tissue.

Her mother sighed. "That is true to a certain extent. He did not, however, pay for women to go to college if he felt their career choices were unacceptable."

"Why didn't anyone try to stop him? It's not 1950 anymore," Roger said.

"It was his money. And he had more of it than anyone else."

"You sound like you're on his side!" Abigail said.

"I'm not on sides, but there was no arguing with him on certain things. Besides, if he got really angry, things got terribly unpleasant."

Mabel reached for one of Abigail's tissues and dabbed her own eyes.

"There, there, dear. Would you like some more tea?" Betty asked. She went to the tea service without waiting for an answer.

Roger came back to his seat. "I remember how unpleasant things got, too. I moved out as soon as I could. That's one reason I

37

never got anywhere in Dad's company. I wasn't 'man enough to take it,' he told me once. Well that's fine. I'm running things now, and they're going to be different."

Abigail fished out another tissue. "I don't know how you stood it all those years, Mother. He could be so mean."

"He could be so sweet." Mabel started to cry.

"Mom, he was a vindictive tunnel-visioned, cheating bastard!"

"Please, don't," Mabel said.

Betty marched over and stood protectively in front of Mabel.

"That's quite enough. I tried to stay out of these family squabbles when Mr. Lemon was alive, and sometimes I just couldn't face him. But you two, I've known since you were children practically, and I won't have you badgering your mother, especially now." She eyed them stonily.

Abigail gave in first. "I'm sorry Mother. It just makes me so angry how he treated you. The other women, the sneaking, I don't know."

Mabel blew her nose. "He always came home to me, didn't he? And I'm the one he provided for now, aren't I? None of the others are in the trust, are they? Are they?" Her children shook their heads. "Well, then. I earned every penny, every convenience, and every humiliation I've got. I think you should go now, but you are both welcome to stay here whenever you wish. The second and third floor rooms are still yours. I don't get up there much. My room and Betty's are on the ground floor now, so you'll have privacy. I'm tired. Betty?" Mabel held her arm out and Betty helped her stand. She pulled a walker to her and painfully shuffled from the lanai. As she reached the door to the atrium, Roger went to her.

"I'm sorry too, Mother. I was unfeeling and rude. I couldn't

38

stop Abigail from blabbing. I didn't know you knew about the affairs and scandal. I'm sorry." He hugged her awkwardly around the walker.

Mabel's eyes filled again. "I've always known. I'm sorry too."

Betty shushed and clucked and guided Mabel to her room between the parlor and the atrium—part of the 70's addition. It also had a partial ocean view, and Mabel sat in a wing chair and looked out the window while Betty turned down the bed and hunted around for Mabel's slippers.

"I wish you'd just put them by the bed like a normal person," Betty grunted as she felt under the bed. "I'm not young anymore. Got 'em." She reemerged and brought the slippers to Mabel who laughed as Betty knelt.

"What's so funny?"

"You have a dust bunny on your head." Mabel giggled. She tried to brush it away, but her watch band caught in Betty's hair.

"Ouch! What are you doing?"

Mabel laughed harder and tried unsuccessfully not to pull Betty's hair.

"I can't, my watch, it's stuck!" She finally gave a small tug and pulled loose. "If you didn't use so much hairspray. . . " She collapsed into a chair.

"Do I have any hair left?" Betty got up and peered into the dresser mirror. "I'll have to use even more spray now. Nice 'do," she told herself and tried to rearrange her hair. Strands kept poking up. "It's hopeless!" She sat on the edge of the bed. "I'm glad to see you're feeling better." She smiled at her friend.

"I am, too. You're good for me, Betty. You always have been. I remember when you first came here, what, almost twenty years ago, after my car accident? You were wonderful. I kept thinking you'd leave, find a better job, get married again, something. As the years went by, I stopped worrying for myself, and started worrying for you."

"What do you mean?"

"Your life is here. And you spend so much of it caring for me, I just wondered what was left for you."

"You're right about one thing. My life is here. After Tony died, I had to go back to work, and the only work I knew was nursing. But I didn't want to be back in a hospital and on my feet all day. I was already too old for that! This job was a godsend. I answered Kimo's ad and it seemed made for me. You became my best friend and your family became my family. I needed you as much as you needed me. I have to say, though, I was never completely comfortable around Kimo. I don't know, something I was never able to put my finger on." Betty stood to help Mabel to the bed. "Enough of the past, now to bed."

"You were always so good with my kids. I always felt you'd make a great mother. Did you ever feel like you missed out by not having children of your own?" Mabel carefully seated herself on the bed and Betty swung her legs up and swiveled her back against the pillows in a single practiced movement.

"That's not entirely true." She busied herself fluffing already fluffed pillows and straightening straight covers.

"What do you mean?"

"I did have a child. A daughter."

"Oh, Betty. Why didn't you tell me? What happened, did she die?"

"No, not exactly."

"Can you talk about it? Is it too painful? We've been like sisters for so long, I want to know. But you said you and Tony never had children."

Betty wandered over by the window. "That's true. Tony and

40

I never did have children together. It's a long story. Are you sure you want to hear this?"

"Of course, Betty. Come sit down." Mabel patted the bed and Betty sat down, one knee tucked up under her, silver hair still askew.

"I think I told you when I was hired that I was a nurse during the war?" Mabel nodded. "Well, I met someone before Tony during the war. I thought we were going to be married, and I had really begun to fall in love with him. We went out one night for dinner and then we went for a drive." She twisted a pinch of bed sheet between her fingers. "I should have seen it coming; he was such a smooth talker. It was all my fault. I led him on, he says. Anyway, he took advantage of me that night." Her lips trembled, the bed sheet a sweaty twist. She continued to look out the window, as if not looking at her friend would make it easier. "He disappeared of course. The next day he got shipped off somewhere. I never saw him again. I went back to check the hospital records for his family and to double check his name, I really didn't know him that well, I thought we had all the time in the world to get to know each other." She laughed humorlessly. "All his records had disappeared. No one knew anything. Of course, I couldn't investigate too thoroughly or red flags would have gone up, but I wondered."

"What was his name?"

"I always called him Jaycee. He was one of those southern boys with a bunch of names, I guess. Anyway, I got pregnant and had a baby girl in 1942."

"That's just before Abigail was born."

"I know. After I met you, that's another thing that made me feel close. You had a daughter the about same age as mine. As I watched Abigail go to college and become a doctor, I was so proud of her. As if she were my own. When my daughter was eight, I met

41

Tony D'Angelo. He opened up that great Italian restaurant in Manoa, 'D'Angelo's'?"

"Oh, yes we've eaten there many times. Who owns it now?"

"When Tony first got sick with the cancer, I knew he wasn't going to make it. So I insisted we sell while he still had some say and ability. He chose the new owners in 1974, and that family still owns it. Second or maybe third generation now. My Tony made a good choice. We travelled a bit, to the outer islands, and he just, you know, tied up loose ends. Tony adopted Margaret after we married and loved her like his own. She was always a hard child." Betty blew her nose. "I loved her to death. She knew Tony wasn't her biological father and I think that was hard on her. I told her that her *real* father left, but I should have made up something like he'd died. It's too late now. Maybe nothing would have changed, but I think she felt abandoned by her father. She loved Tony the best she could, but I guess she always felt her birth father would come back. I don't know. She would never talk about it. I didn't tell her that I'd been, uh, forced, so I guess I came out of the story looking kind of trashy. Since I didn't change my name, she was smart and realized her birth father and I had not been married." Betty sighed, lost in her memory. "But that's okay. Some burdens a child shouldn't have to bear. Anyway, she went off on her own when she was seventeen. I tried to keep in touch, but she made it clear she didn't want that. She did come back to say goodbye to Tony. He was grateful for that. I was too. By then she was, oh, thirty-two or so, and I saw she'd made a mess of her life. She was using drugs, had no job, no place to stay. I begged her to get help. I said she could live with me and I could help her. She would have none of it. I've not seen her since. She has called a few times through the years, but never wanted my help, or even to see me."

Mabel leaned forward to embrace her friend. "I had no idea. I'm so sorry. This makes your staying with me, with us, even more special."

"I haven't told you everything."

"What can be left?"

"Margaret called here the day after Kimo died."

"She didn't! What did she say?"

"She wants to see me. She said she's still homeless and lives in Chinatown. She's addicted to crack and wants to go to a clinic. She asked me to help her."

"Oh, you must. She needs you now. She's crying out for help! For you!"

"I don't know. You need me too now, and you've been a better family to me than she has."

"I'll be fine. I have Roger and Abigail, and you, of course. I have our attorney, Reginald Protheroe to sort out the legal matters. I will survive. See if she will come here. She can have the guest house and you can take her to the clinic and do whatever needs doing. If she'll agree."

"Actually, she suggested it. I was as shocked and surprised as you are. She wants to come here after she gets out of the residential clinic."

"Well, this is quite a turnaround for your Margaret. Did she say what prompted this change of heart?"

Betty stood up and paced. "Yes. She said--she said, now that her real father was dead, she wanted to set things right."

"What does that mean?"

"That's what I asked. She said she will get a lawyer if she has to, but that Kimo Lemon was her biological father."

"What on Earth?" Mabel said.

"I know. I was absolutely dumbfounded. I guess she really was bitter about Tony not being her 'real' father, and what that said to her about me. She just seems to want to hurt me, and those I care about." Betty sighed and finally looked at Mabel. "I thought

43

you should know before you agreed to her coming here. I don't know her anymore and clearly, she's capable of saying anything. I don't know what to think. It could be true, I suppose. That would explain why he made me so nervous. Kimo's face was damaged so badly in the war, I would never recognize him, but there are things, mannerisms, I guess. Patterns of speech I should have picked up on. I didn't though, after so many years. I'm such a fool, Mabel."

Mabel thought for several long moments while she waited nervously. Then Mabel took Betty's hand. "Well, we'll do the best we can, won't we? It's in the past now. We have to think of Margaret. If she really is Kimo's child, she's probably suffered enough. Drugs really change a person I read once. She needs help and she needs you." She squeezed Betty's hand.

"What about Roger and Abigail?" Betty asked.

"I think we'll cross that bridge when we come to it. I just can't see punishing Margaret for what Kimo did. Or you." Mabel squeezed Betty's hand. "Abigail and Roger will always be set even if some of Kimo's estate goes to Margaret in the end. Remember White's Whitewalls! I still have my own money and my children certainly aren't helpless."

"How will they *feel*, Mabel?"

"That I can't say. I'd like to think I raised them to be open-minded and fair, but I guess we'll see. It will all come out in the wash as we say down south. They're not children anymore, and I'll still be there for them. The important thing right now is taking care of Margaret."

Chapter 5

After Betty had helped Mabel from the room, Roger and Abigail stood looking at each other.

"Well," said Abigail, "I should probably get back to the hospital."

"Yeah." But neither moved. Finally Roger pulled a wicker chair close to the edge of the lanai where he could see the white expanse of beach and lapping waves. Abigail sighed and pulled another chair next to his.

"What do you think?" she asked.

"About what?"

"About Mom. What are we going to do?"

"She never signed the release, and if we want LE to really grow, I need autonomy."

"Gee, Roger, my concern at this point is totally on your ability to run the company single-handed."

"Well, it's important that the company make a smooth transition, and it's obvious Mother doesn't want to do it. I'm doing her a favor."

"Some favor. I notice Dad's not even in the ground yet and you're hopping up and down ready to take over. You never got to do diddly before, and now you want to run the show. Kind of convenient, how this all worked out, isn't it?"

Roger reddened. "What the hell's that supposed to mean?"

"You figure it out! Dad dies suddenly and you get to take over everything. I'm just saying things worked out well for you, that's all."

"What are you suggesting? I killed him? Ridiculous. If I were going to kill him, I'd have done it years ago. He made my life miserable, not to mention Mother's. What about you?" He swiveled his chair to face her. "If anyone had motive, it's you! Dad put all these other people through college, but not his own daughter! How did that look in the paper?" Roger laughed. "Dad covered pretty well, but I knew you were mad. And you still are. Dad cut you out of running the company, but you'll get an allowance for Christ's sake." Roger retrieved his glass from the wet bar and fixed a Bloody Mary. "Besides, if Dad treated me like shit, he ignored you. You were a girl."

Abigail sat with her hands clenched and Roger stopped when he saw a tear trickle down her cheek.

Roger said, "I'm sorry. We're both upset and saying things we don't really mean. Motive? I mean, come on." He laughed weakly. "I know I thought about what it would be like once he was gone, but I never thought about hurrying that along. I know you felt the same, right? He was awful to you. I know."

"I know how he treated me," she said softly, "I lived it. And so did Mom. It's true. We were chattel, and not worth the great man's time or attention. You, he expected you to run the company someday, he groomed you for it. But me? I was supposed to make a good marriage and be a breeding cow for his grandchildren.

"Well, we fooled him. Neither of us married or had

children. Why do you suppose that is?"

"I don't know. I guess on some level, I didn't want to create another target for him. And I guess, for spite. I never had a choice about running the company. He made that clear from the start. I was under his control, and I was never going to get out. Well, now I'm out." He sat back in the wicker chair and took his sister's hand. "I'm sorry I never told you this. I always admired you for standing up to him. I could never do that. I guess I didn't have the backbone. Also, after a while, I really wanted this company. It ate at me, that I would have it someday, and I had to wait for him to die to be a real part of it. I could see so many things that could be improved, but years ago I stopped trying to get him to hear my ideas. I was nothing to him. He could just say his son was working with him and would someday be in charge. He thought this day would never come. But it has. And it's my day." He looked closely at Abigail. "And it's your day too, Abigail. Take it. You're free now."

Abigail burst into ragged sobs. "Then why don't I feel free?" Roger got a box of tissues and placed it near her.

They both watched the attempts of an obviously novice windsurfer struggling in waist-deep water. The sail was down, and the surfer tried to right the sail and jump on board at the same time. After several failed attempts, a man from the considerable crowd on the beach waded in and held the board. The wind picked up a bit and the windsurfer began to move slowly away from the beach. He gave his rescuer a huge smile and turned to see where he was going. As the beach dwindled behind him, it became evident to the watchers he didn't know how to turn. His look of utter panic was too much for Roger and Abigail and those on the beach. The roar of laughter was audible from the lanai, and finally the man bailed out into deeper water and swam back to shore dragging his board.

Roger and Abigail smiled at each other. Abigail squeezed Roger's hand and stood up.

"Thanks Roger. He was a real bastard, but I'm sad that he's gone. I guess. I don't know how I feel." She picked up her purse. "I told Mom I'd help her go through Dad's things here at home. Did he have personal stuff at the office? I can help you go through that as well. I don't think we want a secretary or somebody going through that stuff, do we?"

Roger shook his head. "I'm going to do it over the next couple of days. Want a hand with the things here?"

"I'll let you know. Mom seems more together than I thought she'd be. I'll see how she does." Roger followed her to the front door. Abigail locked it behind them and glanced at her brother's profile as he scanned the sky.

"Roger, you've changed. You look different. I do believe you're ready to take over LE. I think you're capable of anything."

*   *   *   *

The executive secretary answered the phone in the executive offices of O'ahu Cane & Pine.

"OC&P executive offices; Mrs. Marsden speaking."

"Gerald Breem, please."

"Who may I tell him is calling?"

"Mick Kau'ula from the *Honolulu Star-Bulletin*."

"What is this regarding?"

"I'm covering the human interest stories on Kimo Lemon, and I'm interviewing his friends and employees. Would you like to contribute?"

Mrs. Marsden seemed flustered. "No, thank you. Please hold while I see if Mr. Breem is available." The phone clicked and a watered down version of Steve and Theresa's song 'Sailing' came on. A moment later she was back.

"Hello? Yes, I'm putting you through. One moment."

"Hello, Gerald Breem here," a gravelly voice said.

"Yes, Mr. Breem, I'm Mick Kau'ula from the *Star-Bulletin*. I'm doing the series on Kimo Lemon and I wondered if I could come in and speak to you."

"I don't have time for an in-person interview. As you can imagine, we're in transition here, but if you want to ask me something now, I have a few minutes."

Mick Kau'ula thought. Interviews were better in person, but it was this or nothing. Oh, well.

"Yes, Mr. Breem. Thank you. How long have you worked for Lemon Enterprises?"

"This makes twenty-six years. I started at O'ahu Cane & Pine, and I never left. I helped groom Lemon Tree."

"Tell me about Lemon Tree."

"It's a job training program started by Kimo in the fifties, part of the Lemon Foundation, which is the philanthropic side of the company. Typical Kimo, he said if you wanted people to work right, they had to be trained right. For him, that meant starting a job training program. If he didn't teach someone how to do a job, then he believed it wouldn't be done right. Probably saved a lot of trouble in the long run, having Kimo do it himself." Breem laughed heartily.

"How did you first hear of Lemon Tree and Kimo Lemon?"

"Well, it turns out he was a friend of my dad's during the war."

"That would be the second world war?"

"That's right. My dad and he were in business together, and then my dad went into business for himself. It didn't do so well. We couldn't afford for me to go to college, but my dad went to Kimo after all those years and asked for me to be placed at Lemon Tree. Best thing that ever happened to me."

"What business was that?"

49

"What business was what?"

"The one your dad and Kimo Lemon were involved in during the war. They were both at Pearl Harbor, right?"

"Right. As to the business, I'm not exactly sure. Kimo lent him some money, invested in him, I guess. I never knew all the details. But it held them together for life, my dad said. Whatever my dad was doing, he never fully recovered financially. Despite that we owe a lot to Kimo. My dad died in 1975, but before he did, he made sure I was secure through Lemon Tree."

"What did your dad die of? He was pretty young."

Breem cleared his throat. "It doesn't have anything to do with your article."

"I won't print this. It doesn't have any direct bearing on my story anyway—just background."

Breem was silent for a moment. "He committed suicide. Hanged himself in our carport."

"I'm sorry to hear that. How is your mom?"

"She sorta curled up and died about a year later. So, you see, since I was taken care of by Lemon Tree, I had a family of sorts to fall back on."

"Tell me about your rise through OC&P, and what interactions you've had with Kimo Lemon."

"After I went through the training program in 1969, I was hired as a gofer. Well, nowadays they'd call it an assistant or something, but I did just about everything but actually cut pineapple!" He laughed loudly. "Kimo personally asked me to work for him in his office. On account of my dad, I always figured, but that was okay with me. I liked it here."

"I understand Lemon Tree graduates have exemplary training; could you tell me about that?"

"I don't remember much except stuff like typing, which I always thought was a girl's job. But it turned out to be handy now with computers. I also learned about all the office equipment, copying and the like, and then the last section of courses was on management. I could have been hired by a couple of other companies, one in Tacoma, but I wanted to stay here. And like I said, Kimo asked me to stay. So I did."

"What has it been like working with him through the years? I understand that even as he got older, he still ran a tight ship."

"Indeed he did. Right up to the last he was directing and running things, and yelling at people."

"He yelled at people?"

"Well," Breem paused and exhaled through his nose, "I don't mean yell-yell. Exactly. I just mean he wanted things a certain way and if they weren't that way, he got upset."

"Upset?"

"He sent a lot of memos."

"What kinds of memos? Did they result in firing anyone?"

"Well, of course people got fired, but you had to do something pretty bad to get the ax. When the company got bigger, he usually only dealt directly with me, the board, and his son, Roger. The regular employees all had managers and people to take care of things there."

"What kinds of memos?" Mick asked again.

"It's kinda funny. He had this old typewriter in his office and for years, memos were the only thing he'd use it for. He wasn't that great of a typist, but that typewriter was known as "The Harbinger" around the office because he never typed good memos on it, only mad ones."

"Mad memos?"

"Well, there was this one time that some secretary or another had let the coffee pot run dry, and it burst the glass pot. He sent her this memo that just about made her cry. No one ever got to see other people's bad memos, because the recipients never

51

shared."

"Did you ever get a mad memo?"

"Yep, about my first week. I tried to make an overhead transparency on the copy machine and fried the copier. I got a major memo about that. I kept it for a while. Now I think it was funny. But I sure didn't then."

"Have you gotten any recently?"

"Noooo, not that I can recall." Evasive.

"Has anyone gotten one recently, that you *can* recall?"

"Hold on, my other line's blinking." More diluted music. Breem came back. "I've got a meeting. I've gotta go. Hope you got enough. I'll look for your article. Bye."

"Thank you for your--" Click. "Oh, well." Kau'ula hung up and sat back to review the notes. The phone rang.

"Kau'ula."

"Hi Mick; it's Yoshi."

"Hey Yoshi; howzit?"

"Not so good. Can you meet me for a drink?"

"Sure, when?"

"Now."

"It's three o'clock in the afternoon," Kau'ula said.

"I know. Meet me at the Japanese restaurant across the street from your building. We'll have sake. I'm buying the first round. Maybe the first couple. See you."

"Yeah, see you." Kau'ula hung up, shuddering at the thought of sake in the middle of the afternoon. Beer, maybe, whiskey, definitely, but sake. . .

Leaving a note taped to his computer saying "Be right back," Mick went downstairs and out into the bright, beautiful Honolulu afternoon. Crossing against the traffic in the middle of the block on Kapiolani Boulevard, Mick headed diagonally toward the little noodle shop gleaming dully in the lowering sun. Pushing aside the fabric strips that formed a curtain, Mick entered and waited for the dim restaurant to come into focus. Yoshi was already there, seated at a corner table with a porcelain bottle and two small cups in front of him. He turned, saw Mick and rose. They hugged hello with a couple of back slaps.

"Thanks for coming, Mick. I really appreciate this."

"You're welcome. Any time. You know that." Mick looked at the older man whose normally dapper appearance had deteriorated. The greying hair, usually so neatly combed, was disheveled and greasy-looking, his loosened tie spattered with oily flecks, the navy blue suit rumpled and frayed. A large ceramic bottle of warm sake and two cups already sat in front of him.

"What's happened? You look terrible. It's not the kids, is it? Or Myra?" Yoshi's son, Shuto, although an adult, was cause for much strife in his life. He doted on his two grandchildren, although he often complained they were not being raised with enough tradition, meaning Japanese tradition. His wife Myra had suffered a stroke some years before, but was slowly recovering through painful physical therapy and nearly twenty-four hour care.

"No, they're all the same." He took a drink of sake and poured some into a second cup and pushed it toward Mick.

"Have you ever found out something that made your whole life a lie?" His chin trembled and he covered it by wiping his mouth roughly with the back of his hand.

"What's going on Yosh? Come on, tell me."

"I just got fired today from OC&P."

"No. Oh, my god. Why?"

"I was forced to take my retirement. I didn't want to. In three more years I'll be sixty-five and eligible for a higher pension, and I know Myra is going to need it. God knows what Shuto and his kids will need by then." He covered his face with both hands.

Mick waved away the waiter.

"Tell me all of it, from the beginning."

Yoshi did. He finished with, "This memo, it's real, I know it is. I remember what it was like when we were little after the war. People were so cruel. I thought all this time, that he was a friend to the Japanese, now I find out he hates us."

"Let me see the memo," Mick said.

Yoshi fished in his breast pocket. "Breem, the guy who fired me, knew all about it. He was happy. He hates the Japanese too, I guess. There are more of those memos. He had a big pile of them. There are more people who are going to be downsized, or transferred or whatever. God, what do I do?"

Mick read the memo and thought. He sipped sake. "Don't go back there for anything. Have someone else pick up your stuff. Here's what you do. Tell Myra you decided to take early retirement to be with her. She'll love it. Tell her it's a surprise. Don't tell her about the memo. I'll work on it myself. I've got plenty of money from investments. I can lend you some if you need it. Just tell Shuto the same story you tell Myra. No more handouts, and get a job!"

Yoshi's red eyes opened wide.

"Not Myra, Shuto!" Mick laughed and Yoshi joined in a little uncertainly.

Yoshi refilled Mick's sake cup. "I'm glad I came to you. Come to dinner tomorrow, I'll do my teriyaki stir fry and we can discuss my retirement and other things some more." He refilled his own cup and swallowed it in one gulp. "I'm really so grateful you could meet me. I feel much better now. More than the forced retirement, I guess the revelation of Kimo's attitude toward us Japanese was what did me in."

"I think there is more to the great humanitarian Kimo Lemon than meets the eye. And you're more than welcome for the advice." Mick poured the last of the sake and they clinked cups

54

together.

"*Kanpai*!" Bottom's up.

Chapter 6

Honolulu Star-Bulletin **Wednesday, September 20, 1995**
Who was Kimo Lemon? Transcripts of Three Interviews.
Part Three of a Series
By Mick Kau'ula
        After the death of businessman Kimo Lemon, this reporter began a series of articles on the impact of Lemon's contributions to our community. Part one covered the Lemon Foundation, the organization that gives financial aid to many, and was one of the original contributors to returning Japanese Americans after World War II. Part two dealt with O'ahu Cane & Pineapple's humble beginnings and rise to become one of the driving forces behind our island economy. In Part three, we discover the man, Kimo Lemon, from those who knew him best. However, the first interview with his wife, Mabel White Lemon, was conducted while he was still alive and part of the Gala Celebration coverage planned for next week. We decided to keep the following interview, and then shifted gears to run a retrospective.
Honolulu Star-Bulletin: What was it like in the early days, before

Kimo had made it big?

Mabel: Well, we had just Roger then. And he was so little. We had a shack near Pearl Harbor, but Kimo was stationed at Fort Shafter. Through some housing problem, we were put over there. It was a two room house and we had a time keeping little Roger off the beach! We were very poor then, a private didn't make much, but still Jim managed to help out his buddies now and again.

SB: How did he help them out?

ML: He lent them money, and they always gave him a little extra when they paid him back. Army buddies are very close that way.

SB: You called him Jim?

ML: Oh, yes. Back then he was Jim. He's from Texas, you know. He just fell in love with Hawai'i. After we decided to stay here permanently after the war, he started calling himself Kimo--Hawai'ian for Jim--a new image and all.

SB: How did he start Lemon Enterprises?

ML: Well, actually, O'ahu Cane & Pine came first. Lemon Enterprises became an umbrella company for OC&P and the other projects.

SB: Tell me about the other projects.

ML: There was Lemon Tree, his job-training division. He also made a lot of private loans, and gave money to other worthy causes. But that came much later. In the beginning, it was just OC&P.

SB: What was that like, starting from nothing?

ML: With what little money we had after the war, Kimo bought a few acres near Wheeler Field.

SB: How many is a few?

ML: I don't know exactly. But enough to plant sugar cane and pineapple. After the first crops did so well, he put every cent back into crops and the business just took off. We bought a nicer house near Wahiawa, to be closer to the fields.

SB: I understand Kimo hired mostly Japanese laborers?

ML: Yes, that's true. He felt so bad about the way the Japanese had been treated during the war, that he hired all these folks who couldn't find jobs. Of course, the pay wasn't much, but then, nobody else would hire them at all. After OC&P really began to turn a profit, he lent money to Japanese businessmen to finance local companies. It almost seems like he lent more money than we had!

SB: Really?

ML: Oh, we never went hungry, but once the word got out, people seemed to come from all over asking for money. I don't know that he turned a one down. And, to show their appreciation, they always made their payments on time, with interest!

SB: Tell me about the last twenty years or so. How has the company progressed?

ML: It seemed like Kimo could do no wrong, business-wise. He bought more and more land, and diversified. He knew he'd need a loyal work force, and it seemed to him the best way to get that was to create it himself. He was a big one for doing things himself. He wanted things done his way, and so he began Lemon Tree Training Division. He gave people without much opportunity an education and business training and later, jobs. Before that, he did the same thing, but on a much smaller scale. He gave jobs to lots of folks he knew from the war. He used to laugh and say he was tied to them so he'd just soon keep an eye on them.

SB: What did he mean by that?

ML: Oh, I'm sure just that he'd helped them in some way, and now they were repaying him, so that tied them together. He always did have a sense of humor.

SB: What do you see in the future for Lemon Enterprises?

ML: Well, I'm not young myself, so I expect Roger could answer that better. I imagine it'll keep growing and helping folks, just like it's always done.

SB: We are all looking forward to the gala and I'll see you there.

Interview Two was with Mitzi Tanaka, one of the earliest graduates of Lemon Tree. Now no longer with the company, she is a housewife and mother in Mililani.

Honolulu Star-Bulletin: Mrs. Tanaka, please tell me how you came to be placed with Lemon Tree.

Mitzi Tanaka: Well, I was very young, and had no money for college. My father had heard of Kimo Lemon during the war, and when I turned eighteen, he suggested that I go to the office and apply to the program.

SB: Did you meet Kimo Lemon himself?

MT: No, not at that time. I was given some aptitude tests, and they asked what I wanted to study, and I filled out an application and financial statement. It was very scary for me. I'd had high school, and my teachers said I was quite bright, but I was raised in a traditional Japanese household, and was not expected to work.

SB: What   was   expected?

MT: That I would marry into an acceptable family and have children.

SB: What happened to change that?

MT: My parents grew ill suddenly. I am an only child, and there were no close male relatives to help us. I needed to earn money. This was toward the end of the Viet Nam war and many eligible young men had gone. I decided Lemon Tree was our only hope, and I convinced my father to let me try.

SB: And the rest is history?

MT: Not quite.

SB: What happened?

MT: I was called several days later to come down to the executive offices for a final interview. That's when I met Kimo Lemon.

SB: Tell me about that.

MT: Well, I was very nervous, and since I was having this interview, I knew I was being seriously considered for training. Up to that point, I had not dared to think I might really get in. I had put on my application that I wanted to be a lawyer, but business was also another interest. I walked into the interview room and a secretary had me sit at a long table with many chairs. No one else was in the room. I began to sweat, and imagine horrible things when that room would fill up with white men in business suits. About ten minutes later, just as I was deciding this was all a terrible mistake and that I should leave, in walks a middle-aged white man in shirtsleeves. His tie was loose and his shirt was rolled up to his elbows. He smiled at me and seated himself across the table. I smiled back, thinking he was a clerk or something. Finally he says, 'Hi, I'm Kimo Lemon, tell me about yourself.' I about died. The interview went really well until the end. He said, 'I see that you put down law as your first choice for college. I need to tell you a couple of things. First, I'll never put a woman through college to do a man's job. Second, never repeat what I just told you, or I'll see you never get a job in any industry of worth in this state. Understand?' And he gave me this terrible smile and stood up. He said, 'So, business it is. I have an opening in the secretarial pool that I'll hold for you until you get your training. You'll work here days and take regular college coursework at night. Okay?' Of course it wasn't okay, but what could I do? I suddenly felt cheap and used. I said fine and thank you and left. I started secretarial school and did exactly what he said. I met my husband at my first job and I eventually left to marry and have a family. I'm glad I never went back."

SB: Doesn't this go against the positive public image Kimo Lemon's cultivated through the years?

MT: Well, now that he's dead, it doesn't matter, does it? Besides, all in all, he performed a service for many people, and just because I didn't like the way he did it, doesn't mean he didn't do a lot of good things. You don't have to print that last part, if you don't want to.

SB: We believe in printing all sides to a story. It seems there are many sides to Kimo Lemon.

Interview with Arthur Sopowski, Executive Vice President of Lemon Tree Training Division

Honolulu Star-Bulletin: How long have you been with Lemon Tree, Mr. Sopowski?

AS: Call me Art. Ten years, next month.

SB: That's not very long, compared to some employees here.

AS: No, I've climbed the ranks pretty quickly. Mr. Lemon saw my potential and helped me out.

SB: How did you come to be with Lemon Tree?

AS: I answered an ad for management training. I went through some interviews and testing, and Mr. Lemon liked what he saw.

SB: Had you already been to college?

AS: Yes, but I needed a few more classes to get my law degree, and Mr. Lemon backed me up all the way. Back then, I had some plan of being a lawyer for Lemon Tree after I passed the bar, but Mr. Lemon encouraged me to go for management.

SB: Encouraged?

AS: Oh, yeah. He was a great one for seeing what a person ought to be doing, and then directing them to that end. He's really, he *was,* really farsighted that way. I'm sorry if I seem distracted, but I'm kind of broken up about his death.

SB: Yet you're here at work.

AS: Oh, yes. Got to keep going. He'd want it that way. I wouldn't want to let him down by letting my emotions get hold. That's another thing. He always was in control. Never saw him cry, or lose a day of work for something he'd call "woman's feelings." No, Mr. Lemon wouldn't want me to cry over him, so all of us here at Lemon Tree are doing him proud.

SB: Is there going to be any kind of memorial for Kimo Lemon by any of the companies he owned or the employees?

AS: I can't speak for the other companies, but here at Lemon Tree, we're having a lobby plaque dedicated, over his bronze bust, and we all plan to attend the service, unless Mrs. Lemon doesn't want us to.

SB: If everyone attends, won't the company close for a day?

AS: Well, I don't mean the clerical staff, of course!

SB: Of course. Where do you see Lemon Tree headed in the future?

AS: We're a subsidiary of Lemon Enterprises, you know, so I suppose Roger will dictate that.

SB: Don't you as Vice President have some say?

AS: Not really. Mr. Lemon ran a tight ship and retained direct control of the business dealings.

SB: What exactly is your role?

AS: I carry out Mr. Lemon's instructions on how the business is run.

SB: Can you give me an example of your duties?

AS: I did the hiring and firing, according to Mr. Lemon's instructions. I arranged all the meetings and documents for his signature, things like that.

SB: It sounds like a secretarial job.

AS: No, not at all. Mr. Lemon often consulted with me on important issues.

SB: I see. Well, I appreciate your time. Is there any last comment you'd like to make to our readers?

AS: Just that Mr. Lemon was a great man, and great boss, and we'll sure miss him around here.

SB: Did you know, now that Roger is in charge, he intends to give each subsidiary autonomy within the company?

AS: Oh. I um, did hear something along those lines.

SB: Apparently Roger voiced this opinion many times during meetings that you attended. It was only a matter of time before he would be in charge, and these changes would be implemented. Isn't that good news? Wouldn't you agree?

AS: I'm sure I don't know. I've got a meeting in five minutes.

SB: Oh, one last thing. Were you aware of any sexist practices by Kimo Lemon in the Lemon Tree Training Program?

AS: I'm sure I don't know what you mean.

SB: I interviewed a past graduate and she claims that Kimo told her directly that he would not train or pay for college for women if they were interested in traditional men's jobs. Do you know anything about that?

AS: That's outrageous! She probably just didn't get what she wanted and was upset about it. Mr. Lemon was a great man and I'll thank you to remember all the good he's done this community. Now, this interview is over.

SB: Thank you again for your time.

*   *   *   *

In Kimo Lemon's opulent office at Lemon Enterprises, Roger Lemon sat at his father's teak desk: a vast surface, polished smooth and nearly black with an empty blotter next to the black marble pen stand holding two old-fashioned ink cartridge pens. One corner held a rippled auburn monkey-pod bowl, and the other, a family portrait in a koa frame, taken when Roger and Abigail had been very young. There were no other remotely personal items anywhere in the office.

On a cherry wood stand adjacent to the desk was the

famous memo typewriter. The rest of the decor was tropical, if slightly impersonal.

Roger sighed. Only if one knew Kimo Lemon loved the islands, would one be able to interpret this office as having a personal touch. He glanced around the room at the large Herb Kane original oil hung behind the desk, depicting Hawaiian gods looming large over an outrigger canoe battling turbulent seas.

Crossed canoe paddles hung on another wall, and antique poi pounders, canoe models, and kukui nut necklaces graced a museum-quality glass case along the other wall. A two-foot border of teak floor glowed around a huge, hand-woven Chinese carpet.

Roger smiled, taking in the memorabilia and Hawai'iana.

"One positive thing that could be said about my father is he truly loved these islands, and overall, has done some good for them," he said to himself.

He sighed again and unlocked the desk, sifted through office supplies and blank forms. None of the usual junk that one would expect to collect in a desk over the years. No photos, no notes from employees, no gag-gifts, no dirt that often collected at the bottom of the little divided spaces for paper clips and rubber bands.

The desk could have been just-shipped from the factory. Roger really hadn't expected to find anything personal or important in the desk, but its sterility surprised him.

"What a sad man," he mused. "Why did he even bother to lock it?" He closed the desk and turned his attention to the double koa filing cabinet behind the desk, also locked. He fiddled with the large collection of keys until he found the correct one. He opened the top drawer to find it absolutely packed with neatly labeled files. He lifted out the first several inches and began the tedious task of sorting and reading. Boring. Interdepartmental memos of the standard and appropriate kind, correspondence, things to do, ideas for future sub-companies, blah, blah, blah. Roger felt his eyes closing and limbs growing heavy as he closed and relocked the file cabinet. One more place to check and then call it a day.

He eyed the office safe squatting in the corner. Small but sturdy, and built into the floor, Roger knew it held petty cash and a few documents. Well, it *had.* Maybe now it held something else? Who would have the combination? Probably no one, he thought grimly. Not even his secretaries or VPs, that's how secretive he was. He rolled the desk chair in front of the safe and tried a variety of standard numbers: his own birthday, his sister's, his parents' anniversary. Nothing. He rolled back to the desk to think. Kimo's ego was well known to be astronomical so he twisted the dial to his father's birthday. 72020. No, that was too many numbers. But he felt he was close. He removed the zeros. 722. Still no. "Crap." He inverted the day and month. He rearranged the year. Roger felt like he should know. He was Kimo's son; he should be able to figure this out. The more he thought, the more he knew it would have to do with Kimo's birthday. The start of the Great Kimo Lemon. Then he tried 7-20-20. Bingo. "Sheesh." Roger was glad no one was around to witness the obvious. "More thinking, and less overthinking," Roger mumbled as he opened the door. He pulled out a stack of memos, known as 'mad memos.' He recognized them since he had received a few himself. His anger rose as he re-read his own as well as other employees'. At the time he'd received them, he'd felt embarrassed and chastised, but not that the memos were necessarily off base. Now, older, and with more experience at the company and around Kimo, he saw them for what they were: attempts to break people down, bits of irrelevant minutiae designed to eat away a drop at a time like acid. Memos kept for a lifetime and used whenever Kimo needed leverage, ego, money? What? Roger's stomach churned as he read deeper into the pile. People he had never heard of as well as those he knew in the company were all victims of Kimo's cruelty. All contained an implied or specified threat if the memo was made public in any way. Incredible information Kimo had gathered over the years and could be used to blackmail the recipients, or held for later use, Roger surmised, since the news about some highly placed officials in Hawaii government had never made the paper. Even dirt on celebrities and Mainland bigwigs. "It just keeps getting better." He wondered at how Kimo had planned to use the memos without coming off like a psycho himself. Perhaps Kimo didn't care in his ambition to climb to the top of the heap. Any heap? He came to a layer of cash. Bundles of bills, stacked under the pile of memos. Seemed like a lot of money for petty cash, but Roger knew he was among the last to understand how the company ran on the inside, kept at arms' length as he'd been. "Not anymore," he said as he removed the money. At the bottom was a startling piece of information. An announcement of the fiftieth anniversary celebration with an addition he'd never seen. He read that Kimo Lemon's tell-all book would be announced. It was not ready for publication Roger gathered, but excerpts would be read and information disseminated that he was sure many people would rather not come to light. No manuscript lay in the safe.

Adrenaline coursed through him as the implications of the discovery raced in his brain. *Why* would he write a tell all book? In fact, on the flyer, the book was even entitled, "Kimo Lemon Tells It Like It Is." And why *now*? Was Kimo's need to hurt people so great that even after years of blackmail, he still needed to expose damaging secrets? Some of the things Roger had read bordered on national security. Not currently, but maybe someone didn't want them revealed at all.

"Oh, God. What do I do now?" Without the manuscript, Roger had no way of knowing what exactly was to be told. Could his father have written a book? Probably. He was smart, obviously. He had been a voracious reader, and in later years, had taken to reading tell-alls other and sensationalistic material. Of course, Kimo was teaching himself to write, just like he'd taught himself everything else in his life. It sounded like the manuscript was complete but no mention of a publisher. Roger hoped that Kimo's ego was so great that he presumed someone would want to publish his pearls of wisdom and salacious tidbits, but hadn't gotten around to acquiring a publisher.

Roger put everything back in the safe, including the flyer, more or less in the order he'd found it. If the manuscript had been in here, too, it sure wasn't now. He couldn't find it, which meant someone else had it. Either Kimo gave it to them, or they had taken it. Before or after Kimo's death, that was another question. And his death. Now that took on sinister meaning, too. Was it really a heart attack? Or had someone killed him? Roger had just found about ten pounds of motive, and motive worth killing for.

His stomach dropped as he realized that if it was murder, the family and employees were going to be watched in case anyone knew about the book, too, and might be willing to pursue it. Now he *did* know about it.

He shut the safe and spun the dial. He needed some air. And some help. He had no idea where he could turn for assistance. Nowhere seemed safe. He was on his own.

*　　*　　*　　*

Back at the Lemon house, Betty the nurse was on the phone with her daughter.

"Margaret, you know you're always welcome here, and after you get out of the clinic, I'll come to get you. It's a little tricky to find the house the first time, and I don't want you to ride the bus."

"Mother, I know how to find the house just fine."

"How do you know that?"

"I've been there. I've seen you."

"When have you been here? Why didn't you come in?"

"Over the years, when I wanted to see you, I just came over. It's not that hard. I'm an addict, not an imbecile. Anyway, I'm due for release in two weeks and then I'm an outpatient. When I'm out, will you help me get a driver's license again?"

"Can you do that?"

"Yes, I'll have an address, and a car. Won't I?"

"Of course you will, dear. I'm just at a loss. It's been so long since I've seen you, and I've missed you so. I always wondered how you were, where you were. And now it seems that you've been quite close by all the time. I just don't understand it."

"I know. It's complicated. Will you help?"

"Of course I will."

"I'll call you next week with my checkout date and time."

Betty slowly hung up, tears welled in an instant.

"Betty?" Mabel stood unsteadily on her walker outside Betty's room. "Betty, I still can't find my glasses. Did you find yours?" She entered and peered at her friend. "Betty! What's wrong?"

Betty shook her head, unable to speak. She reached for the box of tissues on the table.

"Betty, tell me."

Betty blew her nose. "Margaret just called. She wants me to pick her up in a couple of weeks from the residential clinic. Then she wants to come here to live. She told me she wants me to help her get her driver's license again." Betty's nose ran and she blotted it.

"Well, that sounds like good news. You're not happy?"

"Oh, I am. I just never dreamed I'd really see her again. I

guess I thought, maybe she was dead. She was gone so long and has been so lost."

"Well," Mabel started uncertainly, "she is a drug abuser, and maybe she has some mental illness. They say that's common among the homeless."

"It was a little odd that when I tried to tell her about the house, she said she knew all about it, that she had been here!"

"What do you mean, *been here*?"

"She made it sound like she'd been peeking in windows and listening at doors. I've never seen anyone around, have you? She said she'd been here several times over the years, and particularly the last several months."

"Maybe it's part of her delusion?"

"I don't think so. I think she could have described the house if I asked her to. We've never had security or even a dog! It makes me wonder who else could have been around without our knowing. Especially since you and I are here alone so much." Betty shivered, eyes darting around the room.

Mabel laughed. "Well, I suppose no one's under the bed right now."

Betty giggled nervously. "I guess you're right, but it does make you think, doesn't it? I mean we never lock up. Should we check the house?"

"You mean right now?" Betty nodded. "What for? What would we do, hit the burglar with my walker?" They laughed again.

"Maybe they aren't releasing Kimo's body because they're not sure it was a heart attack."

"Oh, pish. It'll work out. I mean, Kimo wasn't well, and hadn't been for a while. You know how he felt about doctors. He could be bleeding in the street and he'd say he was fine."

"Well that's certainly true. He could be stubborn as a

Mississippi mule."

"Texas ass, you mean?" They dissolved into giggles.

"If you want dinner anytime today, I'd better get Teresita to start it. It's not going to fix itself. You okay here, or do you want to move to the lanai?" Betty asked.

"I'm going to lie down, I think. Help me to my room, please."

Chapter 7

That evening, Mick Kau'ula arrived at Yoshi Onizuki's Hawaiian-Japanese style home near the top of Wilhelmina Rise in Kaimuki. An older neighborhood of varied lots and houses, the Rise was a narrow road that went almost straight up a very steep hill. For the less courageous driver, alternate streets zig-zagged over the Rise with a more gradual grade.

Mick always took the direct route, both up and down. Going up required a sturdy transmission and a running start, then flooring the accelerator. At night, it always felt like an ascent into the Hawaiian skies, the stars glowing clearly against the velvet, rewarding the driver with an unobstructed view of what seemed like half the island.

Going down required nerves of steel and good brakes. Mick had both. One of the advantages of driving a VW bug was it could be parked almost anywhere, a distinct advantage on this car-clogged island--especially for a reporter who had to go where there were large numbers of cars already; accident scenes, public events, downtown Honolulu, and particularly Ala Moana Shopping Center, the consumer hub of the island.

Mick edged the nose of the VW off the road and stopped under a drooping tree that promised to drop oozing red-brown pods onto the convertible top. Most of the houses up here didn't have garages, much less driveways. Lots for homes had been carved out of the steep hillsides, usually with enough room for a modest house, and possibly a patch of dirt to park in. A few homeowners had a carport and the really lucky ones had a garage gouged out of the mountain, with the house sitting a level above.

Yoshi was one of the latter. He had owned this house for over thirty years, and although it was not large, it appraised high like the rest of the neighborhood. What it lacked in square footage, it more than made up for in stunning views of the island, down to the white beaches of Waikiki and the distant horizon, including the inside of Diamond Head Crater. During World War II, the slopes of Diamond Head had been used as lookouts for enemy craft, but now it was a tourist attraction and a military training site. If one knew where to look, the concrete war bunkers could be seen from Yoshi's living room.

Periodically, Mick climbed the inside of the crater walls through darkened bunkers, scrabbled up metal ladders in utter blackness, and emerged on the upper and outermost lip of Diamond Head. Reward for the sweaty labor was an ocean view of myriad blues, surfing beaches below, endless sky, and a herd of tourists. Crater Rim Trail provided some solitude for inner contemplation, and sitting on the oddly placed concrete boxes and bunker roofs was a reminder that this beautiful spot had played a part in a horrible war.

Mick climbed the steep stone steps to the front door. Ever-present banana poka—a parasitic vine and scourge of Hawaiian

72

gardeners--strangled Yoshi's trees, and climbed his porch lattice into the dark. Verdigris grillwork with a glass backing centered on the black door. Several pairs of rubber zoris lined up next to the straw doormat. Mick loosened the laces on his scruffy Reeboks and pushed the bell. Mick heard the shuffle of fabric slip-on shoes against hardwood floors. The door opened and Yoshi smiled.

"Come in, come in. Put your shoes here, well you know."

Mick slipped off the loosened shoes and placed them in a wooden shoe-rack just inside the door, replacing them with a pair of soft fabric slippers similar to Yoshi's.

"Hi, Yoshi, howzit?" Mick shuffled down the hall after Yoshi; the only way really, to walk in those slippers.

"I think I'm doing okay," replied Yoshi as he went into the small kitchen/dining room. He patted the shoulder of a small Japanese woman seated in a wheelchair at the beautiful, but well-worn round table. She looked up as they entered.

"Mick! So good to see you! You don't come around enough!" She held up her arms. "Come, give me a kiss." Her speech was slightly slurred; her left arm was shriveled and didn't lift as high as her right.

"Myra! Your arm! You can lift it!" Mick mock-glared at Myra. "How long have you been able to do this? And why haven't you told me?"

Myra hid a little smirk. "Only a couple days. I wanted to surprise you. Pretty impressive, huh?" Myra did a little wave as if holding a conductor's baton. "Soon I'll be back with the London Philharmonic." She chuckled and her eyes squinted unevenly. The left side of her face drooped slightly.

"Myra, you are amazing. Anything else you're not telling me?"

Myra glanced at her husband as he put out glasses of wine. "Should I tell him now, Yoshi?"

"Sure, why not?" Yoshi smiled indulgently at his diminutive wife.

"Yoshi has decided to take early retirement!" She looked triumphantly at Mick. "I never thought I'd live to see the day my Yoshi puts me, or himself, above that company he works for." She poked her husband in the stomach with a stick-like finger. "He says we should start enjoying our golden years. Maybe travel a little, now that I'm getting so much better."

Mick looked at Myra and saw it was true. From just a few weeks ago, her mobility was vastly improved, her chipper attitude and the glow in her cheeks attested to the joy of her husband's retirement. Mick glanced at Yoshi and saw him looking back with a mixture of pride and sheepishness.

"I really should have done this earlier," Yoshi started, but Myra cut in with a heavy pidgin accent.

"See, what I wen' tol' you, you wort'less husband? We coulda been livin' it up in Bali, or somewea!" She dissolved into laughter.

Yoshi tried to continue, "She's been like this since I told her last night. If I'd known it was going to turn her into a crazy woman, I'd never have done it," he said as he bent to kiss her.

"Oh, you." She pushed him away. "Go finish dinner, I'm starved."

"That's another thing; she's been eating like a horse last night and today. At this rate, I can't afford to retire." He moved around the little counter that separated the kitchen and eating area.

Myra wheeled out of the room with, "I'm just going to freshen up; you kids behave now."

Mick sat at the table and sipped the wine. "Wow, what a change. She's a new woman."

Yoshi stirred the tofu and vegetables in the wok, and pivoted to check the large rice-cooker behind him on the counter.

"She's even wearing lipstick. It's a miracle." His lips trembled. "It's like Myra is back. Oh, she's not twenty again, I don't mean that. But her spirit's returned, you know?"

Mick nodded. "I wouldn't have believed it if I hadn't seen it for myself. So, are you really okay with this?"

"I'm okay with what I'm doing, but I'm not okay with the way it happened. I loved and respected that man for years, and now I find. . . I don't know what I've found. I guess I'm not going to analyze it too much. Bad for me." He smiled shakily.

"Have you followed any of the articles I've been doing on Kimo and the business?"

"Not really. 'Til I was bumped out, I thought I was going to help the company get through the transition. Since then, I've been a bit self-involved." Yoshi pulled the wok from the burner and brought it to the table. He set out shoyu and Japanese salad of pickled vegetables. The rice-cooker finished with a loud click and the light switched from *cook* to *warm*.

Mick grabbed napkins and chopsticks. "I've been doing a series of articles on Kimo Lemon and the way his businesses started and their impact on the community, blah, blah, blah," they finished together.

"Yes, the sainted Kimo, defender of the universe," Yoshi said sadly as he rummaged in a drawer for the wooden rice paddle.

"Not exactly, from what I'm hearing."

Yoshi stopped rummaging and looked up. "What do you mean?"

"I'm getting some interesting and possibly conflicting stories. I've been digging into his background and found out some less than perfect things."

"Such as? Catch." Yoshi tossed the paddle to Mick, then brought the rice-cooker to the table as Myra wheeled back in.

"I saw that," she said as she rolled to the refrigerator.

75

"Anybody want juice?" She pulled a large plastic jug of bright pink liquid into her lap and closed the door.

Mick eyed it with distaste. "How can you call that juice? It's just sugar water syrup with food coloring."

"Exactly. I love this stuff. We buy in concentrate by the gallon." She hefted it onto the table. "Then I can have it for every meal, almost." She smiled wickedly. "Yoshi says it's bad for me, but I say, who cares?"

Yoshi shook his head. "What can I do?" He served the fragrant sticky rice and sautéed tofu-vegetable mixture.

"Yoshi, this smells great." Mick poured shoyu liberally over the mound.

"Hey, whoa, you haven't even tasted it yet!"

"Yeah, but I've eaten your cooking before. Always needs shoyu. I'm saving a step."

They all dug in. Myra waved her chopsticks.

"So what were you talking about when I came back in?"

Yoshi and Mick exchanged a glance, and after a moment, Yoshi nodded. Mick filled her in.

"Apparently, Kimo's pristine reputation is a carefully constructed facade. I spoke with some employees and he hired people all right, but there were always strings attached. Pretty serious strings, like he wouldn't help women beyond a certain point. Now it's come to light that he may not have liked the Japanese people as much as he seemed to. I also found out something curious, but I'm not sure what it means yet. His money history goes all the way back to World War II. It was implied to me that he didn't exactly 'help' his buddies with loans and investments. I'm getting the impression he more or less loan-sharked and blackmailed people to get his grub-stake for OC&P. It makes sense, that's how he got enough money to buy those first acres. He earned nothing in the army, had a wife and baby to support, and yet, he gets out of the army with an honorable discharge and immediately buys land and has enough money to start a whole company."

"Wow, Mick. That's a lot of speculation that goes against years of "good works." I'd believe it now, though. Do you have any proof?" Yoshi asked.

"No, but the rumor, from more than just you, I might add, is that Kimo wrote memos for everything, and some of them were quite ugly. It's also rumored that he saved all the memos somewhere. Remember this was before widespread use of computers. If there are hard copies of those memos somewhere I'd like to see them."

Myra took a large swallow of her pink juice. "Sounds like Kimo might have a lot of enemies. Are they sure he died of a heart attack?"

"The Medical Examiner's office hasn't released the body, but there's no suspicion of anything, I don't think. The governor's involved now."

"What does that mean?"

"Kimo's widow, Mabel Lemon, kicked up quite a fuss, and she represents a lot of clout in this town. The governor's office gave a statement of condolence and said they would clear things up."

"Seems to me it might not have been such a great loss after all," Myra said.

"I'm going to do more digging. With this anti-Japanese thing that's developing, and the limiting of women's job opportunities, there's probably more to find out. His daughter Abigail is a pretty well-known surgeon. I'd like to find out about that. If he didn't help women get college educations except for what he deemed acceptable careers, there might be a story there, too. I'm going to go back to the war years. I have some connections, and archival records about Pearl Harbor are pretty copious. I may come up with something else."

"Have you talked to the family?"

"Only Mabel, but that was before Kimo died; when it was a Gala and not a memorial. I hope to interview her again, along with her children, Roger and Abigail. I heard there was some estrangement between Kimo and the daughter. I haven't really been able to find out why, but now I'm thinking it's the college thing. Who wouldn't want his kid to be a successful doctor? Maybe that will come out in the interview. They've agreed to a group interview at the house."

Yoshi began clearing the table, placing dishes in the dishwasher and leftovers in the refrigerator. "You two go in the living room and chat while I do these up. It'll only take a minute." He shooed them from the kitchen into a large, comfortable room where an oversized plate glass window offered a panoramic view of Honolulu.

"After my stroke, we thought of moving, you know." Myra parked her chair between the fireplace and the window. "But I couldn't leave the house where I'd raised my children. At least the house is all one level, once you get up those horrible stairs!" She chuckled. "After I came home from the hospital, we knew there was no way to add a ramp or anything, so we arranged with our upper neighbor, Mr. Yanagida, for us to come and go through our back door, through his carport and out onto the street in front of his house! Mick, you know Mr. Yanagida has had the house above us on Aina Street, since, oh, about 1960 or so."

Mick nodded, having heard this before.

"I'll never forget that first weekend that Mr. Yanagida's children visited him, and saw us roll by his dining room windows! They must have figured we were either lost, or the world's oldest and worst burglars!" They laughed comfortably together.

Myra studied Mick. "I'm going to tell you something, because you're one of my favorite nephews and you're a good reporter, and will probably find it out anyway. Also, you're one of our best friends."

"I'm your only nephew, but do go on." Mick smiled and waited patiently, watching Myra and the view.

"I found something years ago in Yoshi's things. I didn't understand it at the time and forgot about it, but now, in light of what you've said, maybe it makes sense." She took a deep breath. "I found a newspaper clipping, just a blurb really, from December 8, 1941. It was about a young private with a gunshot wound from his own weapon, who was taken to Tripler. He told a wild story about defending the island from a Japanese spy in Red Hill. He killed the spy, he claimed, and that was how he got shot. Defending his country. There was to be an investigation and follow up. But if Yoshi had that second article, I never found it."

Mick completely focused on Myra now. "What do you think is the significance of this article?"

"I'm not sure. I'm beginning to think that private might have been Kimo Lemon. I don't have any proof, just a feeling. The story has a few pieces that correspond to what Yoshi's told me of his father's death. I don't know when he found it, or why Yoshi kept the article, but maybe that's why. He would have been only a boy when this article was written."

"Maybe his mother found it?"

"She didn't speak English, but his sister did."

Mick looked speculative. "It's a stretch, connecting Kimo Lemon with that private. The name of the private wasn't in the article?"

"No. I found that odd. The Japanese 'spy' wasn't named either."

"That gives me something to look for. It may be one

79

connection to the past that I can find."

Myra fiddled with her lap robe. Yoshi trotted into the living room and tucked the lap robe around her more tightly. "It's cold right here by the window, do you want me to add another log?"

"Yes, that'd be nice." Myra smiled as Yoshi wrestled with a log a hair bigger than the fireplace opening. "He does this all the time. You'd think he'd measure, but no."

Yoshi grunted as he worked the log. "It'll fit. Just give me, uh, a minute." He gave a tremendous heave and the wood slithered reluctantly into the gap.

"There. Told you." He dusted off his hands. "Who wants green tea?"

Myra and Mick both said, "Eewww."

Mick said, "What else have you got?"

Yoshi laughed. "Decaf Kona blend with Irish Cream flavored non-diary creamer."

"Sold," said Mick.

"Make it two," added Myra. Yoshi left and returned almost immediately with a tray holding a coffee carafe, two mugs, a full tea cup, sweetener and creamer.

"I knew nobody'd want green tea but me. I just like to ask."

Mick took the offered cup. "I've got to go after this. It's been great, but I've got to get to work early and start my homework."

Myra nodded and blew on her coffee. "Well, don't you stay away so long this time. Did Yoshi tell you part of our retirement plan was to stop rescuing kids? Nelson said he's moving out of the garage apartment, and Shelly is taking that Mainland training course in Computer Science. She says she'll come back after the six months, but who knows? We may get lucky and she'll take another!" Her eyes twinkled. "They are leaving soon, so make sure you stop by before they go." Yoshi and Myra only had one child,

80

Shuto, but wanted more, so they had 'rescued,' fostered and hosted a number of high school and college students over the years.

Mick put down the cup and stood up. "Will do, boss."

"Don't sass me!" Myra held up her arms again. "I really do miss you, you know. Come back soon."

"I will. I can't tell you how great it is to see you on your feet, so to speak. You're really coming back. Your therapy is finally paying off."

"And we intend to see that it stays that way," Yoshi said firmly. "I'll walk you out."

Mick gave Myra one last kiss on the cheek and followed Yoshi down the hall to the shoe rack.

"Thanks Yoshi, for the great dinner. Myra looks amazing."

"No, thank you. You always were the level-headed one in the family. You know, since your mother died, well, you're so much like her. It's almost like having my sister back." Yoshi sighed. "I can always rely on you to take care of things. Of me. I was really gonna lose it yesterday in the bar. It was just a shock. Now I see that it was for the best. Buddha works in mysterious ways." They hugged tightly.

"You take care, Uncle. And Auntie, too. I'll call you later in the week if I find out any more."

Mick carefully negotiated the steep, narrow stairway and wondered if Myra would ever leave her beloved home this way again.

Entering the icy VW, Mick saw that indeed, the nasty tree had shed many blobs onto the roof and bonnet. Mick reversed out of the parking place and headed down the steep road a little faster than was strictly safe.

Chapter 8

Honolulu Star-Bulletin **Wednesday, September 20, 1995**
OC&P Shores Up Sagging Local Crops
By Mick Kau'ula

   After the death of corporate head Kimo Lemon this week, mega company Lemon Enterprises is in executive transition. Business is as usual for the company, despite the all-time low of the local sugar cane and pineapple economy. However, OC&P is still managing to buy up smaller plantations and canneries, offering subsidy and assistance where possible. For small farms like Nakamura Pineapple, the downward trend in the market was a death knell. Nakamura Pineapple was one of several saved by OC&P's buyout. (See accompanying story on B-1, "The End of the Great Pineapple Wars?") Martin Nakamura, 76, has weathered many an agricultural storm. Literal storms, like hurricanes, ravaged his crops while competitors, both small and large, ravaged the market. Mr. Nakamura said, "It's just too bad the world doesn't eat as much pineapple anymore. Used to be we couldn't can it and ship it fast enough. There was smoke all over da island from all the canneries and sugar refineries. I remember one time the dockworkers went on strike, and everyone was panicking, how they going to ship da kine? (sic. *product*) Kimo Lemon offered to ship our pines with his. He had his own shipping line to the Mainland, and for just a little bit more den we coulda shipped before, we could ship wit' him. I mean, we couldn't let our stuff sit there. Cans, yeah, but the fresh? We'd lose so much money. I remember that, like was yesterday.

"You know, more and more land isn't used for crops. Look at Waipahu! It used to be sugar cane as far as the eye could see. The rumble of trucks on the cane haul roads was music to my ears. Now, look. They built that golf course and I knew my pineapples would be the next to go. The Ewa plain is ruined. They building so many townhouses now, where's all that water for all those people going to come from? In ten years, it's going to be *okole* to *okole* out there. Then what do we do? That land's goin' to be gone forever."

One of OC&P's aims is to preserve agricultural lands. Roger Lemon could not be reached for comment, but Gerald Breem, Senior Vice President of OC&P, said he sees no reason to change Kimo's goals. "They were solid and community-driven thirty years ago, and they still are today."

OC&P's buyout of Nakamura Pineapple, among others, preserves those lands for agricultural use, however not all are pleased by the potential monopoly.

Aloha Sugar would not agree to an interview, but released this statement yesterday though their publicity officer, Clayton Addison.

"These buyouts of Lemon's are a farce. He says he's helping the economy by absorbing the mom and pop type businesses. He's virtually eliminating competition. He gets them (the company owners) to agree by telling them he'll preserve their lands for agriculture. They don't get fair market value, or at least what they would if they sold to a developer. They think they're doing good for Hawaii, but I've seen the agreement. The deal's only valid for ten years. Most of these old timers will be dead in ten years, and that's what Lemon's counting on. It stinks. At least the developers aren't pulling any punches." *(The Star-Bulletin* was unable to confirm the contract agreement clause of ten years.)

Whatever the political and agricultural climate of the day, pineapple and sugar crops have been heavily impacted by OC&P.

An influential member of Hawai'i's community is gone, and we will all have to wait and see its effect on the economy.

*   *   *   *

By eight A.M., Roger was at work in his father's office. Yesterday's search had proved fruitful, but he was sure there was more. He just wasn't sure where to turn next.

He worked on company business until lunch, then decided to take a break from the office for a couple of hours. In the parking garage, he slid into the driver's seat of his father's silver BMW, parked as always in his private space. Roger had been driving it since his father's death. He had already checked the glove box and little places where he thought he could find some indication of hidden documents. He began to check again.

He studied the view of the cement wall in front of the reserved space as he contemplated the places he had already searched. He noticed something unusual: Two fire pull boxes on the same section of garage wall. He exited the car and approached the first box. He studied where it met the wall, the writing, the painting, all of it. He was hesitant to pull it. Didn't want the alarm to go off and send hordes of employees and fire department officials swarming through the building, into the garage, looking for a fire. He moved to the second box. Identical to the first, as far as he could tell.

"Maybe they're both real boxes," he said to himself as he stepped back and forth between the two. He tapped the first. Did it seem hollower? Did it sound different from the second? He wiggled them both. The first was definitely looser. He avoided the handle emblazoned with 'PULL,' and wiggled more firmly.

"Definitely loose. It'd be just like my father though, to have the fake one wired to set off an alarm. Here goes."

He yanked sideways and the cover came off in his hand. His force pulled the wires connected to the fire handle to their full extension. He gave the wires some slack. Tucked inside the box was a sheet of paper. He gently lifted it out and unfolded it one-handed. It sagged heavily from one corner. Nothing else was in the box, so he replaced the cover. Just to be sure, he checked the other box. Nothing. He returned to the driver's seat, turned on the interior light and found a key taped to the corner of the paper. The document was a rental agreement for a locker at the YMCA near downtown. His heartbeat quickened as he realized this might be what he'd been searching for. He started the engine, reversed out of the space and headed toward the Pali Highway.

*　　*　　*　　*

At the Lemon house, the phone rang and Betty answered.

"Hello, Lemon residence."

"It's Peg. Come and get me."

"Come and get you? Where are you?"

"I'm at the clinic. I don't want to stay here. I want to come to the guest house."

"I thought you had two more weeks?"

"Yes, but it's voluntary, and now I want out. Please?"

Betty fidgeted with the phone cord. "But don't you think it's better for you to stay there?"

"Please come and get me. I'm out at three today."

"All right. I'll be there."

Mabel looked up as Betty came to the lanai.

"That was Margaret. She wants me to pick her up at three today at the clinic. She says she wants to come here now."

Mabel put down the *Aloha* magazine she was reading and patted the seat next to her. "I thought she had two more weeks?"

Betty sat. "Yes," Betty said nervously, "but, she said she would rather be here. She can stay in the guest house, can't she?"

"Of course, dear. Are you all right?" Mabel looked closely at her friend.

"I think so. I'm just anxious about her coming here without finishing her treatment."

"Do you think she is violent?"

Betty shook her head. "Oh, no. Maybe she is aggressive from all those years living on the street. I guess you have to defend yourself down there."

They fell silent and watched the fluffy clouds scud past. Mabel finally spoke.

"You don't think there is any danger in having her here?"

"She would never hurt you!"

"I meant you. Do you think she would hurt you?"

Betty stood. "No. I think she wants to reconnect. Anyway, she's my daughter. She's asking for help, and I intend to give it if I can." She left the room without her customary bounce.

Mabel sat for a moment before coming to a decision. Mabel recalled a time early in their marriage when Kimo had kept a journal. He used to write at the dining room table each night before he went to bed. After they had become more successful, and he got an office to work from, she seldom saw him making entries.

86

She assumed he'd continued to write there. She asked him about it on two occasions she could recall. The first was shortly after they were in the Pearl Harbor house. She asked if he'd always kept a journal. He'd told her yes, and volunteered that it was mostly daily things he wrote; what they ate for supper, what he'd done at work, weather--things like that. Later when they moved into the Wahiawa house, she mentioned it again.

"Kimo, I haven't seen you write in your journal for a while, do you still?" She'd been standing with her back to him, rummaging for something deep within the refrigerator. The blow took her by surprise.

"What the hell do you know about my journal?" he bellowed at her from six inches away after pulling her out of the refrigerator by her hair. He pounded her in the small of her back and pushed her up to the sink, arching her backward over the faucet. "Well? What? Have you been reading it? You never could keep your nose out of my business, could you? I don't have to account to a woman for anything I do." He rattled her head, still holding her hair.

She trembled, trying not to throw up from fear and pain.

"I don't know. . .anything," she gasped. "I only asked because you used to write so often when we were first married, and I haven't seen you writing anymore. I just wondered." She closed her eyes, waiting for another blow. She found herself without support when he suddenly let go of her hair. Dizzy, she collapsed.

"Well, don't," he said and strode from the room.

Mabel pulled herself up using the cabinet handles and the edge of the sink. She waited, leaning on the counter, until she heard the garage door slam, an engine start, squeak as the door rose up, then down, then the roar of the retreating car. Tears of pain and humiliation streaked her face as she hobbled to their second floor room, and clicked on the heating pad she kept in the bottom drawer of her nightstand. She moaned as she lay back on the bed, waiting for the warmth to relax her bruised muscles.

"I can't live like this." She struggled to push off her shoes. "I hate him. I hate him. I hate him." With each declaration she pounded her fist on the bedclothes and vowed to find the journal.

Mabel hadn't found the journal then, or during the forty odd years since. But she hadn't really devoted much time to it. His reaction to her question told her that he was probably still writing in it. Old habits die hard and she doubted he'd changed much in. She had raised their two children, supervised the move to this house in Kahala, and run the household with the efficiency of a general. Now, in the wake of her husband's passing, she found renewed interest.

"There must be something important in there for him to hide it all these years."

As Mabel stood up, Betty came back in the room, looking uncertainly at Mabel.

"I'm sorry about, well, falling apart, I guess."

"No apology necessary. We'll do whatever needs doing. Now, do you want to help me?"

"What are you doing?"

"I was just sitting here recollecting old times, and I thought of something. Kimo had a journal. I saw him write in it a lot when we were first married, but then he got secretive. I'm sure he wrote in it every night. He kept it at home, I bet, and I want it!"

"How do you know there is a journal to find?"

"People don't change. And Kimo only changed on the outside."

At Betty's raised eyebrows, Mabel said, "Never mind. I'm sure he was still writing. I'm also sure it's not at work. It's not work related, exactly. Well, I don't know what's in it. But if he hid it well enough that I've never found it, he must have thought it was important, don't you think?"

Betty nodded. "Where do you want to start?"

"The office. But we have to be creative. I've looked in the desk already, and so has Roger. We have to be sneaky. Crafty. Like Kimo." The women giggled and shuffled down the hall to the small room Kimo used as his home office.

"Stop!" Mabel thrust her arm in front of Betty like a driver to a passenger.

"What?"

"I just didn't want you to go in the room yet. Let's look at it from here, first."

"Well, you don't have to scare me to death."

"I'm sorry, Betty." Mabel started to laugh. "I'm not being very widowly, or seemly, am I?"

"Laughter and tears are opposite sides of a coin, they say. Where shall we start?"

Mabel looked at the carpeting that had been peeled up around the periphery. There were no papers she hadn't gone through or that Roger hadn't taken. The few bits of furniture remaining looked bereft. The wall safe had been left open, as was the door to the small coat closet. The dark wood paneling looked dirty without the office trappings.

"It'd have to be some place he could get to easily. I remember it as a black notebook, smallish, with three rings and refillable paper. He filled up one notebook, would remove the paper and stash it some place and put new in. The note book isn't very big, but he'd need a box or something for forty years' worth of journals. He always wrote by hand."

"Did you really look through all these books?" Betty eyed the floor to ceiling bookshelves filled end to end with books of all shapes and sizes. "I don't really want to go through them."

"Oh, yes. Over the years, I've looked through everything

like that."

Mabel pulled out a small step-stool and moved it to one end of the rows. The shelves were mounted by ornate wrought-iron brackets. The wide black brackets were on the top of the shelf and mounted to the wall behind, not easily visible from floor level. There were eight shelves of varying heights. Mabel carefully climbed the stool and studied the uppermost bracket. She continued down the wall until she reached the lowest bracket. She turned to move the stool and saw Betty standing in the middle of the room.

Betty had folded her arms and was watching Mabel with a mixture of irritation and pride. "You know you shouldn't be climbing up ladders and poking about the rafters. What if you fall? Do you really think he hid it there?"

"I don't know. But it seems to be the only place possible, short of taking down all the paneling. I guess we could check the closet for a hidden compartment. Why don't you do that while I check the other brackets?"

"I am not taking off any paneling!"

Mabel laughed. "No, I meant look in the closet for a hidden panel or something."

"Well, Nancy Drew," Betty said as she moved to the closet doorway, "how am I supposed to see anything secret in there? That bulb wouldn't light up a shoe box."

"There's the flashlight in the kitchen. Go get it." Mabel waved imperiously and climbed up the stool again. Grumbling, Betty left and returned with a large flashlight. She entered the closet and flashed the beam to the uppermost corners of the shelf. Next she looked at the clothing rail, then the walls. Several chips and knotholes pocked the pine-lined closet, and the joinery seemed shoddy compared to the rest of the room.

"Hey," called Betty from inside the closet, "the

workmanship is terrible in here. Who did it? Roger, when he was ten?" Mabel appeared in the doorway. Betty knelt illuminating a corner constructed of mismatched panels and flawed pieces.

"No, Kimo did it himself. I remember he was quite proud of that project."

"Kimo was an excellent handyman," Betty said dryly. She sat back on her haunches. "Did you see it when he was done, or did he just tell you about it?"

"No, I never saw it. This room was Kimo's and if I was ever in here, or looked in the closet, it was so full of junk, I certainly wasn't admiring his panel job."

Betty smiled. "That might mean it looks like this on purpose. Any luck with your search?"

"I'm not finished. I just wanted to see what you were talking about." Mabel went back to the brackets and Betty continued to look at the flaws, searching for an opening. A few moments later, Mabel was back in the doorway. Betty crouched over a medium-sized knothole trying to see inside it.

"No luck? I may have found some kind of keyhole, if you can believe that." Betty wiggled around for a better view.

"I can believe it. How about a key to go with it?"

Betty turned to see Mabel dangling a small key from a ribbon between her thumb and forefinger. In her other hand was a well-worn black notebook about six by eight inches.

"Oh my god. Where was it?"

"In the bracket on the right, four from the bottom. I should have known Kimo would hide it right at his fingertips. He must have modified just that bracket, because none of the others opened, and that one opened just like a little door. This key was attached to the metal paper rings inside the notebook."

"Well, give it here!" Betty snatched the key and poked it into the hole she'd found. A click opened a large section of panel and revealed a small space behind the wall. Only one thing filled the hole. An office-type box with the cut out handles. Betty hauled it out into the main room. Mabel lifted the lid and saw it was filled with small sections of notebook paper. Each inch or so of paper was wrapped in a manila file folder cut to fit, secured with a rubber band. Mabel lifted out a section, read "1962- January to June." Mabel replaced it, tossed the journal with the black cover in on top of the other journals and closed the box. She looked at Betty still kneeling next to the box.

"And in the box is the beginning, the middle, and the end."

Chapter 9

Abigail returned from lunch and parked her car in its reserved spot. As she threaded her way to the Emergency entrance at Royal Hospital, she admired the beautiful landscaping. The variety of lush vegetation always impressed her. As she entered the Emergency Department, she passed a gorgeous Wiliwili, or Hawaiian coral tree, one of her favorite tropical plants, with its orange blossoms. She had once received a lei made from the seeds. This was a very old tree, dating back to the 30's, she thought fondly, perhaps earlier. Lining the hospital's familiar walls were brown and white photos of the early days; the royal family, the movers and shakers, and the buildings as they expanded to become the Royal Hospital of today. Outside the doors in those old pictures was a young version of this tree. Her mother also had loved this type of tree and had planted one years ago just outside the kitchen door of the Kahala house.

Abigail exited the doctors' lounge, and a nurse waved her over holding out the phone receiver. "It's a reporter from the paper on the phone. Says you're supposed to have an interview at your house later or something. Confirming?" She thrust the phone out again. Abigail sighed and took it.

"Hello?"

"Dr. Lemon? This is Mick Kau'ula from *The Honolulu Star-Bulletin.* I'm just confirming the family interview at your parents' house at four o'clock today. It's especially hard to reach you."

"Yes. Well, I'm working here 'til late. I won't be able to make the interview."

"I'd really like to talk to you. I was hoping for a family outlook, and I know this must be hard for you, but the public really wants to know."

"Well, the public is not privy to our grief. I have patients and other commitments. I do not wish to discuss my father."

"But you're a doctor. I was hoping for your ideas on his condition and his lack of care."

"My father's care and condition is not up for discussion. I need to go."

"Do you know about his condition?"

"If I did, that would fall under doctor-patient confidentiality, and still not up for discussion."

"You were treating your father? I thought he wasn't under the care of a physician when he died?"

"I have to go." Abigail hung up the phone and strode to the elevator. "Shit," she muttered and punched the button for the surgical floor.

"Well," Mick said. "That was an interesting fishing expedition. I think I just got a nibble." Since he was not able to get any information from either the M.E.'s office, or his government sources, he found it intriguing that he had more or less confirmed that Kimo Lemon had not been well. He doodled on his pad as he thought. He didn't have a ton of facts, but he had a lot of loose threads and speculation. By pulling on the Abigail thread, he learned something. *What if,* he wrote, *Kimo was not well due to some outside help? What if Kimo was perfectly fine until someone had enough of the memos? Why now? What changed?* The only thing he knew for sure was different was the gala for the 50th anniversary of the company. It was not to be an intimate affair. Press had been invited as well as celebrities and government heads and bigwigs of other major companies. Villas had been rented to accommodate all the famous guests as well as the Kahala Hilton and other deluxe properties. *Why would someone want to stop the gala?*

"Aaagh. Maybe it has nothing to do with the gala. Something else entirely. Blood diamonds. Coke trafficking. Golf course building." He threw down his pencil and stretched, frustrated. "Jesus. Way to stick to the facts, Ace." He knew absolutely nothing but guessed at quite a bit. Being a reporter for over 20 years, he sensed when he was onto something, or when something wasn't right. He felt that now, but like standing in the eye of the hurricane, he had no single direction to pursue.

* * * *

Roger pulled into the parking lot of the Pali YMCA. Mist that frequented the Pali area had turned into a light rain, cool and penetrating, washing the green mountains with rainbows. He dashed up the short flight of stairs to the covered patio offices, and decided "Youth Services" was not what he wanted. He went to "Membership Services." A young, heavyset local woman looked up from her papers.

"Can I help you?"

"Yes, I hope so." Roger's smile was its most charming. He began helplessly, "I have a locker here and it's been so long since

I've been here, I'm a little turned around. Could you tell me where the lockers are?" He fluttered his hands ineffectually and finally tucked them into his pants' pockets.

She eyed him with the look that said, *another helpless man. What can you do?* She folded her hands on her papers and began as if she were talking to a small boy.

"We have several areas with lockers. We have the residents' lockers. Were you a resident here?" Roger shook his head. At least that part was the truth. "Downstairs," she pointed to a stairway diagonally across the courtyard, "are the men's and women's locker rooms. I assume, you don't want the women's side?" Roger shook his head again. "I didn't think so. Just go down those stairs, and show them your membership card and they'll buzz you in."

"I, uh, don't have it anymore. It's been a really long time." Roger wondered why he hadn't found a membership card among his father's things.

"Okay. I'll take you down and explain." She moved gracefully from behind the counter and out a door to the courtyard. "Follow me."

"I really appreciate this, I just, um, you know. . ." Roger trailed off.

"Yes, I know." They went down the stairs and the buzzer sounded immediately.

"Hi, Hilton," the woman greeted the extremely muscular young man at the desk.

"Hi, Marilyn," he responded with a warm smile. He glanced at Roger. "What can I do for you?"

"Well, he," Marilyn pointed at Roger, "needs to get in his locker." Roger pulled out the locker key as supporting evidence, dangling it so the YMCA logo was visible.

"Okay." Hilton looked a little puzzled.

"He doesn't have his membership card with him, so I came

down to tell you it was okay. Okay?"

Hilton looked even more puzzled. "Okay." He waved Roger in the direction of the "Men's Locker Room" doorway. As Roger entered the locker room he heard Marilyn's voice.

"Thanks a lot, Hilton. You're a sweetie."

Roger looked at the key and saw nothing that appeared to correspond to the locker numbers. He was relieved to see, however, that not all of the lockers had locks on them. Roger started at one end and inserted the key into each lock. Since all the locks were basically the same, the key went into every lock, but wouldn't turn, giving him a few false jolts of excitement until he figured it out. About two-thirds of the way through, a large man entered the room.

"Hey, what chu doin' brah? Das my lockah!" The speaker was over six feet tall, hugely muscled, with the wiry hair and handsome, striking features of a Samoan.

Roger blanched. "I, uh, must have the wrong locker. Sorry."

"Yeah, I guess you do. Where's your lockah den?" The man put meaty fists on his hips.

Roger looked around. "Right here, uh, next to yours. That's why I must have made a mistake." Sweat trickled from Roger's hairline, down through his sideburns, and dripped onto his collar. The man didn't move. He watched as Roger fumbled desperately with the next lock. Roger had never been a religious man, but he prayed as the key slid into the lock. His mouth fell open as the key turned easily and the hasp opened.

"See, I told you." Roger smiled weakly.

"Kay, den." The man moved to his own locker, uncomfortably close to Roger. Roger waited as the man got out his towel and shower kit and moved slowly toward the bay of shower stalls.

Roger sighed and removed the lock. He opened the locker and saw a thick file folder, yellowed with age. He picked it up and read the tab. "Memos." He opened the file and indeed, the familiar font and paper greeted him. If they were anything like the other memos, he definitely didn't want to read them here. He double checked the now-empty locker, slammed it shut. He went back to Hilton at the desk.

"I'd like to return this key and lock now. I won't need the locker anymore."

Hilton took the lock and shut the hasp, put the key in the lock and put them both under the counter.

"Okay. Do you happen to have your rental agreement with you?"

"Why?"

"Because we void your copy and our copy, and then the account is closed, okay? Do you have it?"

"Yes. Here it is." Roger pulled out the yellow copy that had been in the file folder. Hilton checked the name and number and pulled out the Y's white copy.

"Okay, now, I'm going to void these. Oh, you don't get any refund, even though you're returning the key early, okay?"

"I understand," said Roger, resisting the almost compulsive urge to say 'okay.' He watched as Hilton laboriously wrote 'void' and the date and started to refile it. "Can I have those?"

Hilton looked at him oddly. "Okay, but it won't help if you want the locker back. You have to start all over again, okay?"

Roger laughed. "Okay!" He accepted the copies and jogged up the steps to the courtyard, waving jauntily to Marilyn as he passed. The rain had stopped and he went out of his way to step in puddles with his Italian leather shoes. Unlocking his car he saw a huge rainbow, extending from the mountains behind the Y toward Kahala.

"Definitely the pot of gold," he said smiling.

Chapter 10

Betty had just come out of the shower when Mabel knocked at her door.

"Betty, dear. It's almost three. Aren't you supposed to pick up Peg at three?"

Betty came to the door with damp hair and wearing a robe. "I know, I know. I was just so filthy after our search, I had to shower."

"Can I do anything to help?"

"Did Teresita get the guest house ready?"

"She said she did, but maybe I'll just go over and have a look."

"Thanks. I'll be leaving in a few minutes, so I'll see you when I get back. Wish me luck."

"Good luck?" Both women smiled and Betty closed her door. Mabel went out the kitchen door to the path that led to the guest house. The Wiliwili tree she planted years ago was huge now, and shaded the back door. Several clumps of elongated Wiliwili blossoms glowed orange-red.

"That wants a trimming," Mabel murmured as she ducked around a dangling limb. "In fact, this whole garden wants a trimming." Mabel saw that nearly all of the larger plants had overrun their allotted spots. The kitchen garden, too, with its rhubarb, eggplant, herbs and flowers was crowded and weedy. She wondered what the monthly gardeners did when they were there.

As she made her way down the path, the plumeria tree dropped a few of its fragrant blooms onto the shells.

"I wonder if I should make a lei for Margaret?" she mused as she reached the guesthouse, unlocked, as she assumed it would be. She stepped inside and immediately relaxed. This house had been decorated like an old-style plantation house, though it did have all the modern conveniences. Faded curtains at the windows, sepia photos of cane and pineapple fields of thirty years ago hung on white-washed walls. Young Kimo Lemon stood with his arms around his workers in many of the photos. His first processing plants, depicted in grainy shots, hung next to framed newspaper articles. Floor level wooden louvers let warm breezes swirl through the house.

"Hawaiian air-conditioning," Mabel said as she checked the beds--freshly made with a different Hawaiian quilt on each, and a second quilt accordioned at the foot.

Mabel walked over glossy hardwood floors to the kitchen. The distant sound of a wind chime wafted in through the open windows. She could see the garden and her beautiful Wiliwili tree from here.

The kitchen, one of her favorite rooms, although small, was efficient. Lots of cabinets, also white, hung on every wall, even above the stove and refrigerator. The cupboards still had their original pulls. She opened the refrigerator and freezer to find Teresita had stocked them well. As she headed back toward the front door, she stuck her head in the bathroom. All was gleaming, fresh towels on the counter; a vase of fragrant tuberose on the back of the commode. She pulled the front door closed and returned to the house as a car approached. Mabel hurried to the main kitchen and heard Roger.

"Hello, anybody home?"

Teresita was just coming down the stairs as Roger slammed the front door. "Jus' like a little kid, you. You gotta slam the doah ever' time, or what?" Teresita was fond of both Roger and Abigail, and usually treated them as if they were very small.

"Howzit, Terry," Roger greeted her. Then he saw his mother in the hallway and kissed her.

"Hi, Mother. How are you doing?"

"Pretty good. I was just out in the guest house. Betty's daughter Margaret is coming for a visit."

"Betty has a daughter?" Roger took her arm and guided her toward the lanai. "I must have missed something. Catch me up?"

"You're early. What are you doing here?"

"I wanted to see you before the interview. I found something I think you may be interested in."

"I have a surprise, too," Mabel muttered.

Roger said, "Well, Mother, what's with Betty?"

They sat in wicker chairs as Mabel briefed Roger on Margaret's visit. She omitted what Betty had told her about Margaret being Kimo's biological daughter.

"So, we'll have to see what happens, whether or not she really wants to get cleaned up," Mabel finished.

"Are you sure you want her staying in the house with you?"

"She won't be in the house; she'll be in the guest house. Betty feels she'll be fine, so I do too."

"Well, all right then. I have more news, and I wanted Abigail to hear it, but she has to work late and won't be here for the interview." At Mabel's inquiring look, Roger laughed.

102

"I'm not psychic. I called her before I left to confirm she would be here. I'll have to catch her up later. Anyway, what I found could have great importance to us and to the company." Mabel didn't respond.

"I found Dad's memos. The ones no one could find. At least some of them. Probably the first 20 or 30 years. I looked everywhere for them, but the most recent ones, or what I guess would be recent, I can't find. Not in the filing cabinet at his office. I'm sure he didn't stop writing them, and he must have kept them close at hand, but I don't know where to look. Safe deposit box?"

"We have one at Bank of Hawai'i, but I don't think the memos are there. I have access to that, too. Did you look in his office safe?"

"Yeah, it's not big enough to hold much, but I found a lot of cash and an interesting flyer about the company anniversary celebration."

"What's so interesting?"

"Did you know Dad was writing a book?"

"What book?"

"Apparently, a tell-all book based on his memos and his life. He doesn't come off too well in the memos I read. Why would he want to advertise that to the world?"

"I have no idea what you're talking about. He wrote a book? I never heard a thing."

Roger scooted over and hugged her. "It'll be alright, Mom. Really. We'll get through this. It's not published as far as I can tell; more of a manuscript, I suppose. From reading the flyer, I gathered he was going to read excerpts from it at the gala. Can you imagine that? All those people there, to celebrate the company, and he reveals that he is practically a criminal, black mailing people, I assume, all these years."

Mabel started to cry. "Oh, my God, it's so much worse than

I imagined."

"What did you imagine?" Roger pulled back. "And why would you imagine anything, anyway?"

Mabel looked at her son. Other than a few times when Roger was very small, Kimo had been careful to hide his physical abuse and keep it exclusive to Mabel. That had tapered off over the years as they both aged and Kimo spent more time away from home--also, as Mabel learned to avoid him and his triggers. Roger, it appeared, did not remember that part of his life. She was thankful for that. She diverted him.

Mabel blew her nose and straightened her spine. "I was talking about the secret safe behind the Herb Kane painting. Not the small safe in the corner."

"Secret safe?"

"No one's supposed to know about it. I came early to have lunch with him one day and saw him closing the Herb Kane painting behind his desk. It was on hinges, like a door. Later I checked what was behind it. It was a wall safe, but I don't have the combination. I never asked about it, and never let him know I was aware of it." Mabel recalled the results of her inquiry about Kimo's journal writing and had no desire to repeat that.

Roger's eyebrows had risen considerably. "Of course, another safe! He would want those memos close to him. He makes me think of a goblin with his gold. He likes to take it out and fondle it every once in a while." Roger blew out a breath, shifting gears. "He wrote some terrible things. I can see why people hated him. The last couple he wrote just before he died, a few days, I guess. I found those in the small office safe. He wrote one to Gerald Breem, and told him he'd always been a no-good schmuck, his work was substandard, and the only reason he was hired at all was Kimo felt sorry for him and for his useless father, who Dad bankrupted during the war. I gathered the father never recovered

104

financially. The other part of that one was a reminder to Breem that another employee, Onizuki, was coming up to retirement age, and if I can get it right," Roger shuffled through the memos from the Y in his briefcase, "here it is. 'Tell that crappy Jap he's out on his ass, and no loss to us.' He made a reference to an earlier memo to Onizuki, I guess telling him the same thing. I haven't found that one yet, but I haven't had time to read everything."

"Why didn't anybody sue?"

"You didn't sue back then. You were just happy to have a job. Besides, some of these memos, like the one to Onizuki, were not supposed to be revealed for many years, so a lot of people didn't know what was coming."

Mabel put her face in her hands. "I knew Kimo was, oh, prejudiced inside, but I had no idea the hate he held. I knew about those memos, but I thought the rumor about how awful they were was an exaggeration. Disgruntled employees griping. I had no idea they were so cruel. I really thought they were just interoffice business."

"I guess not." Roger held out a sheaf of papers, some yellowed and brittle, others newer and white. "Here, take a look. I can't believe someone didn't kill him long before now, if this is any indication of how he treated people."

"No one killed him. Don't talk that way, Roger."

"Mother, all I'm saying is, hell, I thought about killing him myself, just didn't see how to get away with it."

"Oh, Roger. You don't mean that." Mabel took his hand in hers. "Don't say things like that. Someone might hear you and think you're serious. What about now? Will people sue retroactively, or whatever you call it?"

"I don't know. I suppose they could. I'll try to do some damage control on that while I'm putting out other fires."

Mabel picked up the memos. "I suppose I'd better see what

these are all about."

"Let me handle it. I'll keep you informed. This could affect the company, if it gets out."

"Then we'd better make sure this doesn't get out." Mabel's eyes were wet, but her jaw was firm.

Sometime later, Mabel and Roger finished skimming the memos. Her eyes had still not dried, and she trembled.

"I can't believe I was married to that fiend. If I hadn't hated him before, I would now," she mumbled.

Roger sat up. "You hated him?"

"I shouldn't have said that." Mabel sighed and dried her eyes. "I hated him. I loved him. It's all mixed up. I needed him. I couldn't be without him, but now that I am, I'm getting used to the feeling, and it's not bad." She hugged her son. The sound of crunching shells heralded the arrival of Betty and Margaret.

The front door opened and Betty said, "Margaret, welcome. I hope you'll be comfortable. Let me show you the main house, and then I'll take you to the guest house, all right?"

Silence. Then footsteps toward the lanai. Betty called out, "Mabel? Are you here? Is that Roger's car?"

Mabel and Roger answered, "In here, the lanai." Roger slid the memos into his briefcase as Betty and another woman entered. The woman was dressed in clean, but obviously cast-off clothing. Much taller than her mother, Margaret's wisps of greying hair poked from under an aqua ski hat with an incongruous pom pom and framed her weathered face. Betty came to Mabel and Roger, but the other woman remained standing just inside the door.

"Mabel, Roger, this is my daughter, Margaret. Margaret, this is my dear friend Mabel and her son, Roger."

"Nice to meetcha," Margaret said staring over their heads.

"If you need anything, don't hesitate to ask," Mabel said.

"Thank you," Margaret mumbled.

"I'm sure you're tired. I'll take you to the guest house now." Betty said. Margaret followed her mother back down the hall and out of sight.

Roger turned to his mother. "Well, isn't she the party animal?"

Mabel nodded. "I can see why Betty's so worried about her. I hope they sent her home with some medication."

"Do you want me to stay for a while? I can." Roger started to snap the locks on his briefcase.

"Could you leave those? I'd like to look at them again. If you want to stay, you know you're welcome to. But I feel all right about things." Roger smiled. "Well, as all right as I can when I just found out I was married to a bigger monster than I thought."

Roger took out the memos again and put them on the coffee table. "I'm going to go relax until that reporter gets here, okay?"

"I'm going to lie down. Ask Teresita to call me when he arrives." She kissed her son's cheek. "Thank you for coming, Roger. And thank you for finding those papers." She picked up the memos. Together, they left the room, parting at the staircase.

In the guest house, Teresita had already placed Margaret's few belongings on the bed. Betty nervously showed her daughter the small house, and they stood at the kitchen window, looking toward Mabel's large tree outside the back door.

"Do you know how long I've waited for this?" Margaret asked.

"No. I don't know anything about you," Betty said carefully. "But I'll listen to whatever you want to say."

"Did you know Wiliwili is poisonous?"

"What?"

"About half the things in the garden are poisonous. Did you know that?"

"No. I, uh, didn't. How do you know?"

107

"Research. On my previous visits, I checked things out."

"Why would you research that? What does that have to do with anything?"

Margaret didn't answer.

"Will you tell me about your visits? Why didn't you ever see me? I've missed you so."

"I saw you, but I couldn't. It was for both of us that I stayed away."

"What do you mean?"

"There's so much I can't tell you, but you have to have known." Margaret sat on the bed and patted it. Betty sat.

"Known what?"

"Why on earth would you take a job from the man who raped you, fathered me, all those years ago?"

"Oh, my god." Betty stood and moved to the kitchen table. Margaret turned to watch. "That's not true. What would make you say that? How do you know?"

"How do you *not* know? Just look at him!"

"I looked at him every day. Granted, I never liked being in the same room with him, something I couldn't put my finger on, but. . . that's not the same man."

"Of course it is!"

"Kimo's face was disfigured. From the shrapnel injury during the war. It's not JC. I would know." Betty's eyes filled. "Wouldn't I? Wouldn't I remember a thing like that?"

Margaret's weathered face softened. "Mother, when something bad happens to us, sometimes the mind just re-frames it, so it can cope. I'm sorry, but Kimo Lemon is the man who raped you and is also biological my father."

"Are you sure?" Betty whispered. "How can you know a thing like that? How can you be positive? It was such a long time ago. A long time between—between what happened to me and my getting this job."

"I know, Mother. But I am sure, because of several things. On one of my visits to his office, I went through Kimo's wall safe. I found--,"

"You went through the wall safe? How did you get into it? How did you even get into his office?"

Margaret sighed. "I didn't always look like this. I can fit in. Anyway, I found a copy of my birth certificate, for one thing. I also found your work records at Tripler, and I found his patient record at Tripler."

"I, I went back to look for those, after he shipped out. After I found out I was pregnant with you. They were all gone. No one seemed to remember him. I was so afraid. I knew I'd never hear from him again, and I'd be raising a baby all alone."

"But you did hear from him again, didn't you Mother?"

Betty slumped at the table, emotions flitting across her face as she recalled those years.

"No."

"Yes, you did. What about this job? You don't think it was a coincidence, do you? Kimo always kept everyone close to him. That's where you keep your enemies, isn't it? Where you can keep an eye on them?"

"What do you mean enemies? All the people he had near him were family, friends, co-workers. . ." she trailed off as she recalled Mabel's story, the journals, the possibility of more deceit.

"Of course you were all enemies," Margaret said softly. "The great Kimo Lemon was a fraud and a coward. He built his empire on the backs of everyone he ever met. And to keep the truth from getting out, he tied those people to him with threads of their own weaknesses, frailties and lies."

"Oh, Margaret, that can't be right! How can you possibly know?"

"I know it, Mother. You know it too. When Daddy Tony died, I was so angry at him. I hated you for having me without a father and Tony for leaving—I know he died and couldn't help it, but I left." Margaret finally sat opposite her mother. "I was still a child then. I did a lot of wandering, and I began searching on my own. I didn't know what I was looking for at first, but I found out that nothing to do with Kimo Lemon is an accident. He probably orchestrated everything in his whole life, down to the day he died."

"I don't think the last part is true. Kimo never planned on dying. He left an awful lot of loose ends. He certainly didn't expect to die anytime soon."

"I can just bet. Tell me how you got this job."

"Well, I answered an ad in the paper."

"No, tell me exactly, *how you got this job*," she repeated firmly.

"Let's see. Tony had been dead only a little while, but I knew I had to work--to do something. I missed him so. The money from insurance and the restaurant sale wasn't much; wouldn't last forever. His medical bills ate up so much. The only thing I knew how to do was nurse. I started checking the ads in the paper, reading the boards at the hospital, you know, things like that. It's been so long. Is this really necessary?"

"Yes, it is." Margaret took her hand.

"Nothing on the job boards seemed right. But I put my name and phone number on a few, asking for work. I really didn't want to go back to hospital work. It's so grueling, but I didn't think I could get private nursing care. Those jobs are so precious. I was getting desperate. I read about Mabel's car accident in the paper. It's kind of funny; I found out later that it was a hit and run at the entrance to the driveway there. It shattered Mabel's leg. They didn't find the other driver." Betty sighed. "Anyway, the next day I saw an ad in the paper, and I just knew it was for Mabel. It seemed perfect for me."

"Yes. Kimo wrote it only for you."

"You don't know that."

"How many people did he interview?"

"I was the first, he said, and he liked me so well, he hired me."

"You were the only one he interviewed. He had watched you all those years. While Tony was alive, you were no threat. But when Tony died, who knew? You might connect things, come after his money, run down his reputation. So, he had to get you close to him."

"But Mabel's accident, I mean I might not even have answered that ad!"

"You had to Mother, you were out of options, and he knew it."

"I don't believe you."

"Kimo saved the ad."

"He saved the ad?"

"Would you like to see it?"

"You took those things out of his safe? I thought you said you just looked at them."

"I made copies. I didn't want Kimo to suspect anyone was onto him until I was ready."

"Ready for what?" When Margaret didn't answer, Mabel said, "Show me the ad." Margaret went to the bedroom and retrieved a large manila envelope. She sat again and laid out the items, one by one. Her birth certificate. Her mother's employment records. Kimo's patient record. The newspaper wedding photo of Tony and Betty, with little Margaret. The ad for Mabel's nursing care. A memo. Several other papers she shoved back into the envelope and sealed with the metal tab.

"The ad reads, 'wanted: skilled private nursing care. Long

111

term care may be necessary. Mandatory: Female. Live in. Military hospital experience. No private nursing care experience. No family ties. Generous salary and advantages for right applicant.'

"Oh, my. That's it all right."

"Why didn't he want previous private care experience?"

"He told me because other families have their own way of doing things, and he didn't want someone who had 'bad habits,' is how he put it. He would have to retrain them, I think. It didn't matter anyway; I didn't have private care experience then. Except for Tony. He told me that didn't count. What's this?" She picked up the memo and read.

"'Have just hired nurse for Mabel. I wanted that little tease from Tripler. Got her. Had a daughter, probably my kid, but nobody knows where she is right now. Start looking. Name's Margaret Elizabeth D'Angelo, but god knows what she's calling herself since she ran away from home. Lost track of her. The guy she calls daddy died. Big C. Hope I don't go that way. I've got the mother, now you find me that kid—hell, she's all grown up now. Even more reason to find her. I don't want trouble. And if I've got trouble, you got all kinds of trouble.'"

The memo was old, yellowed, and trembled in Betty's hand.

"Who is the memo to?"

"It doesn't say. That part ripped off. I assume some of his goons."

"That bastard. All those years. He knew! I didn't see it right under my own nose, and he's flaunting it at me! He was looking for you!"

"I know. He sent guys asking all around my old hang outs. I was scared. I knew wherever you went, he'd be there too. I didn't know why he wanted me. Maybe I'd have a little accident like Mabel? Maybe I wouldn't have just a broken leg?"

112

"That's why you stayed away? All those years? How could you think I'd put my job, even though I loved Mabel, over my own daughter?"

"I knew you wouldn't. But I also knew Kimo would never let you go. It would be too dangerous."

"Too dangerous?"

"For him. Kimo Lemon was poison, and I'm so glad he's dead. You're finally safe."

"You lived on the street, so I could live in luxury. I will never..." Betty couldn't finish. Margaret went around the table and hugged her mother. The first in over thirty years.

*   *   *   *

In the main house, the front doorbell rang, a rare occurrence. Teresita ushered the reporter, Mick Kau'ula, to the lanai. Roger was already there, pouring lemonade. Teresita went to rouse Mabel.

"Mick Kau'ula, *Honolulu Star-Bulletin*."

"Roger Lemon." They shook hands. "Have a seat. Would you like some fresh lemonade? Our tree's been particularly prolific this year."

"Yes, thanks. Beautiful view."

"We like it." Mabel entered. "Mother, this is Mick, from the paper." Mick stood and shook hands with Mabel. "Lemonade?" Mabel nodded. When everyone was seated, Mick began.

"I really appreciate your seeing me during your time of grief." Mabel and Roger exchanged a look. "I'll try to be brief. I've covered all the stories on Kimo and the company, and I've done the company history. What I'd like to do now is get a little family perspective for our readers. What's happening now, at home and in

113

the company—the plans for the gala—if it's going to be a life celebration. How things are affected by the loss, okay?" Nods. "Do you mind if I record this for accuracy? Thanks. Let's get started. Tell me about Kimo as a leader and a patriarch."

An hour later, Teresita ushered the reporter out, and Roger turned to his mother.

"Do you know anything about that 'ten year clause?' the reporter mentioned?"

"No. I know almost nothing about how your father ran his business. Do you know what it was about?"

"No. This is the first I've heard of it. What the hell is going on? Just when I think this company is making sense, something new comes up."

"What does the 'ten year clause' mean for us?" asked Mabel.

"It doesn't even have to be true, but it probably is. It could have a devastating impact if enough plantation owners, past and current, compare notes. We could be in for lawsuits our assets can't handle. It also opens up a whole new batch of enemies. I should have known. Every time that man did something that seemed good, it was just a layer of green over a rotting corpse."

Mabel looked shocked at Roger's analogy. However, she was no longer surprised by the things she was discovering or hearing. There were things Roger would never learn from her.

Roger left for the office, and Mabel sat on the lanai, waiting for Betty. Teresita rang the guest house to ask Betty and Margaret if they'd like to come to the main house for dinner.

When Betty arrived alone at five, Mabel asked, "Where's Margaret? I thought she was joining us?"

"No, she's tired, and we're both more than a little overwhelmed. I have a lot to tell you."

"Dinner will be in half an hour or so. Would you like some

tea before we eat?"

"I think I need something stronger than that. Want some wine?"

"Sure. There's a nice chardonnay, or I have that merlot."

"Either. Both." Betty poured and brought the glasses to the wicker lounge set. "Are you warm enough? The breeze is nice but getting a little chilly." She tucked a blanket around Mabel and got one for herself. She was about to add water to a flower vase when Mabel stopped her.

"All right, already! Sit down so we can talk. I'm dying to know how Margaret is."

Betty sat. "I have a lot to tell you."

Chapter 11

Honolulu Star-Bulletin **Thursday, September 21, 1995**
Where to Now, for Lemon's Legacies?
By Mick Kau'ula
    I interviewed the family of the late Kimo Lemon in their spacious Kahala home. The view was wonderful and the lemonade delicious on this side of the tracks. Although the family must be grieving, they graciously consented to this intrusion. Business continues at Lemon Enterprises, as I've covered previously, but what I wanted was the family's take on their patriarch. This is the transcript from that interview. (Daughter Dr. Abigail Lemon was not available at this time.)
SB: How has Kimo's death impacted you as a family?
Roger Lemon: We will miss him a great deal. It's a big hole in our lives.
Mabel Lemon: It seems my whole adult life I've lived with Kimo running things. Now I'm learning to do for myself.
SB: You still have your staff and children, don't you?
ML: Yes, but he affected me emotionally, and I'm having to adjust

to that.

SB: Of course. How are things here at home?

ML: He was a big man, with a big voice, and the house is suddenly so quiet. His favorite room, his office, for one thing, is so different with all the changes.

SB: What changes have you made? And to clarify, this would be his home office, correct?

ML: Yes, that's right. I haven't *made* any changes. It's just that things have changed. He left many business things here, and Roger's taken them all to the main office. I've had to go looking for accounts and things like that. Kimo took care of me. Of everything. It's been hard.

SB: Surely, you have accountants, a business manager?

ML: Kimo was a private man, and he handled much of our home business himself.

SB: Any surprises?

RL & ML: No.

RL: The business is fine; better than ever, so no worries there.

SB: Well, let's shift gears here a little. Roger, where do you see yourself in five years?

RL: Probably married to the company! (Laughter.)

SB: Well, that takes care of the personal end I was getting to next. But, seriously, do you see yourself running the company until you retire?

RL: Yes, of course.

SB: You're not married?

RL: No.

SB: Children?

RL: Not yet.

SB: Mrs. Lemon, who would inherit the company, if Roger has no children?

ML: I'm not prepared to discuss that.

SB: Do you plan to continue the outreach programs Kimo started? Lemon Tree and the community programs?

RL: We don't plan to make any changes immediately.

SB: Will there be any firings or employee changes?

RL: No. No job losses due to my father's death. We plan to offer bonuses to long term employees. Anyone is free to leave if he or she wishes, but all jobs will continue as always.

ML: Yes, bonuses. We will offer job security and thoroughly review each department and company, looking for. . .

RL: Ways to improve, upgrade, advance into the new century.

SB: Can you confirm the rumors about the memos Kimo used to write?

RL: What about them?

SB: So Kimo did send memos?

RL: Of course. Every company uses memos.

SB: These memos were supposed to be of a particularly degrading or shocking nature, beyond interoffice communication.

RL: I have no comment on that.

SB: Do you have a comment on the buy-outs of the small plantations by O'ahu Cane & Pine?

RL: We've been helping smaller business who would have gone under anyway. Sometimes we offer financial assistance, and in other cases, the owners are elderly with no one to run it for them, and they want out.

SB: What about the 'ten year clause?'

RL: What 'ten year clause?'

SB: Aloha Sugar claims OC&P buys up smaller companies with the promise the land will not be developed. They further claim the contracts have a hidden clause which stipulates the land protection only lasts ten years. Just long enough for the old-timers to die off.

RL: I have no comment on that either. I thought this interview was about our family life?

SB: Of course. What was it like growing up with Kimo Lemon as your father?

RL: He wasn't around much when I was young, and when I was a teen, I began an apprenticeship at the company.

SB: Did you always want to work for your father?

RL: Yes, I did. It's a wonderful opportunity and anyone would be lucky to have it.

SB: What about Abigail? Did she want to work for the company?

RL: No, she always wanted to be a doctor. It's great that she fulfilled her dream.

SB: Was Kimo supportive of Abigail's choice not to join the family business?

RL: Anyone who knows Abigail knows she does what she wants. You'd better ask her, though, about her career choice. I have my hands full with Lemon Enterprises right now.

SB: Mabel, I understand your long-time nurse and companion Betty is assisting you?

ML: Oh, yes, I couldn't do without Betty. I need to rest now, so I'll have to end the interview.

SB: Is there anything you'd like people to remember about your husband?

ML: Kimo's helped a lot of people, and I would hope that they'd remember all the good he's done.

SB: Just one more thing, Mrs. Lemon. Do you have any comment on the Medical Examiner's office's refusal to release your husband's body for burial?

ML: No, I don't. The governor has been very kind and I understand the problem's been cleared up and we'll have services soon.

SB: Of course. Thank you for your time, and again, I'm sorry for your loss.

The interview closed on that note. Kimo Lemon left some

big slippers to fill, some questions to answer, and the family seemed stunned at the sudden loss.

*　　*　　*　　*

Roger awoke with a plan. He called his sister and asked her to meet him at their parents' house.

Abigail arrived to find Roger pacing the drive. "Remember what I told you. We're here to find out if this Margaret person is legit and not some schemer to take advantage of Mother and Betty.

"Yes, you told me a hundred times already," Abigail said impatiently and crunched down the walk to the guest house.

Margaret answered their knock, silently ushering them in without an explanation from Roger or Abigail.

"Well?" Margaret sat with arms folded. Roger and Abigail also sat. Roger had already lost control of the interrogation before it began.

Abigail started. "We have some information and we wanted some clarification from you."

"Why should I say anything at all to you?"

Roger continued. "My mother told me you claim to be Betty's daughter from a previous relationship."

"Previous relationship?" A sardonic smile.

"Well, previous to your father, Tony."

"Tony is not involved in this, even slightly. He was a good man. Let's leave it at that."

"Uh. Okay. But are you, in fact, Betty's daughter?"

Margaret assessed them, tucked her feet under her on the sofa, and sighed. "Yes. I have some things to tell you too, and it might as well be sooner than later. It's all going to come out in the wash anyway. Doesn't matter to me how dirty the linen."

Roger and Abigail exchanged a glance at her matter-of-fact

tone, and lack of anticipated hysteria.

"Go on," said Abigail.

Another assessment. "All right, but remember you asked first. I am Betty's daughter from a 'previous relationship' as you so carefully put it. I am the product of a rape. Not only am I a guest in your father's home, but I am also his daughter."

"What!" from Roger.

"Oh, my god. I knew it," said Abigail.

"You *knew* it?" said both Margaret and Roger.

"Well, not *knew* knew, but I expected something like this."

"Jesus. Go on Margaret. Where's your proof, and what do you want?" Roger's tone was decidedly hostile.

"Our father raped my mother during the war. All's fair in love and war, right? My mother has an excellent memory of my conception. A young, naive nurse at Tripler, thought she was in love, duped by a slimy toad."

"Oh, sure, your mother was completely innocent, if what you say is true," Roger said.

"Roger," Abigail began, but was cut off.

"No, I want to hear all of it. Out with it."

"I told you that you might not like it," said Margaret.

"Yeah, whatever. Where's your proof?"

"I have hospital records, both patient and staff, and I have my birth certificate."

"Big deal. I have my birth certificate, too." Roger paced agitatedly.

"I found all these documents and more in your father's hidden office safe."

Roger scrambled for control. It might be true after all. His mother and he were the only ones to know about that safe, and he had just found out about it. "Oh, that's just great. A liar and a criminal."

Abigail shushed him with her hand. "I believe you. I don't know why, but I do. How did you get those documents?"

"I learned a lot living on the street. Things come in handy. I knew Tony wasn't my biological dad. When I was little it was okay, but as a teen, I couldn't handle it and ran away. I decided to research my roots. It took years. I didn't know about the rape until later. Kimo wrote memos about everything."

"You're saying he wrote a memo about the rape?" Abigail asked.

"I'm saying I have a copy of Kimo's memo about the rape. I also have copies of the other documents, and I'm willing to give you copies."

"I'd want to see the originals." Roger sat again, thinking furiously. If she'd only made copies, and the originals were still in the safe, he could find out. If he could get into the safe. And if he could get in before someone else did.

"I know. But I don't trust you yet." Margaret's expression was almost sympathetic.

"Yeah, well I don't trust you either. You just come here, fresh from a mental ward, claim you're what? Our step-sister? Half-sister? Christ. This is a bit much. If you blab to the papers, I'll sue."

"First off, it was a residential treatment clinic for drug abuse, not a mental ward. I can blab all I want since it's true. And yes, it does make us related. Not by choice, I might add."

"You got that right."

"Roger, give her a chance." Abigail turned to Margaret. "All right. Assuming what you say is true, and I'm not saying it is," a sharp look at Roger, "what *do* you want? Is this blackmail?"

"I want a blood test to prove his paternity."

"What? You're out of your mind!" Roger leaped to his feet.

"Why, Roger? Afraid it might prove something?"

Margaret mocked him. "Someone like me could be related to someone like you?"

"Yes," Abigail turned to Roger, "why wouldn't you want this? It would prove once and for all if Margaret is Dad's daughter. If it's true, all of this is not her fault. She does deserve something for what's happened."

"Oh, sure. Want to adopt her, too? Let her move in with you? She's already living here, and for who knows how long. Where has this gooshy side come from? I've certainly never seen it before."

"Roger, don't be an ass," Abigail said. "First off, it's only fair. Second, if it's true and we are open about it, it can't be used against us in the press and maybe we can work something out and she won't sue."

"Not now. Not with the company in transition."

"I'm still sitting right here," Margaret said.

He leaned over to whisper to Abigail. "Think of Mother! We thought we knew Dad, and we knew he did awful things. Now it looks like it's worse than we imagined! Have you read his company memos? No, of course not. He was a bastard. Every time I turn around I find another group, race, company, something or somebody he screwed. I just found out he was duping the pine and cane competition to get the land. I'm amazed he lived as long as he did!"

"He died of a heart attack, Roger, get a grip."

"So you say. I'm beginning to wonder."

Margaret interrupted. "Hey, it's rude to whisper."

"Yeah, well it's rude to. . ." Roger began.

"To what? Be illegitimate? Be homeless? Want better for myself?"

Abigail asked, "But why now? You've obviously known about this for a while, but why are you coming forward now?"

"Because Kimo was never dead before."

"What does that have to do with it?"

"When I ran away," Margaret took a deep breath, "Kimo had me tracked, hunted. I lived a secret life for years. Once in a while I'd think I was safe, and then up would pop some of his goons. I never knew for sure if he was out to kill me, hurt me, or what, but I knew he wasn't looking out for my welfare. I stayed away to protect my mom. As long as I was no threat to Kimo, if I didn't come forward and claim to be his daughter, an heir, my mother was safe. He trapped her, held her, just like he did all of you. I wasn't going to let that happen to me." Margaret's eyes filled. "Now he's dead. I want a piece of him. He raped my mother. He made me hide. God knows what else he's done, but I suspect I'm not the only one he's been slowly strangling over the years."

Abigail moved to the couch and took Margaret's hand. "I lost all respect for my father when he told me he would never pay for medical school for a woman, especially his daughter. I hated him then. All the things, subconscious from my childhood, came pouring out. I put myself through medical school and threatened to go public if he tried to stop me. He didn't help, but he didn't stop me after that. I didn't exist anymore for him. Maybe that hurt most of all."

Roger's face showed how little he had known of his sister's agony.

Abigail patted Margaret's hand and moved back to the chair. "So. Roger and I both will support your desire to have a DNA test. It might be tough though. Kimo hated doctors, and hadn't been to one in years. The medical examiner's office is supposed to release his body today, and technically, as next of kin, Mom, has to approve a sample. I don't think she will. But, I can pay the ME a little private visit, and I know a lab. . . DNA results can take months, though, I have to warn you. This won't be resolved definitively anytime soon."

"What do you hope to gain from this? I'm not giving up Lemon Enterprises no matter what," said Roger.

"Legitimacy. And an end of struggle. I want freedom." She held up her hand, palm out, stopping him mid-breath. "I don't know exactly, except to prove I exist. All the years of Kimo denying me that."

"How is Mom going to take this?" Abigail asked.

"I'm discovering sides to Mother I never knew existed," Roger said. "I have a feeling she knows. But I don't want publicity, and that's my final word."

Margaret smiled; a little of the earlier steel reemerged. "I've got news for you, *brother,* that's exactly what I want."

*   *   *   *

Mick walked downtown and headed for the county records building after already hitting both the *Honolulu Advertiser's* and *Star-Bulletin's* morgues, the newspapers' records' storage. Without too much trouble, Mick retrieved the article Myra had mentioned. Dated December 8, 1941, it contained disappointingly little information, just that a soldier had been found in the Tripler parking lot bleeding from a gunshot wound in the leg after claiming he shot a Japanese spy in Red Hill.

Following that, an interesting phone call had come this morning from a woman named Margaret D'Angelo, claiming to be the illegitimate daughter of Kimo Lemon. She had told an amazing, but believable story, given what Mick discovered about the county, no *state*, icon who was fast becoming an enigma. She had offered a number of records for verification of her story, after explaining she had found them in Kimo Lemon's safe, and they, therefore, could not be found in public record. At best, Mick knew information that old would be difficult to find, and many fruitless hours might be spent before discovering the records she claimed to have copies of, and access to, were indeed missing from the county. Absence of records might mean anything and nothing. Nonetheless, Mick was up to the challenge. A beautiful sky, warm breeze and clacking palm fronds added to the adventure.

After some fast talking, a press card, and one overburdened supervisor later, Mick glumly surveyed a dusty storage area crammed with ill-marked boxes.

"I'm sorry I can't help you look," the records clerk apologized, "but I just don't have time. Remember, you can't take anything out, but the copier is down the hall. Ten cents a copy, yeah?" She added the pidgin all-purpose "yeah" that ended almost any sentence.

"Thanks," Mick muttered, reading faded labels, pulling likely candidates from shelves and already wishing for a bottle of water. Or scotch. Whatever.

Honolulu Star-Bulletin **Thursday, September 21, 1995**
Family's Grieving Sours as Lemon's Body Finally Released
By Mick Kau'ula

The family of Kimo Lemon will finally be allowed to fully grieve when, later today, his body is scheduled for release to an unnamed mortuary. The battle over the community's lost icon fomented this week when the Medical Examiner's Office refused to release the body to the widow, Mrs. Mabel White Lemon. Only after threatening a law suit and the intervention of the Governor's office, did the M.E. release the remains.

Because of the family's no-publicity policy, and lack of comment from the M.E.'s office, speculation has risen regarding the delay in release. The M.E. still has no comment, but the Governor's office said it was simply a mix up in communication.

A source close to the family revealed an autopsy was hotly opposed, but the official word is that none was ever in question. The family's public outcry and the Governor's stepping in have been deemed a sign of privilege for the rich. The final services time and location remain undisclosed at press time.

*   *   *   *

Abigail pushed open the morgue door after being buzzed in. She headed to the body storage area. Although she was used to death and dying on a professional level, she had to steel herself for what she was about to do.

She had purposely chosen the lunch hour for her mission, in hopes that most of the staff would be gone. She lucked out. No one was in the autopsy room or refrigerators. She by-passed the large "file-cabinet" drawers television shows were so fond of, knowing they held homicide victims. She read the labels on the three walk-in refrigerators: Incoming, meaning she supposed, awaiting autopsy; Outgoing; and the third was unlabeled so she opened the door and stepped inside. The racks held trays, and on several trays were literally *remains.* One tray held a burn victim so charred it looked fake. Another tray held pieces that did not resemble human parts so much as cuts of meat. Old, rancid meat at that. She quickly backed out and closed the door and turned to "Outgoing." Opening the door she saw several uncovered bodies lying on metal trays. Two women and one man. The man was her father, but she barely recognized him. Death had shrunk him and weakened his hold on her. His waxen skin, half-closed eyes and limp limbs could in no way be mistaken for sleep. She took a deep and unexpectedly shaky breath and brought out the syringe from her pocket. She quickly drew blood. She also took hair and skin scrapings. She tried not to look at him, and to remember him as she

127

had hated him most of her life. Death was the great equalizer, and tears spilled over. She did something she never would have believed she could. She began to grieve.

Samples stowed safely in her pocket, she pushed open the refrigerator door, startling the lab tech returning from lunch.

"Hey, what are you doing in there?" He read her name tag. "Oh, sorry Dr. Lemon. Your dad, huh?"

She nodded weakly; now glad for her tears and that she'd kept on her official 'doctor' gear for her visit to the M.E.'s office. "I just wanted to say good-bye."

"That's okay. Here." He handed her a tissue.

"Please don't tell anyone I was here. My colleagues, well, you know how it would look." She continued to cry, not completely contrived.

He nodded sympathetically. "You got it, doc."

"Thanks." She stepped out of the morgue and into the sticky, slightly smelly air of the Iwilei industrial district. She breathed deeply, and tried to rein in her emotions as she unlocked her car and dropped into the driver's seat. It didn't work. She leaned her forehead on the steering wheel and wailed; wrenching sobs from her core for all she had lost, all she'd never had, and all she could never have with her father. Even in death, Kimo Lemon did not let go.

In the basement of county records, Mick was frustrated and no further enlightened. Hours of pawing through dusty, ill-marked boxes and files had yielded nothing. Of course, that could mean Margaret D'Angelo was right. It could also mean she was wrong. Mick was hungry, thirsty, tired and disgusted. A couple more boxes and then a well-deserved, extremely late lunch. Two more likely candidates on the highest dirtiest shelf. In the back. Of course. Mick crawled along the shelf just under the flickering fluorescent lights to reach his quarry. Pulling the boxes ungently to the floor, Mick opened the first. Rifled the contents and started to put the lid back when a file seemed to leap out. Opening *'Miscellaneous, '1942'*, Mick excitedly skimmed the documents and then pulled out a Birth Certificate for Margaret Elizabeth Miller, born to Elizabeth Lynn Miller, September 19, 1942. Father unknown. The surname was different, and that meant something, but he wasn't sure what. The rest of the information seemed correct. By misfiling it and with different names, as well as omitting the father, it seemed possible that someone was trying to hide this in a way that drew less attention than the absence of the document altogether might. Mick had to presume Kimo had provided for the possibility that someone would come searching during the past fifty years. Mick quickly checked the rest of that box and the next, finding nothing else relevant. Mick quickly fished out a dime and copied the birth certificate, replaced it, put the boxes just as they were, and fantasized about an extra-large plate-lunch.

*   *   *   *

In the executive office of Lemon Enterprises, Roger's appointment had just arrived.

"Come in Aaron, have a seat." Roger shook hands with the head of his corporate law department. "Thanks for coming up so quickly."

"No problem, Roger. What can I do for you?" Aaron Goldberg adjusted his palm tree tie against his navy silk shirt.

"I've been hearing a few things, Aaron, and I need some clarification from the legal department."

"If you'd have told me on the phone what this was about, I could have brought any relevant documents with me."

"I wanted to see you in person." They both knew that meant Roger wanted to gauge his reaction without any warning. Although Roger had been in charge less than a week, already his reputation as a no-nonsense, but unlike his father, honest, leader was emerging.

Aaron casually tried to cross his legs, but his enormous gut prevented it. "Yes, well, just what do you need to know?"

"It is my understanding that the contracts my father made with the various smaller sugar and pineapple companies contained a certain clause. Since you have been the company attorney before there were other attorneys to boss around, you would be the one my father would have come to." Roger waited. Aaron's only reaction was a weight shift to a different buttock.

"So, is it true? Is there a certain clause, called I believe, 'the ten-year clause'?"

"I'd have to go back in the records. I can't remember the details of every contract. . ."

"Cut the crap. Do you or do you not have knowledge of this clause? Before you answer, consider this. If you did it at my father's request, that's one thing, but if you lie about it now, and I find out, you will find yourself looking for work. Now. Answer the question."

Aaron Goldberg's sweat beaded his forehead like a headband. A fleshy pink tongue wet his chapped lips. "Yes. I did arrange those contracts at your father's request."

"That's what I thought. How can we fix it? I want damage control. The paper's already printed it and blind-sided me once. It's not going to happen again. The farms that my father absorbed that have remained fallow are to be made into a conservancy. The 'ten-year-clause' crap is going to be made out as a misinterpretation and a mistake to be corrected. The only way to save ourselves from millions in lawsuits is to go ahead and preserve those lands."

"But that's millions we could be making in profits for land deals to developers!"

"I'm sure my father realized these farmers might have heirs. Heirs who would quite possibly rebel at the outcome of these buyouts. However, since he's not here, and I've found no indication how he would have handled it, this is what we're going to do. Get the word out to legal and make a new set of papers, for *each* farmer he bought out using the 'ten-year-clause' deal. Plantations purchased without it, the deals can stand as is. But go over those contracts as well. No loopholes. When this hits the fan, I want it already to be taken care of. No back-pedaling. Got it?"

Aaron Gold looked exceedingly unhappy, but was too smart and too old to go looking for another job. "Got it. I'll get right on it." He left the room, his short legs moving too fast to be graceful. More of a quick waddle. Roger smiled briefly at the penguin image that rose to mind.

Roger ran a hand through his hair, truly feeling as though he had dodged a bullet. How many more surprises were there going to be?

Chapter 12

Mick entered Royal Hospital through the doctor's parking lot near the Emergency Entrance. He threw his press pass on the dash and snagged a doctor's spot, albeit one far from the doors. At least it wasn't a named spot, so maybe he'd get away without a ticket or a tow. HPD could be generous to the press, but he wasn't so sure about the hospital. He'd already called ahead to make sure Abigail was working, and he'd not identified himself, but had opted for an ambush to get his interview. She could continue to duck him, but his message said basically that he'd pull a story together from what he'd heard and discovered if she didn't cooperate.

The rush of cool air after the downtown humidity felt like someone poured iced tea down his back--so good it was almost painful. He allowed himself to slow down now, out of the heat, and found the elevator to the floor where she worked.

Facing the elevator was the nurses' station and like spider legs, several halls branched from there; to patient rooms, he presumed. No one would escape the nurses' sharp eyes here, like they did in movies. Well, not to the elevators, at any rate.

He approached the nurses' station and quickly concocted a lie for the nurse who was seated writing chart notes, slightly turned away. As she swiveled to greet him, he noted a patient name on a chart still open on the desk.

"Can I help you?" she asked.

"Yes, I'm here to meet with Dr. Lemon? I'm Irma Antonio's nephew."

"Oh, yes. We were just talking about her. She's doing really well. Let me page her." As she picked up the phone, she added, "I didn't know Irma had a nephew. I'm glad someone's here for her. Her husband only came once, poor soul, and he's so old and frail. . ."

Mick smiled weakly. He hoped his lie didn't get him into trouble. Or Irma for that matter. His lies usually *did* get him into trouble of varying degrees. Lying is part of the job, he thought, but he really didn't want to hurt some little old lady. *Maybe she was senile and would really think he was her nephew when this nurse inevitably told her about him. Crap.*

As he envisioned some karmic punishment, a figure in a white coat swept into view. He recognized Abigail Lemon from a few stock photos the paper had. She really looked like Mabel must have in her youth. Mabel would have been a looker, like her daughter. Glossy dark hair pulled into a slightly messy but professional bun, no make-up, but maybe some lip gloss? He couldn't tell for sure and now she was on him. Naturally black lashes framed brown eyes, the same shade as her hair. They narrowed as she got closer and he figured the jig was up. He walked to meet her, not wanting a dressing down in front of the nurses' station.

"Dr. Lemon," he whispered. He told himself it was out of consideration for the patients, but he was suddenly a little nervous.

133

What was going on? He was never nervous. She was as tall as he and looked very strong and more than a little angry.

"You're that reporter. I told you I didn't want to discuss my family."

He dragged up a little bravado. "I remember, but I'm going to write something, and the paper is going to print something, so don't you want a say in that?"

They had a bit of a stare down. "Fine. Come into the lounge. It's early enough so we should have some privacy." She turned, led him to an unmarked door, and pushed into a light, airy room with windows that faced downtown, swaying palms and blue skies. No one else was there. She sat in a single chair and indicated he should sit. She folded her arms across her chest and crossed her legs. *Classic defense posture*, he noted. *Or she's really mad.*

"Well?" she asked after a moment. "Let's get this over with. I have patients."

Mick stalled by taking out his tape recorder. "So I don't make any mistakes," he said.

"Right. We'll see about that."

"I've gotten a lot of perspective from employees and from your mom and brother and I wanted your input. Frankly, I have conflicting information and was hoping you could clarify."

She was a no BS lady, so he hoped she'd appreciate the direct approach.

"What conflicting information?"

"I've been a reporter for over twenty years and all I ever read or heard about Lemon companies was how great they were. I know companies aren't perfect, and neither are people, but now that your father's dead, it seems like some of the dirty linen is coming out."

"What on earth are you talking about?"

Maybe he wouldn't get anywhere with the direct approach.

134

After all, it was her family.

"Kimo wrote all these memos to employees. Mad memos, they called them, because he was angry when he wrote them, or it seemed that way and also because it usually made the recipient mad, too. Any comment?"

Her face paled. "No. I don't work for my father, or his company. In fact, I have nothing to do with his company. Why would I know about internal company business?"

"Well, it's the family business, isn't it?"

"I never worked for him or any of his subsidiaries."

"Why not?"

"I wanted to be a doctor. Period."

"Period? Didn't you have to earn money to get through medical school? Didn't you work for the family at all?"

"No. I wanted to make my own way. I didn't want to work for my father."

Now we're getting somewhere. "Why not? Didn't Lemon Tree put people through college? Didn't Roger intern there?"

"Roger wanted to work for the company. I didn't."

"Your father put a lot of people through college. Why not you?"

"I didn't want that." He noticed she looked exhausted, and sitting in the recliner-type chair, she had begun to relax.

He spoke cautiously, like he was trying not to spook a horse. "I heard he wouldn't put women through college if they chose what he deemed unsuitable careers."

She looked down at her hands, clasped in her lap. She exhaled and seemed to give in to some inner battle. "He told me once that if I continued on this ridiculous course, not only would he not help me, but he would do everything he could to stop me."

The reporter in Mick was jubilant, but the man wondered how Kimo could do that to his own daughter. His thoughts flashed

135

to Yoshi and Myra, taking in complete strangers, nurturing them as their own, helping them with college. What happened to Kimo Lemon to break him of everything that was human and compassionate?

"I'm sorry to hear that. But you did it. I don't know you, but I'm getting to know Kimo Lemon, and that is quite an accomplishment. And from the medical write ups, you aren't just any doctor; you are a star in your field."

"I guess I do have my father to thank for that." She half smiled.

He cocked his head. "How so?"

"Genetically, in part. I am every bit as stubborn as he is. And also, because once I realized I would get no help from him, just roadblocks, I was determined to be successful and publicly successful. I do care about my patients. They are my priority, of course, but their healing and care adds to my stock of armor against my father. I never knew what he would do next and I always wanted to be ready." She looked directly at Mick and he felt like he was being x-rayed.

He cleared his throat, feeling hot again, like he was outside in the downtown heat, not sitting in a comfy air conditioned lounge. "That's pretty much the story I heard from someone else. Not about you, though. It is just so different from what we've all thought all these years." He mumbled the last part, but she heard him.

"That's what everyone thought. My father was an amazing showman. A lot of flash but you never knew what the left hand was doing while you were busy keeping track of the right." She seemed to realize she was talking to a reporter and re-gathered herself. "I know you're going to print what you're going to print, and a juicy 'not what we all thought' story has more reader appeal than a 'gee what a great guy' story, but he also did a lot of good."

"You believe that?"

"Can I say something and not have it in the paper? Can I have something off the record, I guess is the phrase?"

Mick would have agreed not to print pretty much anything except her confession to her father's murder while he was mesmerized by her dark eyes.

"Sure. Go ahead. Unless it's your confession," he tried the lame joke.

"No, it's not my confession. I know it's your job to ferret out information the public 'needs to know' but I want to tell you something. You, not the paper, not the public, okay?"

"Sure," he repeated, his throat now completely dry. What was happening to him?

"Life with my father was not pleasant, most of the time. He learned early on to be a chameleon and this super public figure. I still have some pretty bad memories from when I was little. It got better as I got older. We had more money. Dad was gone most of the time, making it, I suppose. He also was smart enough to realize that as we got older, my brother and I, we might just talk, so he gave us less ammo. Less to talk about. I was never happy or comfortable in that house when my dad was in it. My mom protected us and as an adult, I see now how much she protected us, and what that must have cost her. I love my mother dearly, she's my best friend in some ways, but I always thought she was sort of a wimp, you know? Why stay with a man like that? Now that he's dead, I see how strong she was. Is. And she is also responsible for my becoming a doctor. We had a conversation once, before I moved out on my own. She helped me out financially, by the way. My dad never knew. She had her own money and we agreed not to tell him. So, I didn't really do this all on my own, but we both thought it best not to let that out *ever*." She sighed and seemed lost in her memories.

"What was the conversation you mentioned?"

Abigail re-focused on him and he felt weak. He saw the tendrils escaping from her bun and imagined it all loose and falling around her shoulders. What was *wrong* with him? *Don't forget, she's Kimo's daughter, and just as capable of deceit as he was.* That admonishment didn't help. Something chemical was happening. He needed to finish and get out of there.

"One day after a particularly bloody argument with my father about college," she saw his face and added, "not literally bloody. I don't remember him ever hitting me, but I always thought he could. That he might. Anyway, after he'd told me I should be a secretary or something, okay, he'd conceded, maybe a nurse, and if I wanted a man's job he sure as hell wasn't going to be a part of it, and he would cut me off financially, and on and on in that vein, I totally blew up. I wasn't really shy as a kid. I mean, I'd say what was on my mind, but not like this. I went crazy yelling at him. Who was he to determine someone else's life? Who did he think he was, God? You know, on like that until I was just exhausted. Our screaming match had my mother running into the front room to break it up. I don't know what she thought she would see or how she thought she was going to do it, maybe get the hose and squirt us like fighting dogs?" Abigail chuckled, actually enjoying this recollection. "You've seen her. She's not very big.

"My dad just shook his head and walked out of the room. That was one of the last conversations I ever had with him. But then my mom took me aside. We went upstairs to my room and without even discussing it, she helped me pack. She told me she would always be on my side. That's exactly how she put it. My side. And that she had money and would support me through medical school, with an apartment, through astronaut school if that was what I wanted. She actually said astronaut school and it made me laugh, just like she knew it would. That made all the difference in the world. Having her on my side. I don't think he ever found out about that. I worked at Anna Banana's restaurant so I'd have an income if he ever checked. I got loans and grants and she helped me quietly pay them back."

Her eyes locked on Mick's. "That is the real reason I don't want the Kimo Lemon life story to come out. It would change not only his image, which I could give a shit about, but it would change hers and I couldn't bear that. She risked everything to help me and I won't repay her by having it up for debate."

She leaned forward and he got the faintest whiff of her Halston perfume, combined with her own scent. Heady. "So, off the record, right?" When he didn't say anything, she added, "Please?"

"Yes. I'll stick to the agreement. Nothing about your career as it relates to your mother."

She rose. He gathered his recorder, which he had already turned off, his bag of reporter crap, and also stood.

At the same time she said, "Thank you for being so understanding," and he said, "Will you have a drink with me?"

They each processed the other's words.

"You're welcome."

"Yes."

He left the hospital after agreeing to call her soon. The oppressive heat smacked him in the head as he pushed out the glass doors and into the parking lot. He barely felt it. No ticket and his car had not been towed. He would have a date and was euphoric for no discernible reason. He had not had a date in years. Well, not one that had gone well at all. He unlocked his car and slid inside. It was a thousand degrees. Mick didn't care.

*   *   *   *

Roger had been waiting for an opportunity to get into the secret safe behind the large Herb Kane painting. It was odd how he never suspected a second safe in the same room. All those years and he just *assumed*, like everyone else probably did, that the visible safe was the only safe. He knew his father had been a cautious man, always locking his office, even during the day if he was gone for more than a few minutes. It had a private restroom and he had a cleaning crew come in only while he was present.

Roger pulled at the edge of the picture frame and nothing happened. It was firmly attached. He tried the other three sides and the same thing. Stuck. "You can't make anything easy, can you?" he said. Some kind of catch. A release. He studied the frame and ran his fingers around it. All smooth. He tried pulling once again, just to be sure it wasn't some sort of extra strong magnet. Nope. He slapped at the frame in frustration and the whole right side separated from the mitered corners and a muted click was his reward as the frame released from its position.

The large hinged painting swung out easily and exposed the safe. Embedded in the face was a four wheel combination lock. He knew his father would spin the dials to relock it after any opening, but nevertheless, he had to try. He pulled the handle, but of course, it was firmly shut. He spun the dials. They were deceptively large, hidden as they were inside the door. The numbers ranged from zero to ninety-nine. Great. Times four. It was not a computerized safe so even if he had access to a computer, it would do no good. It was an old-fashioned Fort Knox. Once again, he had no idea of the combination. His father would never write down any codes, combinations, or passwords. It was always something that had meaning to him and that he would not, could not forget. That security measure juxtaposed with his predilection for journal and memo writing puzzled Roger. "I guess he felt safe with it locked up if he never wrote down the passwords or codes anywhere. What a guy." He was back to the beginning with trying all known birthdays, anniversaries, and holidays. He even tried the Kahala address and the address of the business. No soap. He flung himself into the office chair and swiveled idly as he thought.

Roger glanced about the room once again. On one wall just above the small corner safe, hung a well-known, framed black and white photo of Pearl Harbor on the day of the attack, plumes of smoke rising from the ships that had been damaged or destroyed. Roger mentally sifted through the information about his father, and what had changed. It seemed that Kimo's career really had started because of the war. His buddies, the loans and repayments... the beginnings of OC&P. He dialed 12-7-19-41. The safe opened. Roger was so surprised that it actually worked that he just stood there a moment. He pulled open the door and saw a stack of documents. He quickly pulled them out and flipped through them. He did *not* find a manuscript or anything that looked like a book. A birth certificate for Margaret with a hand written note in Kimo's distinctive scrawl clipped to it: "Original document." The father was only listed as "Jaycee." *Maybe James Carter Lemon,* thought Roger.

Another document of an employment record for Elizabeth Lynn Miller, a nurse at Tripler during the war. Who was that? He flipped back through the papers and saw that the nurse was also listed on Margaret's birth certificate as her mother. Okay. Then he found his dad's hospital records from Tripler. Before the devastating facial injury that got him out of the war, he had also been treated for a gunshot wound to the leg which occurred on December 7, 1941. Roger had not known of his father's first wound. He was surprised his father went back to active duty. Maybe they didn't give you a choice back then. If you got shot but could still serve, you went back. Roger didn't know.

Also in the pile were more memos. Current memos and

141

going back a few years. Typical of previous memos, they included the 'ten year clause' issue as well as a memo to Gerald Breem. He jaw dropped as the memo regaled poor Gerald with a tale of Kimo's winning poker dealings, begun during the war, which sent Gerald's father into depression, poverty and finally death. The memo detailed how and when, and also the implication that Gerald's father was weak and stupid and not a real man to let a habit ruin his life. *However,* Roger thought, *Kimo was not man enough to help a buddy out, or not to take advantage of a situation that got him a dollar, no matter how unsavory.* He made a mental note to check on Gerald and see how he was doing financially. Perhaps Gerald's mother could use some help. It wouldn't bring back Gerald's father, but Roger felt he had to make amends however he could.

Roger felt he needed a shower to wash off some of the mental dirt. It wouldn't really help, and it was not a pleasant feeling. He rechecked the memos to see if he'd missed anything he needed to take care of right away. He would check with employee records for most of them. He was a little embarrassed that he knew so few so little about the employees. Lemon Enterprises was huge, but people he worked with in this office he wanted to know. In fact, he wanted to know a lot more. He promised himself to fix that.

Nothing else was in the safe. He returned everything and locked it.

Chapter 13

Betty stood in the doorway of the atrium. "Mabel dear, are you all right?"

Mabel had just hung up the phone. "They're releasing Kimo's body today. I think I'm all right."

Betty hurried to comfort Mabel. She hugged her and patted her hand. "Well, that's good news, isn't it?"

Mabel nodded slowly. "Yes. It is. I guess we should plan something?"

Betty nodded, too. "Did you two ever talk about 'arrangements' or last wishes, or anything like that?"

"Kimo thought he was never going to die, remember? So, not for him. But when I had my car accident, we talked about me. Ironic, isn't it?" She gave Betty a wan smile.

"Well, we'd better do something. Do you want to call the children? Do you want me to?"

Mabel shook her head. "No, we should get the ball rolling, I suppose. Roger will have to take care of things at the company end. I should call Reginald Protheroe, our family attorney. If Kimo made any arrangements, it would have been through him, but I doubt it."

"Should I call him for you?"

"Thank you, dear. I have to do it. Next of kin and all. Can you get the number for me, though? It's in the address book in my nightstand. Then maybe a cup of tea and we'll plan based on what Reginald tells me."

"Of course."

Betty returned with the address book and left Mabel to her phone call.

Mabel dialed. "Mabel Lemon for Reginald Protheroe, please," she told the girl who answered. While she waited to be connected she smiled to herself. What good was being the wife of an important man if you can't throw it around a little? Almost immediately Reginald picked up.

"Mabel. My condolences."

"Thank you, Reginald. I'm calling about a couple things. Did Kimo leave instructions for his funeral arrangements with you? I don't have any, or at least I haven't found any."

"He did not want to discuss that. I kept after him, but you know how he could be. He only left his will and trust about his assets. But his body, either he was never going to die, or he just didn't care. Couldn't get a word in edgewise about it. I'm sorry."

"No, that's fine, thank you. What about the reading of the will and trust? The children need to know. Well, I do, too."

"We don't really do the family gathering in the library anymore, but we can meet in my office if you like. You know I only handled yours and his personal estates. The corporation is a different kettle of fish and I'm not a corporate attorney."

"Yes, I'm aware of that. Roger is running Lemon Enterprises now and I'm sure he has been in touch with the Board and the attorneys. I suppose I should follow up, but I just haven't had the energy."

"Oh, Mabel, I'm so sorry. We can do the reading next week, whenever it suits you, all right? Just call me to set it up. I have to notify all the heirs and a couple of them I'm not sure who or where they are."

Mabel was surprised by that. Even if Kimo left money to universities or charities, surely Reginald would know how to contact them. Who would Kimo leave money to besides family?

"I appreciate that, Reginald. I'm sure Roger and Abigail can find time for this. Shall we say Monday at 10 AM in your office?"

"Tentatively, yes. If I can contact everyone. Sometimes people are out of state and just want to be informed, so having everyone physically present isn't necessary."

"Fine. Thank you." Mabel hung up. Betty must have been hovering because she brought in a tray with a pot of tea and some cookies she'd made earlier.

"How did that go?" Betty asked as she set the tea tray down.

"The reading is Monday in his office at 10, provided he can reach all the heirs."

"What about funeral arrangements?"

"Nothing there. So, it's up to us. You will help me, won't you, Betty?"

"We've come this far together. Of course I will. Now, one cookie or two to start?"

"I think two. We've got to keep our strength up, after all."

The two women silently shared a few moments as they sipped their tea and ate. The day was clear and the view spectacular. The short yard and garden sloped gently down to the lava rocks that made a rocky cliff leading to a small beach. Not terribly high, but enough to discourage lookee loos and curious tourists. As with most of the homes in this area, there was beach access from the house and Mabel fondly remembered she and the children scrambling down with beach things and picnics several times a week when they were still young enough to do things together. Together without Kimo, of course.

Betty had opened the glass doors so the view was unobstructed and a warm breeze blew in a light perfume of brine and plumeria blossoms. Plumeria was one of Mabel's favorite flowers and scents and she had the garden filled with them over the years. Not directly in front of the windows of course, that would obstruct the view. Fronting the atrium, the yard contained the short, tough Hawai'ian grass and was planted only with a low-growing border hedge of naupaka.

"Well, should we start?" Mabel asked.

"I suppose." Betty sighed. "I know this is hard. What mortuary do you want to get Kimo's body? I mean, who should I call to pick him up?" Betty's eyes were warm and comforting.

"I am going to Hawai'i Memorial Park, so I suppose Kimo can go, too."

"What?" Betty seemed surprised. "You already made your plans?"

"Of course. Kimo may have been the businessman, but I am quite practical." Mabel smiled.

"Yes, you are. Quite." Betty took the phone book from the drawer under the phone stand and looked up the number. "Here, I'll dial for you and you tell them what you want. I'll sit right here and take notes and be supportive. While I have another cookie. This was a good batch."

"Yes, it was." Mabel knew her friend was trying to cheer her up. She didn't think this would be so difficult. She thought she was prepared for this day. Neither of them was young, but somehow, the details of it were harder than she'd imagined.

Her face must have shown some of what she felt because Betty said, "Afterward, when we have all the information, I'll call the Medical Examiner's Office and tell them what you want. You stay with me though, in case you have to verify anything, okay?" Betty gently squeezed Mabel's hand and dialed Hawai'i Memorial Park. She carefully watched Mabel's face as she answered questions and repeated information so Betty could write it down. Mabel seemed to shrink in her chair and her voice grew quieter and quieter, but eventually, all the questions had been answered.

"I'm so tired, Betty."

"I know. Let me just call and pass on what you said, all right? Then I'll help you lie down. This will only take a moment and it will be done." Betty called the M.E.'s office and passed on what she had written. She told them to expect Hawai'i Memorial Park to call and arrange a pick up. Toward the end they did ask to speak to Mabel for verification, but they seemed very kind and were brief when Betty handed over the receiver. Mabel passed it back and Betty heard the dial tone, so she hung up.

Without any further words, she helped Mabel to her room and to lie down. Mabel seemed a little deflated. She had lost her bounce and energy. Betty quietly closed the door and went to clear the tea things.

*   *   *   *

When Mabel arose an hour later, she felt better. She had not expected to feel anything but relief when she made funeral arrangements for Kimo. After years of abuse and neglect, she thought she would maybe even feel happy. Strange. She and Betty had told Hawai'i Memorial Park to cremate him and put the ashes in a koa wood urn. He loved koa. Why did she care what he loved when he so clearly did not care what she loved? And why now,

147

after he was dead? A family interment would be arranged when the children were available. It did seem odd to plan things without checking with Kimo. A lifetime of checking with Kimo and a fifty-fifty chance that whatever she did would displease him was now over. She felt a little tingle of jubilation at that thought.

"I can do whatever I want. I am the boss of me," she told herself. It was a little joke between her and the children. Young children so often say, "You're not the boss of me," when they don't like a decision or request an adult makes. When they grew older and were clearly their own bosses, all three of them would say it to express what they wanted. Also, a little defiance of Kimo. None of them really outwardly defied Kimo until Abigail went to medical school, so that little phrase offset a lot of hurt feelings. It was the way they consoled one another.

Mabel opened her bedroom door and shuffled to the kitchen in her rubber slippers. They weren't fancy, purchased from Long's Drugs store, but they had little honu--turtles--on the bands between her toes, and that made her smile.

"Betty? Where are you?"

"In here." Betty backed out of the pantry. "Just looking for something to give you for a snack."

"Where's Teresita?" Mabel referred to their housekeeper who also did a lot of the cooking.

"She's cleaning upstairs in case the kids want to stay. I didn't want to disturb her just for a snack for you."

"For me?"

"Okay. For us." Betty smiled. "Teresita's making fish and rice for dinner so I don't want to spoil our appetites." She smiled. "How are you doing?"

"Much better, thank you."

"Would you like anything in particular? Are you hungry?"

"A little. How about a yogurt and some granola. Feel like

148

reading some journals?"

"Absolutely." Betty put bowls of yogurt and granola on the little kitchenette table that sat by the window to the side garden. More of the hardy Hawai'ian grass that rarely needed cutting, but dotted with mature plumeria trees. The open window let in the sweet scent of the blossoms while they ate.

"Onto the journals," Mabel said as she rose from the table.

"You get started. I'll just put these things in the dishwasher. Don't want to interfere with Teresita's fish for one second. It's so *onolicious!*" They laughed comfortably together at Betty's use of the local term for delicious—an older *haole*—white lady—saying that was just funny. Especially because she had mastered the local pidgin accent.

Mabel opened the closet door in the office and picked up the flashlight Betty had left on the floor. The box of journals was far too heavy for her to lift, or even pull out of the closet. She marveled at Betty's strength in getting it out of the hidden cubby in the first place. She flipped off the lid and shined the light into the box. The most recent journal sections were on top, but the most current, the one Kimo'd still been writing in, was the one she'd found in the bookshelf bracket. She'd only glanced through that one, but a lot of it was boring. The same sort of stuff Kimo had told her he wrote when they were young. When they still talked. Sort of.

Got a haircut today. Bought stock in company on the rise, Veri-Fone. Had snapper for lunch. Boring. She knew she'd have to read all of them and it would be hard to decipher Kimo's scrawl. He wrote with a fountain pen when he wrote by hand. The slant of the script and the nib of the pen made it difficult to read. She heard Kimo's voice throughout, and that helped her when the actual words were difficult.

"Where would you like me to start?" Betty stood behind

149

her.

"What's your opinion? I don't like this room. It's so..."

"Kimo?" Betty finished for her.

Mabel laughed. "I was going to say dark, but you're right. Can you get a dolly from the shed so we can move this box to the atrium? The light is great in there and we have a lot to go through."

Betty bent over and picked up the box.

"Betty, don't! That's so heavy."

"I don't have to go far. Besides, I want to get into this. Find some dirt." Her eyes sparkled with mischief.

"Fine. Don't come crying to me for Tylenol later, then."

In the atrium, Mabel said, "They are in chronological order, most recent being on top. I think we should go in some sort of order, don't you? So we don't miss anything?"

"That's a good idea. I know. I'll get a second box. When we've gone through one, we'll put it in the 'done' box. That way, we don't necessarily have to go in the order he wrote them."

"Good idea." While Mabel decided where to start, Betty went to get a box. Mabel dug down to the bottom and grabbed a section, pulled off the rubber band holding the manila folder, and started to read. Betty placed a box next to the first. "Grab a folder. I went down as far as I could to start."

"Then I will, too." Betty dug and started to read.

All was quiet in the atrium, just reading and breathing and flipping of pages. After a while, Betty dropped her head back onto the wicker chair. "I'm sorry but this is *so* boring," she whispered. "I thought it would be, well, more interesting. Trade secrets or something. More 'dirt'-related."

"I know. Me, too," Mabel whispered back. "I haven't found a single thing that is remotely sinister. He seems to go to the dentist a lot."

"Wow. Fascinating."

"Why are we whispering?" Mabel asked.

Betty laughed. "I don't know. I didn't want anyone to overhear. You know, in case the kids came in and we didn't hear them or something," she said in a normal voice.

"You mean like, gee kids, I hate for you to hear this, but your dad, well, he went to the dentist *and* got his haircut in the same week."

"That is pretty damning," Betty said. "I know we have to do this, but do we have to do it now?"

"We most certainly do not." Mabel glanced at her watch. "It's late. Time went by quickly, despite our reading material. I'm getting hungry."

"I'll check on dinner. What should I do with the box? Should I leave it here so we can go through it whenever we like?"

Mabel thought. "No. Just because we haven't found anything yet, doesn't mean there isn't anything to find. We should put it back, at least in the closet. Roger has already cleared out that office of company related things, so I doubt he'll be back. I don't think Abigail cares one way or another. Besides, the risk of someone reading it and dying of boredom seems to be the greater danger at this point." They both laughed.

Betty sobered. "I hate to say it about my own daughter, but what about Margaret? She's already angry; I don't think we want her to see this, do we? Just in case?"

"No. You're right. Let's put it back in the hidden space. Just to be safe. It's not too much for your back is it?"

"Not at all. I'm used to lifting heavy things as a nurse. You weigh a ton."

Mabel mock slapped at her. They both knew Mabel was tiny and fairly frail. "We can try again tomorrow, okay? After you've man-handled me to breakfast, that is."

Mabel still got around on her own for the most part. She needed help in and out of the shower, but just for safety, not necessity. Betty stayed in the outer room of the large bathroom, the dressing area, while Mabel showered, leaving the door open. The large shower had a bench and grab bars. The toilet area also had an intercom and telephone in case Mabel got in trouble. Those were installed after Mabel had broken her leg but were never used.

Dinner and bedtime came and went. Mabel called Roger and Abigail to meet at the house in the morning for coffee before they went to work. So much to discuss.

Chapter 14

The next morning Mabel and Betty had already finished their first cups of coffee and breakfast when Roger and Abigail arrived. Teresita showed them to the atrium, where as usual, Mabel and Betty were seated, chatting over the morning paper.

"Don't get up Mother," Roger admonished as he came around the chair to kiss her hello. Abigail followed suit and they greeted Betty as well.

"How are you doing, Mom?" Abigail asked. She had always been less formal with her mother.

Mabel wondered if their closeness, forged when she helped Abigail through medical school, sustained that term from her daughter, and if Kimo had influenced Roger to keep the formality, or in her opinion, distance from his mother. Kimo had always viewed his son as 'his' and the girl—his term—as hers. She had a vague memory of Roger calling her Mommy as a young child and Kimo chastising him for it. The word had slowly faded from family use. Sad, she felt.

"Mom?"   She was brought back to the moment by

Abigail's voice. "Are you all right?"

"Mother?" added Roger.

"Yes, I'm fine, just woolgathering." Mabel smiled. "I wanted to discuss a few things with you two about your father's arrangements and felt it easier than over the phone, back and forth."

"Sure. What do you have in mind?" asked Abigail. She sat close to her mother, leaning forward, fully attentive. Roger, on the other hand, Mabel noticed, busied himself pouring coffee from the service on the wicker table between them.

"Sounds good. Ab? Coffee?" Roger asked.

"Sure, thanks."

Mabel thought the use of this nickname was a good sign. No one else was allowed to use it, including her. She had wanted her children to be close to each other. Especially if Kimo outlived her and they had to rely on each other after she was gone. She knew they wouldn't get much support from Kimo in any case. However, she didn't have to worry about Kimo outliving her now.

"First, can we all meet in Roger Protheroe's office on Monday at 10 AM to go over the will and trust?"

"Monday is a full surgery day, but I can push some things," Abigail said. "As long as they're early in the week, both my patients and I feel better."

"Roger?" Mabel asked.

Roger had opened his briefcase and was looking through his planner. "Same. Monday's always busy but I can push some stuff. 10 AM, okay." He noted it in his calendar.

"Also, we need to discuss the funeral or memorial arrangements. He'll be at Hawai'i Memorial Park where I also have a plot. He's already been taken there and should be ready by the end of next week."

"Is it going to be open casket?" Abigail asked.

"No." Mabel and Betty exchanged a look Abigail caught.

"What, Mom?"

"Do you really think your father would want everyone to see him like that?"

"Absolutely not," Roger said. "How big is this shindig going to be?"

"Roger!" Abigail said.

"What? It's not a party. Or a 'celebration of life' or whatever you call it--whatever normal people have. He was a jerk. I just want to see him in the ground and be done."

Mabel carefully sipped her coffee with a shaky hand. "I understand your feelings, Roger, but we do have to keep up appearances."

"What does that mean?"

"It means, unless we want the papers printing what a horrible, money grubbing family we are, we need to appear a grieving, *private* unit."

"What do you mean by unit?" Abigail asked.

"I mean, a solid, unbreakable unit, who loves and misses the paternal leader."

"Whoa, Mom. That's kind of, I don't know. Weird for you." Roger finally was focused completely on her.

"It's not a shindig at all. Just family. A grieving family," she repeated. "What is the company doing? We need to discuss that, too."

Betty noticed Mabel's hands shake and the tightening of her lips as she struggled to remain composed.

Mabel knew Betty noticed the change in topic, but neither Roger nor Abigail seemed to care. After so many years of caregiver and patient relationship, and that morphing to true friendship, she and Betty were very aware of each other's mood and appearance.

Roger said, "The Board has decided to keep the structure of the Gala but add a memorial piece. We've commissioned his portrait and a bust for the lobby of the building. The Gala was too much to reschedule. It's set for next Saturday, so after the Monday meeting with your lawyer, I'm pretty much unavailable until this is over. You're coming to the Gala, right? All of you? Our *unit*?" Roger smiled.

Mabel chuckled. She didn't know how, but both her children had managed to hang onto a sense of humor. "Of course, Roger. We'll be there. 7 PM right? On the grounds of Lemon Enterprises?"

"No, the Open House part of the Gala is at Lemon Enterprises all day Saturday and open to the public, but we are thinking of adding a separate memorial in a larger location. The anniversary dinner and ball is at the Hyatt Regency in Waikiki at 7 PM. We have the ballroom, but that's not big enough for a public memorial. We're thinking of renting the Waikiki Shell for that. I know, I know. It seems weird, but we can't change all the other stuff at the last minute. This has really thrown a monkey wrench into things."

"Roger, he didn't die on purpose!" Abigail said.

"I'm sorry. But it's so typical of him to make things harder on everyone else."

They all burst out laughing and Roger looked up from the notes he'd been perusing.

"I'm glad somebody's having fun," he grumbled, but he smiled, too. "Yeah, I guess that does sound pretty funny. He couldn't have waited two weeks to have a heart attack." He sobered immediately as he remembered the surprise manuscript Kimo had planned to unveil at this Gala event. "Jeez." He ran a hand through his hair.

"It's all right, dear." Mabel reached across the table and

patted his knee. "We're all at sixes and sevens over this. We'll just muddle on the best we can."

"Mom, you say the weirdest things," Roger said.

"I know. It's my British roots. Especially when I'm under stress." Mabel's family was from England and she had grown up around elderly relatives with distinctly British slang. The children had heard all the stories while growing up. Mabel had been an 'oops' baby—the surprise to older parents—and so was pretty much alone in the world but for a few cousins scattered around the Mainland and England with whom she only exchanged Christmas cards.

Betty had been taking all this down. "So, let me recap," she said. "The company Gala celebration is at Lemon Headquarters," everyone smiled at her pet name for the company, "all day Saturday, pretty much, for employees and the public. Food, drink?" She raised her eyebrows in question.

"Yes. We have that in the lobby along with different bands and entertainment all day. Tours will be given hourly for the public."

"Okay," Betty noted that. "Then, when is the Waikiki Shell Memorial thing?"

"We haven't confirmed the venue, but we don't think the same day. That will be too much. We'll let the papers know because it will be a public memorial along with the employees of all the companies and the subsidiaries. We have no idea who will come to that. Everyone from the sugar and pine companies to the graduates of Lemon Tree—we just don't know. We're getting a kahuna to do a blessing and chant and the company heads are all saying a few words. Then we are asking if people want to speak, they request it in writing first so we don't have a million speakers."

"Where will they request that?" Betty was writing fast.

"We're going to have a press release drawn up. We hope to

do this all fairly quickly so we can get back to business."

"What about that reporter?" Abigail asked. "Are you going to ask him?"

"What reporter?"

"The one who's been doing all the coverage on Dad and the company. He interviewed me. I thought he interviewed you, too?" Abigail looked a little pink.

"Oh, yeah. I forgot. He'll get a press release, too, I suppose. Are you okay?"

"Sure, fine," she mumbled.

"What's next?" Betty asked.

Roger pulled out a sheet of paper and handed it to her. "This is the schedule of events in the Hyatt ballroom for 7 PM. You guys have to be there, okay?"

"You won't care, you'll be busy," Abigail said.

"I have a table reserved for you. Oh, Betty. I didn't count Margaret when I started this. Do you think she'll want to come? Should I put her name down for the door?"

Both Mabel and Betty shook their heads no.

"This says 'head table' for Mabel and Abigail." Betty showed them the paper.

"No way. I'm not sitting up there for everyone to gawk at," Abigail said. "I'm not kidding Roger. I won't come if you do that."

"Okay, okay. I'll change it. Mom? Will you sit up there with me?"

"Isn't that for the company bigwigs?"

"No, it was supposed to be for the family and just the top guys of all the companies, and Dad, of course was supposed to be in the center. Now, I guess it's me. I don't want to sit up there alone. I mean, with no family."

"Somebody needs a girlfriend," Abigail said.

"Yeah, well, if I had time for one." Roger smiled at his

sister.

"Since Abigail doesn't want to be up there, I will, if Betty can sit next to me," Mabel said.

"No, Mabel," Betty said. "I don't belong up there."

"Yes, you do," Abigail and Mabel said together.

"I see I'm out numbered. Okay. But I can't make any promises about my behavior once I start drinking."

They all laughed because they knew she didn't drink much at all. A glass of wine, maybe champagne in celebration occasionally, but that was about it.

"Just keep your tube top on, is all I ask," Roger said.

"Like I said. I can't make any promises." Betty winked.

Roger continued. "Cocktails and light music from 7 to 8, then dinner. Speeches, brief ones I hope at 9 and dancing is supposed to start by 10 and continue until 1 AM. I guess some of those speeches will be memorial stuff, but I'm going to let everyone know to save the big memorial speeches for the Shell event."

"Sounds good. I have to get to the hospital. Anything else I need to know right now?" Abigail asked.

"I wrote this all down, Mabel. Can you think of anything else?" Betty asked.

"Not right now. I know you have to go too, Roger, so thank you both for coming. I'll see you Monday at 10. Do you know where Roger Protheroe's office is down town? Off Fort Street? You can park in the building but it's expensive. We usually park in the public lot by St. Andrew's Cathedral and walk down the mall."

"Mom, you're wealthy and you park in a public lot and walk to save five dollars?" Abigail asked.

"I like the exercise. Besides, some of the best food is downtown and I'm going to get a green papaya salad for lunch. So there. You are all welcome to join me." Mabel stood to kiss her children good-bye.

*   *   *   *

Abigail did want to get back to the hospital, but not for a specific patient. For the lab tests she'd run on her father's blood.

She hurried to her box where confidential documents were delivered. All patients had a number to protect their confidentiality, and only a few places, like the patient chart, had both name and number. That prevented someone from identifying a patient's test results.

She had ticked off a number of boxes on the sheet and run some of the more basic tests herself. Absolutely nothing had come up to indicate foul play. Kimo's cholesterol had been high and given his temperament, she presumed his blood pressure as well. Based on his blood tests, his organs showed no unusual wear for man of his age. His hair clippings had not revealed anything so Agatha Christie as arsenic poisoning or even hair dye. She sighed.

She dropped her head in her hands. What had she expected? Why did she even care? It had all came to nothing anyway. So many conditions and toxins were undetectable unless you knew what you were looking for. Now his body was gone to the mortuary and once filled with formaldehyde, would be even harder to find anything in tissues or marrow.

It must be some weird form of grief, she decided. It's clear Kimo probably had enemies. You don't become a world-wide businessman without making a few along the way. She smiled thinking back to her "motive" conversation with Roger. They had decided they both had motive. Ridiculous.

She made her way back to her office and plopped in the swivel chair. "What a dope," she scolded herself. Now a little embarrassed at her suppositions. Her phone rang.

160

"Dr. Lemon."

"It's Mick Kau'ula. Is this a bad time?"

"Not at all." She felt the smile in her voice and her heart rose a little.

"Wondering about that drink. You free after work? And when is 'after work' for a doctor, anyway?"

Abigail laughed. "Yes, I am free. And today, that would be about five o'clock after late rounds and a mountain of paperwork. I got a late start today." Why did she tell him that?

"Oh, I see. Late night?"

She thought she heard more than just casual interest. Reporter or man speaking? "No, not at all. Early meeting, so I'm a little late getting to my mountain of paperwork. I'm sure you must have meetings in your business."

"Way too many. 'Let's talk about what we're going to do, discuss why it's a good AND bad idea, then maybe get around to actually doing it.'" Mick mocked his meeting protocol in a silly voice that had Abigail giggling.

Abigail was surprised at herself. Giggling. She pulled herself together. "That sounds like around here. Should we meet somewhere?"

"I'm going to come clean. I have no idea what kind of place you'd like. I hang around reporter dives for pleasure or skulk in classy joints to eavesdrop, so I'm flexible."

"My hospital and your newspaper are not too far apart. Someplace in the middle? How about a place neither of us goes. We can keep up the sneaking around part." Abigail realized that sounded like they were having an affair. "Uh, not that we, uh, I, sneaking around. . ." she trailed off.

Mick laughed. "I know what you mean. Neither of us wants our colleagues to start the rumor mill. Gotcha." Abigail silently chastised herself. Well, she was out of practice, she reasoned.

"How about Pontoon Pete's on Ala Moana?" Mick suggested. "That's a little bit dive-y, a little bit touristy. We should be safe. Best part, a parking lot behind it. Even our cars will be incognito."

Abigail agreed and hung up feeling absolutely giddy. She hoped he wasn't just out to report on the heir of the great Kimo Lemon. She really didn't think that's all there was to it, but she had to suppress the thought. She told herself, so what? He's tall, dark, handsome, unattached and not gay. How many of those men fell off the trees for someone her age? She knew she was older than he, but not sure how much. She was in pretty good shape. Being a doctor kept her out of the Hawai'ian sun and her skin was lovely and clear. Only a few laugh lines and crinkles, she mused, because she hadn't had much to laugh about. Since she'd met Mick, she'd laughed more than she had in a year. She had always vowed not to get involved with someone at work. The doctors she worked with were either married or so egotistical it completely put her off. There had been a guest doctor she'd cozied up with a time or two, and she'd only allowed that because she knew he'd be off to the Mainland as soon as he'd presented whatever technique he'd come to share.

The day dragged by and she did her rounds, chatted to colleagues and patients but found herself unable to concentrate. She finally left work, deciding she wanted to shower and change before meeting Mick.

She arrived at Pontoon Pete's five minutes early. The day was hot and humid and she didn't want to wait in her car and have her carefully constructed casual look melt in the heat. She entered and was relieved to see that it was not as dive-y as she'd anticipated, but lit with skylights and decorated with the currently popular brass and fern decor. She released the breath she didn't know she'd been holding and approached the bar. As the bartender turned to take her order, she heard her name called.

Mick had a booth in the back that afforded some privacy and he hailed her over. He stood as she approached.

"What'll you have?"

"Miller Lite," she said. "I know, but calories count," she amended when he made a face.

"Be right back." He smiled to show he'd been kidding about her drink choice. She'd barely gotten seated and squeezed in a fast make-up check when he was back with her beer.

She explained. "I don't like it that much, either, so I don't drink as much."

"That makes no sense at all," Mick said. "Cheers." He clinked his glass to hers. "To a rough week."

"Amen to that." She took a drink. "Not so bad when the beer's this cold."

"If you say so."

They chatted amiably and fairly comfortably for a first date, if that in fact was what this was, Abigail thought.

"What's going on with the funeral plans? How you holding up?" Mick asked.

"Reporter asking?"

"Nope, just me. I'm off duty. I decided drinks with a beautiful woman was well-worth missing a breaking story. Well, it's probably worth it," he added with a smile.

She loved the little silly things he said. And the beautiful woman part didn't hurt either. On her second drink, she switched to something equally as disgusting according to Mick—rum and Diet Coke.

"Family funeral next Wednesday. Just us. I think. . . I think I'm okay. I have come to realize I didn't like my dad much and that's okay, too." She wondered if she'd said too much. Was he really off duty? Was any reporter ever off duty? She guessed she

163

had to listen to her gut on this one.

"I know what you mean," Mick said. "I'm not too crazy about all my family members either."

"On a better note, the Gala is still going to be all day Saturday starting at 10 AM. Lots going on. They're not postponing it since so many people already made plans to come for it. I guess Dad knew some pretty famous folks. The dinner and dancing part are at the Hyatt that night."

"Oh, yeah. I'll be there for that. I've been covering this for months, so I'll be there working. We have a press table and everything."

"So, I'll see you there?"

"You bet. I even rented a tux on the paper's dime. Given the paper's budget, I think it's left over from the seventies and powder blue, but hey, it's a tux."

She was just imagining him in a black tux, starched white shirt and black bow tie when the powder blue image replaced it, and she laughed out loud.

"Just kidding about the powder blue. Got me a real one. I won't embarrass you." His smile was gentle, but something more. An attraction.

"I'm not worried about that. I can embarrass myself just fine. I don't wear heels too much, so I'll have enough problems skidding from my table to the ladies room without falling on my face. Speaking of, I'll be right back."

She picked up her purse and weaved through the tables to the ladies room. She looked in the mirror and decided she still looked okay. Maybe even a little pretty with the flush of being close to Mick? More like a rum flush. But Mick sure looked good. He was charming in an unconventional sense. She hadn't realized how much she had missed being around people who not only were smart, but were funny, too. Her family and co-workers were smart, but not terribly funny. Roger could be, but he'd been so tightly wound with things at the company. Until her father died. He should have been even more stressed by that, but he seemed more relaxed. Like he had planned for it. She mentally shook herself and remembered a handsome man waited for her.

She returned to the table and scooted in a little closer to him on the banquette seating. He did the same.

"This is nice," she said.

"Yes, it is," he agreed. "Would you like to continue it over dinner?"

"I think so." She leaned in. His eyes were so brown and the lashes so long. She smelled soap and *him* and the warmth of his skin met the warmth of hers as she touched his arm. He leaned toward her and their lips met, gently at first. Tentatively. Her grasp on his arm tightened, she felt the muscle and fine hairs. He pulled her closer with his other arm and their kiss heated. Her skin tingled and she felt a shiver from the top of her head all the way down, warm and spiky. She pulled back and looked into his eyes. He looked as surprised as she felt.

"Wow," he said.

"Yeah." She was breathing heavily. "I think I should eat something."

"Yeah, that's probably it. You're just hungry." His smile was so bright and lit his eyes completely. She noticed it had gotten darker in the bar.

"Where should we go?" he asked, pulling away. He pulled his heat and his smell with him and she was a little disappointed.

I gotta relax and calm down, she told herself. Even with her occasional affairs, she had not felt this, this chemical reaction, was the only thing she could name it.

"Aloha Tower Marketplace just opened. It has lots of places to eat. We could try there." She was still diagnosing her

165

unusual behavior. Another strange expression of grief?

"Sounds good. Take both cars or you trust me to drive you? You can control yourself, can't you?" he asked.

"I'll do my best," she said. Her stomach flopped and she wondered if she could. She barely knew him. He was a reporter on her father's Gala and now memorial. Was this a good idea? She prayed he wasn't using her for information, but part of her didn't care. It had been so long since she'd been held, and even longer since she'd cared. This first gentle kiss went beyond any of her recollections of her sporadic sex life. She would have remembered if it had been the Fourth of July in her stomach. She decided to let go.

They left her car at the bar and Mick drove them to Aloha Tower. They decided on a steak place. She didn't remember the name of it, or what she ate. She was hyper-aware of everything to do with him. How he looked, how he smelled. How he felt.

After dinner the conversation stopped altogether in the car. "Where should I take you? Back to your car?" Mick asked.

"I guess so." She felt she was vibrating with need, but also knew it was a bad idea to jump in bed so fast with someone who could potentially damage her or her family. She was torn with desire and loyalty. She needed a little more time. She hoped he'd grant it.

Mick was also quiet and she hoped she hadn't put him off. Was she being a tease? Was she a conquest?

At the bar parking lot he parked and came around to open her door. The night was warm and clear and smelled of motor oil and plumeria. Music and light spilled out of the back door of the bar into the dark lot.

She got out feeling awkward. What to say? What to do? He solved that problem by pressing her against the car and kissing her again. Gently, enquiringly, with his whole body aligned with

166

hers. Her skin was electric and tingled everywhere he touched. Her eyes were closed but she felt she'd see sparks on contact if she looked. He ran his hands down from her shoulders, pressed her palms flat with his, then locked their fingers, kissing her neck. She moaned and moved to kiss him back, her tongue seeking his. She felt him grow against her hips and that ignited her. She pulled her hands free and ran them through his hair, then pulled him harder against her. She bit his neck and he gasped.

"Stop, stop," he said. "I don't want it to be like this and if we don't stop, I won't be able to. I can barely say that now." He pulled back to look at her, both of them panting.

"What do you want it to be like?" she asked, not sure what he meant.

"I want... I want," he gently cradled her face in his hands. They were rough and gentle at the same time. How does a reporter have rough hands? So much to discover.

"I want it to be in a bed. I want it to be where we can take our time. I want, maybe, to wake up with you and hold you in my arms." He kissed her gently.

She didn't know what to say. Her body throbbed but her mind agreed with him. She'd never heard those words before.

Mick continued. "This feels. . . important. I don't know. I haven't felt this way and I'm not sure how to handle it."

"We could go to my house," she ventured. "Or yours. They have beds."

He smiled. "Indeed they do."

"This feels strange to me, too. This also feels good. Right. Maybe it's only right for one night. For tonight. I don't know that either. But I am sure it's not a mistake. Does it feel like a mistake? If it does, we'll say good-night and call it good."

He leaned in and kissed her again, his hands molded to her hips. It left her breathless.

167

"No. It's not a mistake. I have a really important question to ask you before we decide."

"What?"

"Whose place has guest parking?"

She burst out laughing, still feeling like she could jump him right there. "I live in a tiny house in Makiki with a long driveway. And there's street parking. You?"

"I have a tiny house in Manoa, also with street parking. Your choice."

"I have a queen sized bed," she offered. "You?"

"Me, too."

"Your place. I'll follow you. I need my car in case I get paged."

"Done." He kissed her once more and drove slowly to Manoa. She had no trouble following him.

She did stay all night.

Chapter 15

In his office, Roger was adrift in a sea of details for the Gala and now the memorial. At the back of his mind, as he answered the phone and drafted his own memos, he thought about his father's memos and what to do about them. They should not come out, that was certain, but he had no idea who else knew about them besides the recipients. Did anyone else have all of them? A fifty year span could mean a vast collection. He shuddered to think about them put into book form and unleashed for the world to see. And why? He just didn't understand why Kimo would want to do that. And why now? Perhaps he would never know, but someone might have a copy of that book and Roger had no idea what the intent was. To publish it posthumously?

Maybe Kimo was never going to publish it? Maybe it was just another noose in his blackmail lynching scheme. But he said he would read excerpts at the Gala. Would he really?

Roger dropped his head in his hands. So much he didn't know. It would be so like his father to threaten someone just to achieve or attain something. Squashing people like so many bugs to get another dollar, or just to cause pain or embarrassment. It was too much to hope that the book was a hoax. He had to assume it was real and it was somewhere, perhaps even with a publisher. It would sell millions of copies, he was sure, from the memos he'd read. Extortion, sex, power, greed, his little collection of poisonous words had it all. He had no idea where else to look for the manuscript. He'd seen no letters from a publisher or agent, and at this point, he thought he'd exhausted the number of safes in Kimo's office. The home office held nothing of interest and the YMCA locker was empty. Roger supposed he could have left it with someone for safe keeping, but who would he trust? Even if he told the person not to open it, curiosity was a powerful tool and now that Kimo was dead, it might all come out.

This circular thinking was giving him a headache. He looked at the piles of work on his desk, including the speech he was to write for the Gala. So far it read, *Thank you all for coming.* "Probably needs a little more," he said. He'd put it off as long as he could. He pulled it to him and began jotting ideas and notes. Because he knew there would be other speakers, he kept it brief.

Throughout, poking at him was the manila file of memos. Well, one of them, he thought grimly. He opened the folder and began to skim through. The name Elizabeth caught his eye. A memo regarding his mother's newly hired nurse--also Margaret's mother. It seemed Kimo had chosen her specifically, for some reason. Maybe Abigail's story was true. Well, parts of it.

He read further and was stunned to find that his mother's accident was no accident. It seemed to have been orchestrated for two reasons: to keep Mabel at home, dependent and under Kimo's control and also to hire Elizabeth, Betty.

Why Kimo needed to hire Betty was another thing, but Roger imagined it also had to do with controlling her. Kimo had to control every aspect of his world. And his world kept getting bigger.

It was clear to Roger that neither woman knew the history of the other. How terrible. He wasn't going to be the one to tell them. He had to make sure those memos and the manuscript did not get out. He was glad they were not in the group he'd given his mother.

If Kimo hadn't died now, this would all have come out, Roger was sure. A wedge of doubt evolved. He died now. Timing was perfect. Murder cloaked in a heart attack? Can't prove it. His body had been removed to the memorial park. What if he *could* prove it? Would he?

"Ah, shit." He didn't know. So many people would be hurt, had already been hurt by Kimo. And then if his so called tell-all book came out. What a mess. Roger's conscience rose up. *Can you live with that? With not knowing? Can you live with it if you do find out something?*

He checked the clock and the day had flown by. Although it was the weekend, so much was happening next week that the offices were as busy as if it was Monday. People passed his door and snatches of conversations drifted by. Excited plans being reviewed. Kimo was gone, but the company wasn't and people seemed okay with that. Roger was okay with that, too.

*   *   *   *

Mabel and Betty had committed themselves to reading every journal section before destroying it. They wanted to be aware of any bad news coming down the road via those pages.

Mabel looked up from her section of journal. "I guess he saved the juicy stuff for the memos. This is deadly dull."

"I know. But we agreed to go through it all, just in case." Betty perused her section. "I've been thinking. Maybe we shouldn't destroy them? They are pretty benign. Do you think the children would want them as a reminder of their father?"

Mabel raised her eyebrows.

"You know, that he wasn't always that way? This way?"

"Well, he was. Always this way, and the children know it. They lived it, too. Besides, who cares if he got a haircut in May of 1956 and had breakfast at the diner on A'ala Street?"

"Ohhhh, Mabel! What if it's a code? What if all this boring stuff is encoded with state secrets or something?"

"Right. I think Kimo is really a double agent. I doubt it's a code, Betty. But maybe we should hang onto it for a while." She smiled at her friend. "Just in case."

They continued to read until Teresita called them to lunch. And then to dinner. Mabel didn't even have her nap.

"I'm so stiff," Mabel said.

"I know! A little walk around the garden will help. Look at all we've accomplished."

The box with the 'already read' sections was fuller than the 'to be read' sections. "That does feel good," Mabel said. "Yes, a walk will be nice. Can you get my shawl? The breeze seems cool."

The two old ladies linked arms as they had so many times before, and set off around the garden, admiring the lovely plants in the setting sun.

*   *   *   *

Honolulu Star-Bulletin **Monday, September 25, 1995**
Lemon Gala To Go On As Scheduled
Family Plans Private Service
By Mick Kau'ula

The fiftieth anniversary celebration of Lemon Enterprises

will continue as planned this Saturday, September 30, at Lemon Enterprises corporate headquarters beginning at 10 AM with entertainment and pupus. No host cocktails. It is open to the public and tours of the building and subsidiary companies on site will be hourly. Free.

That evening, by invitation only, there will be a gathering of Lemon bigwigs and guests; celebrities to multi-millionaires are expected to attend the black tie affair. Dinner, dancing and honors will continue into the wee hours. Roger Lemon, President of Lemon Enterprises, said that the memorial speeches will be presented at the Kimo Lemon memorial event at the Waikiki Shell the Friday before, September 29, at noon. That is also open to the public. He wishes to focus Saturday's event on the company his father built and carry out his last wishes for the fiftieth anniversary of the founding of Lemon Enterprises.

The family is planning a private service this Wednesday before the Gala. Condolences can be sent in care of Lemon Enterprises or to this paper.

*   *   *   *

Monday at 10 AM found the family in the conference room of Reginald Protheroe, Kimo's estate attorney. Mabel, Betty, Roger and Abigail sat around the large table.

"What are you waiting for, Reginald?" Mabel asked. "We're all here, let's get this over with."

"Not quite," Reginald began and was interrupted by a ruckus in the outer office. "One moment please." He opened the door and they all could hear, "I'm *supposed* to be here. He told me to be here, *today, now.*"

He returned with Margaret in tow. "Now we're all here."

The four around the table just stared. "Are you sure?"

173

Mabel said carefully.

"Let's begin." Reginald pulled a sheaf of papers to him. "I will skip all the legal language, but as heirs you are all welcome to peruse copies of the will and trust at your leisure. I will get right to it. To my wife, Mabel White Lemon, I leave lifelong financial interest in Lemon Enterprises, the house in Kahala, all my assets in the house and half my stocks and bonds. She also will retain our joint bank accounts and contents of the safety deposit box.

To my son Roger James Lemon, I leave my interest and position at Lemon Enterprises. He will retain this financial and management control for no less than five years. At which time the Board and he can make another arrangement. I also leave $100,000.00 in cash and one quarter interest in my stocks and bonds.

To my daughter, Abigail Mabel Lemon, I also leave $100,000.00 in cash and one quarter interest in my stocks and bonds.

To Elizabeth Jean D'Angelo, I leave $25,000.00 for your serving my family's needs.

To Margaret Elizabeth D'Angelo, I leave $25,000.00 and my good wishes for your future."

The conference room was silent for a moment. "Is that it?" Roger asked.

"Well, no. There are other distributions such as to the Warriors baseball team and to charities, but that is all concerning the family. I have been in touch with your corporate attorney, Aaron Goldberg, and he will meet with the Board to discuss the company details. Does anyone have any questions?"

"I don't understand why Margaret was included?" Betty asked. "I am happy for her, of course, but curious?"

"I'm curious, too," Margaret said. She looked like someone had punched her in the gut.

"I was given a specific response to that should I be asked."
Reginald cleared his throat. "I am quoting here. 'I have to leave her
something or she'll sue. I know her. I know what she's like. Like
father, like daughter.' I'm sorry that was so, uh, crass," Reginald
added.

Several gasps around the room. They looked at each other.

"Well that certainly sounds more like him," Margaret said.
"Covering his ass to the end. If that's all, I'm out of here. If you
need me, I'm staying with them," she hooked a thumb at Mabel
and Betty.

Now Reginald looked surprised. "You knew each other?
About each other? I was told to keep my mouth shut until this
occasion because you all *didn't* know." He was completely
bewildered.

"It's been an enlightening week, hasn't it, everyone?"
Margaret asked.

They all kept glancing at one another, finally realizing they
all knew, but had withheld it from each other.

Numbly, they stood and left the room. Reginald gathered
his papers, prepared to begin his end of the process, still reeling
from the fact that the years' long secret he'd kept, was apparently
no secret at all. For the first time, he thought, maybe someone had
gotten a leg up on Kimo. That made him smile. Just a tiny bit.

Chapter 16

Tuesday morning found Mabel and Betty back at the journals.

"Meetings, department meetings, budget committees, this is horrible reading. A day in the life of Kimo Lemon. If I didn't know about those memos, he would seem the most boring man on Earth," Mabel said.

"We both know that's not true," Betty said as she flipped through her own set of journal pages. "Why did he save all this? It can't be because he wanted everyone to think he was such a great guy. He saved the memos, after all."

"I'm not sure. I think it's part ego, and part in his nature to journal. If he'd been a normal man, this might have been a nice chronicle for future generations."

"What do you mean?"

"You know how when we go to Bishop Museum or someplace and they have journals from the Missionaries early days? What their life was like?"

"Sure."

"Have you actually read them?"

"Um, not really. Skimmed a bit, I suppose," Betty said.

"I have. They're pretty ordinary, like these entries, only they're not, because they revolve around what their regular life was like at the time. A long time ago, I went to Gold Rush country and a little museum had a journal from a man named Horace. He wrote letters to his friend Charlie back east. He pretty much wrote ordinary things, but because he was a young gold miner in 1854, they're interesting."

"Give me an example."

"He writes what time he gets up. He goes to the creek to bathe. He is actually a very good descriptive writer so you get a sense of what is around him. But still, mostly everyday events."

"I guess Kimo thought he'd be immortalized by his fascinating words." Betty slapped another section in the 'done' box. "I need a break. Want some tea?"

"Sure. We're almost finished. I want to keep going just to be sure."

"I'm not reading as carefully anymore but I don't think I've missed where Al Capone is buried or anything." Betty stood stiffly and stretched.

"With Kimo, you never know."

"I hope there are no more surprises. I hope we can just move on after this week."

"Me, too. When the memorial and the Gala are all over, maybe I can have some peace."

"That would be nice. Once everything is laid to rest once and for all, we can put it out of our minds." Betty headed to the kitchen.

Mabel held her journal section, but stared blindly out the atrium windows. "Kimo, why did you have to be this way? Things could have. . . should have been so different." She felt tears rise

177

and angrily wiped them away.

Betty returned. "Tea water's heating and Teresita left us a snack. Hey, what's wrong?" Betty sat next to Mabel.

"I guess I'm just tired. Overwhelmed. I want it all to be over so I can finally relax a little."

"I know. As soon as we make sure there's nothing unexpected or more damaging in the journals, we'll let it rest. Okay?"

"If I can get through this week, I think I'll be home free."

"We will. It'll be fine. Maybe we can even share these with the children someday, like you said. Maybe they would want to read about their father. You have to admit, this is a pretty benign light for Kimo to be in." Betty smiled.

"I suppose. Good for them to know there was another side, maybe."

"I think I hear the kettle. I'll go finish the tea. Teresita was cleaning and I didn't want to stop her. I can manage some tea."

"And cookies. Could you manage a cookie or two?"

"I think so."

Mabel was no longer in the mood to read journal entries. She was in the mood to bury Kimo and let him and all his secrets stay buried. "One more week," she said to herself. "I can do this."

* * * *

Mick and Abigail had agreed to have lunch after her family's meeting in the lawyer's office the previous day, but both their schedules had interfered. Today they had managed and met at Monterey Bay Canners restaurant in Ward Warehouse. A little out of the way for both of them, but the second story view across from the beach was lovely and worth the traffic and heat to get there.

Abigail arrived first and ordered two iced teas. She had just begun to read the menu when Mick came in, stopping at the hostess podium to scan the room for her. She raised one hand and smiled, enjoying watching him before he saw her. She still found him handsome, with a tiny bit of gray starting at the temples. She hadn't seen him since "the morning after" and hoped she didn't remember incorrectly how he looked and how she felt when he looked at her. Or touched her. He wore a wrinkled Aloha shirt and slacks, the all-purpose wardrobe of businessmen in Hawai'i. He spotted her and weaved his way through the tables to theirs by the window.

He bent and kissed her cheek. "You look great."

"I feel hot and sweaty, but thank you. I was thinking the same about you."

"That I look hot and sweaty?"

"No." She laughed. "That you look great." Her cheek felt warm where he'd kissed it.

He sat and took a big drink of the tea. "Thanks for ordering this. It's a hot one out there. Know what you're getting?"

"Same thing I always get. Seafood salad and a cup of clam chowder. I love their clam chowder."

"Me, too. I'll get the same."

A server came and took their order.

"How are you holding up?" Mick asked.

"All right, I suppose. The hospital is keeping me busy, so that's good. I was going to take a few days off, to help my mom you know, but she seems to be doing pretty well. Betty is wonderful. She's my mom's caregiver, but they've been together so long, they're like sisters. Where ever one is, you'll find the other nearby. I think Betty's been a great help to her.

"I offered to help make arrangements or clean or go through papers, but they seem to have it handled." Abigail sipped her tea.

"I know Kimo was not the nicest guy it seems, but he was your father. Are you doing okay?"

"Surprisingly, I am. Maybe it just hasn't sunk in yet that he's really gone and not coming back. He would disappear for days when I was young. After we had that big blow up when I wanted to go to medical school and I moved out, I hardly ever saw him. Only the last few years did I make any sort of effort to be around him. That was really for my mother's sake. I'd go to the house occasionally for a meal, tea in the garden, whatever."

Mick laid his hand palm up on the table in front of her and she put her hand in his. "It's going to be okay. Betty does seem like a very good friend. A solid person. What's her last name, by the way?"

"D'Angelo. She was married to Tony D'Angelo. They had that great Italian restaurant in Manoa."

"I've eaten there. It's fantastic."

"It was amazing when Tony was alive. I remember my father taking us all there for some birthday or something. It must have been before our big fight. It was actually a good evening for once. I didn't know Betty then, or that it was Betty's husband who cooked and ran it."

"It's still pretty good, but I bet it was incredible when Tony cooked. I didn't live in Manoa then. That's going back a ways. I might even have still been in college. I think we went there for a family celebration."

"Do you have family? We always talk about my family, but what about you?"

"My parents are gone. Car accident when I was about 30. But I'm close to my mother's brother, Yoshi and his wife, Myra," Mick said.

"I'm sorry about your parents. It's nice you're close to your Auntie and Uncle. Here on O'ahu?"

"Yes, Kaimuki, up Wilhelmina Rise."

Their food arrived and they dug in. "Cousins? Other folks?" she asked around a mouthful of salad.

"Uncle Yoshi and Auntie Myra had one son, Shuto. They also fostered other kids over the years and hosted foreign exchange students. There were always kids around their house when I was growing up. My parents' house was close to theirs so we could play together." Mick took a sip of tea. "I sold the house after they died. Too many memories there."

She reached over and touched his hand. "I'm sorry."

"Hey, who's the reporter here, anyway? I should be grilling you."

Abigail smiled and resumed eating.

"That reminds me," Mick said. "I want to show you something. Get your opinion."

He took a folded piece of paper out of his shirt pocket and handed it to her.

"What is it?" She opened it.

"A birth certificate. Do the names seem familiar?"

"Well, Elizabeth Lynn is Betty's formal legal name, but the surname, Miller, isn't right."

"What is it?"

"I'm not sure, but I thought her maiden name was Connor. I might be mistaken. But it's odd that the daughter's name is the same as Margaret's. Betty's daughter. She's staying with us for a while until she gets back on her feet. She's a strange one. Her last name is the same as her father's, Tony D'Angelo, but this says Miller here, too. Father listed as unknown."

Abigail felt a little queasy as she recognized the similarities between this certificate and what Margaret had told her and Roger. So, there was a birth certificate. But why were the last names different? And why no father listed?

"Are you okay? You look a little green," Mick said.

"I guess the heat's just got me all of a sudden." She pushed her plate away. "Maybe I'll take this to go and have it for dinner."

"I'm sorry. Did I upset you?"

"No, of course not. I should probably get back to the hospital anyway." What she was going to do was to call Roger and ask about the birth certificate he had.

"Want to have dinner later?"

"Sure. That sounds nice," she said absently, her mind whirling with possibility. Even though she had stuck up for Margaret, now that there was a birth certificate of sorts, it meant that her father had indeed had an affair. Affair—but then it probably meant the forcible conception of that baby was true, too. She couldn't wrap her mind around that part of it.

"You really look sick. Are you sure it's just the heat?" Mick asked.

"I think so. I should go." She fumbled with her purse for her wallet.

"Lunch is on me. Should you drive?"

"I'm fine. I'll call you later, okay?" She fled, brain swirling.

She'd been lucky enough to park in the structure so the car was only five hundred degrees instead of a thousand. The seats and metal handles were sizzling. She started the engine and let the A/C cool the car enough that she could touch the controls.

Abigail pulled into her reserved spot at Royal Hospital and made her way to her air conditioned office. She had calmed somewhat since leaving Mick at the restaurant. Heavy traffic and heat helped focus her. By the time she reached her office, she was ready to face confirmation of the worst news to date. She dialed.

Roger's, well, her father's, secretary answered on the first ring.

"It's Abigail. I need to speak to Roger. It's very important."

"Hello, Abigail. He's in a meeting now. Everyone is working toward the Gala and the memorial as well as keeping this ship on its course."

For a moment, Abigail had no idea what she was talking about. The company. Right.

"Please leave a message for him to call me at my office. It's urgent."

"I will. Oh, wait. He's heading this way. Let me see if I can grab him for you." She was put on hold.

"I have to remember to get her a nice present," Abigail mumbled. Secretaries were better than guard dogs sometimes. Could be your best friend or your worst nightmare.

"Hey, Ab," came Roger's voice, slightly out of breath. "What's up? I'm between meetings."

"I just had lunch with Mick Kau'ula," Abigail began.

"The reporter? Whatever for?"

Abigail forgot that everyone was used to her lack of social life. Besides, a reporter might not be the best choice of 'new special friend' as far as the family was concerned.

"Um, just talking, you know. Remember when Margaret told us she had a copy of her birth certificate? And that the originals were in Dad's office?"

"Yes, I know. What about it?"

"Well, did you ever find it?"

Roger was in a quandary. Abigail had a right to know, especially after the meeting with the lawyer. It would all come out anyway. But did it have to come out now? When everything was so. . .

"Crap."

"Roger? You all right?"

"Yeah. Fine. And yeah, I found it." He decided to continue

183

to keep the flier about the book to himself, as well as any additional information about the memos. He felt protective of his sister and mother. They didn't need more grief right now.

"Is it true? I assume it is, since Margaret was at that lawyer's office."

"I think so. Why?"

"Mick showed me a copy of the birth certificate he'd found at county records and something is weird about it."

"What?" *What now?*

"The dates seem to match, and of course, the father isn't named, although Dad pretty much admitted it, but the last names are different."

"What do you mean?"

"Do you have the copy from Dad's safe?"

"Well, not on me. Kinda busy here. What's your point?"

"I'm not sure. Betty's maiden name was Connor, right? Do you remember if that was on the birth certificate? And because the father was 'unknown,' that made baby Margaret Connor also, correct?"

"I think so. They're calling me. What's going on?" Roger did not share that the father line on the birth certificate he'd found read: Jaycee.

"On the one Mick found, it read Miller as the last name for both. Also, he found it in a box marked 'Miscellaneous 1942,' and not with other birth and death records for that year. Don't you find that odd?"

Not really, since Roger had found the memo detailing the fake and the switch. Again, to tell her or not? Not. At least, not right now. If he could just get through this week and keep his mother and sister from really knowing what kind of person Kimo had been. He'd like to bury these memos with Kimo at Hawai'i Memorial Park.

"I'll look into it, okay? I don't have time now. Without seeing the documents, I can't say for certain that it's not a coincidence or a mistake. We were in the middle of a war then, so I can't imagine record keeping could be held to be accurate, right, Ab?"

"Okay, Roger. I guess I could be making too much of this. It just shocked me, seeing it in writing. I guess I don't want to think our father raped someone."

"Just because one thing is true, or even might be true, doesn't make another true as well." Roger tried to console Abigail but he knew it was *all* true. The very worst was all true. He would do his best to keep it from her and their mother. He would be the man his father never was.

"I really have to go. We'll talk later. I'll see you tomorrow at the cemetery, right? 2 PM?"

"Yes, I'll see you there."

Abigail spent the rest of the day with patients and paperwork. An emergency surgery came in, so she had a nurse cancel Mick. That raised a few eyebrows, but the patient was critical and she had no time to take care of it. She stayed on the floor until close to midnight, monitoring. She didn't need to, but she was avoiding going home or talking to anyone. Although she had asked Roger to check into the birth certificate thing, she knew it was true, and just wasn't ready to admit it to herself. Keeping busy was one way to do that.

Chapter 17

Gerald Breem sat in his office chair, back to the desk, idly swiveling back and forth as he looked out the window. A file folder lay open in his lap. Every time he'd looked in the folder over the years, his anger had grown until he felt he could no longer contain it. Carbon copies of all the 'mad memos' handed down. Memos from way before his time, paper yellowed, purplish blue type-written messages with varying degrees of venom, a legacy no one would want.

Gerald had wondered why Kimo had given him copies of them. At first, he had been honored that the big boss, the owner, entrusted him with such leverage. He hadn't even read them the first several years until rumblings at the company made him dig out the file and really study it. It was horrible. Filled with racism and hate, misogyny and brutality, thinly disguised as company discipline. In later years, as Kimo aged, the memos were less couched in disciplinary terms and more direct and leaning toward extortion.

For the first ten years or so of his career, Gerald had

idolized Kimo. Thought of him as a father figure, especially after his own father died. Then he got a few memos of his own. Although they were cruel, they weren't litigious or even worthy of reporting to the police. What could he say? "My boss was mean to me?"

Kimo was smart and never came right out and admitted he committed any crimes, but looking back, Gerald was sure he had. He was thrilled that Kimo was no longer around, no longer his problem. Roger probably would run the company for a while, but like all kids, well, he wasn't a kid per se, but he'd been treated like one his whole life... like all kids, he'd get tired of doing real work. Gerald hadn't taken all of Kimo's crap all these years, covered for him, done his dirty work so he could *still* sit on the sidelines. He'd take matters into his own hands. Once again. Make sure Lemon Enterprises was run the way he wanted. There was very little he wouldn't do for his company. Now that the head of the snake had been lopped off, the body would flop around and he'd swoop in. Just like he'd always planned.

The family's services for Kimo were at 2 PM and he'd been invited. He'd declined. No way. He wasn't family. He knew that. Especially after he'd found his own special memo from Kimo detailing his father's spiral into debt from gambling. Money owed to Kimo as far back as when they served together in the war. Debt Gerald's father had never been able to repay. He had seen suicide as the only way out. Kimo had not only enabled him down that path, he'd pushed him right off it. All the while, treating Gerald like he was something special; being a surrogate father to him. It made him sick to think of it. His father never once told him or his mother the truth. Taken it to his grave. Then one day, fairly recently, a new memo had appeared in Gerald's file. A new *old* memo, written after he was hired, explaining the situation. He might never have seen it because it was placed in the section of the early days of the company. He wasn't supposed to find it until. . . until what? When? But he did. He'd gotten a new filing cabinet for his office and was transferring files and dropped one. The memos had spilled out and he'd seen his own name on this one. Everything changed for Gerald Breem.

*   *   *   *

The windward side of O'ahu was wet and overcast. At 1:45 PM, as the family all pulled into the Hawai'i Memorial Park lot, a rain shower had just finished.

Mabel hoped it would stay dry long enough for the service. She was not looking forward to explaining to her children that it would not be a burial, but an interment. She and Betty had kept that to themselves.

Margaret had declined to attend. Just as well. She was unpredictable. Justifiably so, but still. Mabel just wanted this over with. Betty helped her from the car and into the lobby, dodging puddles.

A woman came to greet them. "Hello, I'm Edith Gomes. I'm so sorry for your loss. You are here for the Lemon services, correct?" Mabel nodded. "Well, then, just step into our sanctuary and sit anywhere you like. Your husband is already there."

Mabel was a little startled to hear it put that way. Betty met her eyes and shrugged. The music was meant to be soothing but came off sounding like elevator music. They made their way down the aisle to the front pew. On a pedestal was an urn, presumably where Kimo waited. *Or rested. Whatever,* Mabel thought. She felt a little bubble of giddiness rise and struggled to squelch it. *Am I grieving? It doesn't feel that way. I feel like I did when I was six years old at my grandmother's funeral. Had no idea what was going on and lay under the pew for a while until I decided to roll*

188

from pew to pew to see how far I'd get before some adult stopped me. Not very far as it turned out. Her grandmother had been a lovely woman with many friends and relatives whose legs and feet hampered the experiment. Also, her mother's swift swat on her bottom set her behavior straight.

She wondered what would happen if she were to lie under the pew right now. Thankfully Betty never had to hear what Mabel was thinking because Roger and Abigail rushed in.

"Hi, Mom," Abigail said, and kissed her cheek. "Hi, Betty." Abigail sat on Mabel's other side.

"Hi, Mother." Roger also kissed her cheek, then sat next to Abigail. "Wow, this whole room just for us." He looked around. "When are they bringing out the casket? I thought it'd be here already."

"Yes, well," Mabel began. "Your father wanted to be cremated, so I followed his wishes." She and Betty had discussed how to handle this question. Since Kimo refused to discuss end of life plans with his attorney, Mabel felt she could tell the children that Kimo had discussed it with her. The funeral home had not quibbled at all once they confirmed with the attorneys there were no conflicting written instructions.

Roger and Abigail looked at the wooden box atop the tiny pedestal.

"That's it?" Roger asked.

"Mother, you didn't even tell us," Abigail said.

"There was nothing to tell. It was what your father asked for, so that's what I did." Mabel set her jaw and stared straight ahead. A man dressed in a simple black suit entered from a side door and approached them.

"Hello. I'm Robert Davis, the chaplain and kahuna here at Hawai'i Memorial Park. I understand this is a non-denominational service with a Hawai'ian blessing? Is that correct Mrs. Lemon?"

"Yes, that's right," Mabel said.

"We'll begin in here and then if you all would follow us to the site for the actual interment, we will conclude there."

"That's fine, thank you."

"Will others be joining us today?"

"No, just the immediate family," Betty said. "A large memorial will be held later in the week and a more public service as well at his corporate headquarters. This is just for them, you understand." She indicated Mabel, Roger and Abigail.

"Of course. Let's get started, shall we?"

The children said nothing throughout the service. Mabel's mind wandered to different times in her and Kimo's life together. This moment, this final piece, somehow did not seem real. She expected Kimo to step through the doorway, spread his arms and say, "Ta da! Just kidding."

Although she had found him, slumped over his desk, not breathing, she somehow expected him not to be dead. For that not to have killed him. Nothing else had. None of Kimo's actions, hideous as she knew they had been, and would have continued to be, had finished him off, so, could he really be gone?

"Mom. Mom." Abigail nudged her. "Do you want to say anything? He's asking you." She pointed to the kahuna.

"No. I don't. You go ahead. Or Roger."

"I don't have anything to say, Mom," Abigail whispered.

"Mother I am going to have to speak in front of hundreds of people on Friday at the Shell and then on Saturday at the Gala dinner at the Hyatt. I'll be talking enough. Pass," Roger also whispered.

"Betty? Do you have anything to say?" Mabel asked.

"Nothing I can say in front of the children," Betty whispered.

"No. I guess I'll wait until we're at the grave site," Mabel

190

said to the kahuna, suddenly feeling as if she were a very bad widow indeed. *He must have seen it all by now*; she thought grimly and watched his poker face.

"Very well. If you'll all follow me."

They did follow him to the parking lot and got in their cars. Abigail and Roger had driven separately, claiming work commitments immediately following the service. The kahuna got into a golf cart-like vehicle and drove around curving well-manicured lawns and gardens to the site where Mabel had bought her plot years ago. She didn't remember it at all.

They gathered at the edge of a small square of AstroTurf and the kahuna place the koa urn with Kimo's ashes next to it.

"Is it all right to begin the blessing?" he asked.

They all nodded. He held a small bowl of water and used a ti leaf to sprinkle water around the site. He chanted in Hawai'ian and sprinkled some more. They stood solemnly, silently. Mabel held onto Betty on one side and Abigail on the other. Abigail linked her arm through her brother's.

"Would anyone like to make any final remarks?" the kahuna asked.

Mabel cleared her throat. "I just want to say, this was a memorable life, Kimo Lemon. Thank you for my children. I hope you find peace and happiness, wherever you are."

No one else said anything. The kahuna waved over a man they hadn't noticed. He pulled back the Astroturf to reveal a small hole. He knelt and set the urn inside the hole and covered it with dirt, then replaced the AstroTurf.

The kahuna said, "If you would like time for reflection, you may stay here as long as you wish, or we have a reception room with refreshments if you prefer."

"Are you all right, Mom?" Abigail asked.

"I have to go," Roger said. He hugged his mother. "It's

going to be all right," he whispered.

"I know," Mabel whispered back. "I love you, son."

"I love you, too, Mom. I'll call you later. Betty, you'll see she gets home all right?"

"Of course, Roger."

Abigail embraced her mother tightly. "It's over, Mom. I think it's finally over."

"I hope so, love."

"I have to get to the hospital. I love you, Mom. Call if you need anything."

"I will."

Mabel and Betty watched them get into their cars. "Do you think they'll be all right?" Mabel asked.

"I think they are more than all right. You ready?"

"I certainly am. I've been ready for this day for a long time."

The two old ladies got into their car and drove out into the mist.

*　　　*　　　*　　　*

Abigail should go to the hospital, but she really needed to see Mick. She couldn't just show up at the Star-Bulletin offices, could she? That would be odd. The daughter of Kimo Lemon asking to speak to a reporter. They didn't need any more publicity, good or bad. She opted for the hospital in the end, because she figured maybe Mick was actually working and might not be able just to drop everything to see to her emotional needs. He did say to call after the service if she needed anything. She did. Need something. Him.

The drive over the Pali Highway took forever in the mist. As she came out of the tunnel a rainbow arced from the valley toward downtown Honolulu. Perfect. The mist had disappeared by the time she hit the H-1 then exited the freeway for the hospital. *The sun did amazing things for one's mood,* she thought.

She felt a bit lighter as she entered the hospital, what she thought of as her domain. She checked her patients' charts and all seemed to be on track. Everyone on her floor knew about the family's services today, but no one said anything. A high profile family, a celebrity doctor of sorts, and of course, Mick's articles hadn't really helped keep her out of the public eye, but the staff were respectful of her privacy. She'd never been a chatty co-worker anyway.

She did feel okay. She still wanted Mick, but her equilibrium rebalanced as she fell into familiar routine in a familiar place.

In the doctor's lounge she checked the notice board for anything new, then she took a chocolate old-fashioned donut. Something she almost never did. It was a little like cake, and she felt like celebrating. *Hmmm. Better not let that get out.*

In her office she dialed Mick and sure enough, he was out on a story. That was okay now, too. Surprising what a few miles and a few minutes could do. She left a message, first name only, for him to call her.

When he did several hours later, she was just wrapping things up. He'd been at Lemon Enterprises, or Lemon Central as he'd called it, following up on the arrangements for Friday's memorial at the Waikiki Shell and Saturday's Gala at the Hyatt.

"I was just leaving. Why don't you come to my house and I'll cook something for dinner?" Abigail asked.

"Sounds good. I have to write up my notes first or I'll forget. An hour give or take?"

"Great." Abigail gave him her address and some directions to her little house set back from the street. She warned him it was almost camouflaged by plumeria lining a long drive amid a sea green lawn of hardy grass. A short Hawai'ian style lava rock wall flanked her drive at the sidewalk, further disguising the house.

"If I can't find it, I'll just stand in the street somewhere and yell for you," Mick joked.

"I'll keep an ear out," she said.

She grabbed her bag and headed out. Just enough time to stop at Foodland and grab a quick shower before he arrived. He could help cook. It pleased her to think of them doing something domestic together, then sharing their day with each other. Then perhaps the night.

Chapter 18

Honolulu Star-Bulletin **Thursday, September 28, 1995**
Lemon Enterprises Squeezes In Memorial At Waikiki Shell
By Mick Kau'ula
Preparations continue for the memorial for Lemon Enterprises head, Kimo Lemon, who died of heart failure September 16, at his home in Kahala.

Already in the works was the fiftieth anniversary Gala for his company, scheduled for Saturday at the Hyatt Regency Hotel in Waikiki—by invitation only. However, a memorial will take place at noon this Friday at the Waikiki Shell, which is open to the public. The *Star-Bulletin* has been running stories on Lemon's various companies and philanthropic works since his death.

Continuing in that vein, according to OC&P Executive Vice-President Gerald Breem, the company wishes to give back to the community once again, by allowing them to say good-bye to the founder of such companies as O'ahu Cane & Pine, the Lemon Foundation and Lemon Tree Training, among others. So far the program includes an overview of Kimo Lemon's life, a musical tribute by Sheila and the Shells--one of Kimo's projects--and testimonials.

A private service for the family was held yesterday. What's next for the corporation now that the reigning monarch is gone? Only time will tell. New head of Lemon Enterprises, Roger Lemon, son of Kimo Lemon, says business will go on as usual and will continue or even expand its philanthropic efforts.

*   *   *   *

Roger was in a tizzy at Lemon Enterprises. He hadn't gone home the night before, but had changed into a clean shirt this morning just before his morning coffee. Then he changed it again after he immediately spilled his coffee down the front. His hair stood out despite a combing and he couldn't remember if he'd eaten since his father's interment yesterday. That had been a shock. He'd been expecting a funeral and a casket and all he'd seen was a little wooden urn on a tiny table.

Why didn't his mother say anything to him? Or Abigail? She'd seemed as surprised as he'd been. *I guess it doesn't matter in the long run.* His father certainly had never discussed those things with him. *Still dealing with the shock and grief, I suppose. Didn't think there would be any grief at all. Strange. I'm probably just tired.*

He'd been working on his speech and making lists most of the night. He had people helping him of course, assistants and event coordinators, but this was no ordinary corporate event. Not only was it the fiftieth anniversary of the company his father had built from the ground up, but it was also his first major event after taking over the company. Throw onto that a very public memorial and—no wonder he wasn't sleeping.

His father's secretary—*his* secretary now—knocked at the

open doorway.

"Mr. Lemon?"

"Yes, Mrs. Marsden? And please, call me Roger."

Mrs. Marsden was somewhere in middle age, Roger wasn't sure, but she'd been there at least twenty years. In fact, she looked about his age, attractive, efficient, professional. He realized he'd seen her around most of his working life there, but knew nothing about her.

"Uh, Roger," his name seemed to stick a bit, "I have a list of all the event contacts for you. I know you were working on so many aspects of both events, so I compiled a list. I can confirm their duties and time requirements if you like."

Roger realized she had probably been one of the people who just *did* things for his father. That was how they magically got done. *She* did them.

"Are you a Lemon Tree graduate?" he asked her.

"Excuse me?" She was caught off guard.

"Are you a graduate of my father's training division?"

"Yes. Your father was very good to me," she said carefully. "Why do you ask?"

"Just curious. Can I ask you something in complete confidence?"

"I suppose."

"No, really. I've been here in this office a week now, more or less, and you are amazing. You just get everything done. I don't know how you do it without blowing your top."

She smiled now, a bit more relaxed. "It's better to stay calm and focused. Gets more done in the end."

"Did you want to go to secretarial school twenty years ago, or whenever you wanted to go to college?"

She looked wary again. "Not really. There weren't a lot of jobs available, so. . ." she trailed off.

197

"Was it more like my father said he wouldn't help you unless you became a secretary? It will stay between us, I promise."

"He was very good to me. I don't like to complain."

"You're not complaining. I'm asking." Roger thought fast. "I'm asking all the employees for their self-evaluations to see if they're in the best place in the company for them and for us." Now that he'd said it, it wasn't a bad idea.

"I wanted to go to business school. Thought I could run my own company. I did know a lot about the documents end of things, and I'm an excellent organizer."

"That's true. Are you still interested in running your own company?"

"I think. . . I think I'm too old to start over. I mean, I don't want to start from nothing."

"What if I sent you to business school and you ran one of our subsidiaries? What would you think of that?"

"I don't know what to say."

"I'm thinking of expanding Lemon Tree. It's 1995, Mrs. Marsden, not 1965. Would you help me?"

"Anything Mr. Lemon. Roger."

"The way you can help me is with this experiment. You can be my guinea pig. What do you think? You will still work here, but I'll send you to school and we'll figure out a better fit for you in the company. I think you're wasted here as a secretary."

"I, I'll think about it." The color had drained from her face.

"Don't worry, if you don't want to do it, you'll still have this job."

"It's not that. Maybe we can talk about it after the Gala. Maybe next week? I'm so filled with details right now, Mr.— Roger. Thank you."

"You're welcome. Okay, so yes. Here is the list, well, *stack*

198

of stuff for the Memorial tomorrow. If you can cross-check it and get back to me that would be great."

"Do you have the Gala list, too? I can double check that while I'm at it."

"Both?" She nodded, holding out her hand. He gave her the files and smiled. "I have meetings all morning--lawyers, the board. I was wondering how I was going to do all this, too. I just didn't want to pass it off. He was my father. This last thing is for him."

"I understand. I'll email you updates. If you think of anything else, let me know."

"Did you email my father updates?" Roger couldn't imagine Kimo emailing.

"No. He was more of a memo person." She smiled, but bitterness edged her mouth.

"Yes, he was. But I'm not."

She gave him a genuine smile and left the room, closing the door behind her. For the first time in several days, Roger felt that he'd gotten a hold on the company. He might just survive this week after all.

He changed his tie and decided he needed food before he could face all those meetings. Did he have time? It wasn't even 8 AM. What was Mrs. Marsden doing here that early? Either she was a real gem or . . .? Or what? Food and sleep. That was his problem. Seeing things that weren't there, imagining conspiracies. Get a grip. He went downstairs and out to Pop's Diner--a favorite of his--and got a Portuguese sausage, eggs and rice breakfast. Perfect.

*　　*　　*　　*

Mick did indeed wake up in Abigail's bed. Their second

199

night together had not lessened their chemistry. The simple task of preparing dinner together and the resulting domesticity, in fact, seemed to intensify it.

Abigail was already making coffee in the kitchen as Mick could attest by the delicious aroma wafting his way. Her side of the bed was messy and he pulled her pillow to him and inhaled.

"Hey," she called. "I have to get to the hospital. Do you want some toast?"

When he didn't respond, she came to the doorway. "You up?"

"Yes," he said into her pillow.

"Don't drool on that. I'm going to need it later."

"I'll try." He released her pillow and saw she was already dressed. How had she managed not to wake him? He must have been tired from all their activity last night. His lower back ached a bit. He smiled at the memory.

"What are you smiling at?" she asked.

"Just reviewing last night's events."

"Oh, yes. Dinner was good, wasn't it?" She smiled back. "Coffee's here and I'm making sourdough toast. Want some?"

"Sure. When are you leaving?"

"In five minutes. Don't hurry, though. Just lock up on your way out. I have to get to the hospital."

Mick mulled over her allowing him to stay in her private space without her. Seemed significant, but without coffee, he couldn't be sure. "I want to take a shower. Will you still be here?"

"Probably not. Let me say good-bye now." Abigail came over to the bed and kissed him firmly. "Good-bye. Have a good day. What are you up to, anyway?"

"Is today Thursday?" She nodded. "Then I'm going to the Hyatt and the Shell and nose around. Get some comments and info on the preparations for tomorrow and Saturday."

"Okay. Talk to you later?"

He nodded and watched her leave. He lay in her bed a few more moments, enjoying the memory and smell of her. The room was cozy and personable, but not cluttered. Her graduation picture with her mother and Roger flanking her; a dried lei draped one corner of a small mirror over a worn but well-built bureau; a wicker chair by the window with a view of a tiny backyard. The house was set far back on the lot with an enormous, skinny front lawn and driveway and a microscopic back area. The shotgun-style house had the living room and kitchen facing the street with a nice front lanai. The kitchen side door opened onto a carport, and two small bedrooms in the back were separated by a bathroom just wide enough to contain a tub/shower, sink and toilet.

He wasn't a 'yellow' guy, but the pale, sunny shade of the rooms with their white trim brightened the house and made it seem bigger. Dark wooden floors, polished to a rich hue added to the plantation-style flavor. The second bedroom was a guestroom/office with computer and small file cabinet. He stopped himself from searching it. *Reporters' inquisitive habits die hard,* he thought.

Must be love, he joked to himself. What did he just say? *Since when had a potential source not been utilized to the max? Since Abigail. Shit.*

He showered, dressed and locked up. The advantage of her long skinny drive was that it easily fit two cars. Five cars. The advantage of the tough, flat Hawai'ian lawn was that you could drive over it, no harm done. When he was a kid, he'd had a dog who was a digger. Holes appeared in the family lawn, but the grass just kept coming back. Eventually the dog passed away, and the lawn returned like nothing had happened, except for smooth rolling bumps in places. He sort of missed those gopher-like mounds.

He backed out carefully onto the busy street. It was a lovely day. A little humidity said it might rain later, or it could just as easily dry up. He checked his meter for rain, the Ko'olau mountains, as he drove toward the Star-Bulletin offices. Just a wisp of cloud lay over the back of the Manoa valley today. Probably dry and hot, then.

After checking in, he left the building again and drove to the Waikiki Shell bandstand. He'd already called to be sure someone was available to talk to him. He had to do some convincing to get some time, since everyone was in a frenzy about tomorrow.

The heat was worse in Waikiki. He parked near the zoo and walked over. He was a sweaty mess by the time he reached the Shell office. At least the Hyatt would be air conditioned, he thought as he tramped around looking for his contact amid the buzz of activity.

*   *   *   *

Mabel and Betty awoke to the same heat in Kahala. Although both were early risers, the usual breeze was absent, making the house and gardens close and oppressive.

"When that wind shifts to off-shore, sometimes I think it'll be the death of me," Mabel said.

"I know. I don't even want coffee this morning." Betty was helping Mabel to dress. Mornings were always difficult with her arthritis and the old broken leg stiffening up each night.

"Betty, tell Teresita to make a big batch of iced tea and keep it coming. I can do this last bit." She grunted into house slippers. "I always feel so, I don't know, informal and underdressed in a muu muu, but on days like this, boy am I glad they were invented." She sat panting on the edge of the bed. "Go on, I'm okay. Tell her."

Betty, also clad in muu muu and rubber slippers, slap-slapped down the tiled hall to the kitchen.

"I'm going to need my cane today, dammit," Mabel mumbled to herself. The cane made her feel so *old* and incompetent. It was somehow worse than the walker which she still occasionally used. She prided herself on days she needed neither, saying she was a 'normal' person again. She sighed, staring at the cane lurking by the nightstand. She'd gotten a 4-footed cane after she'd transitioned from the wheelchair to the walker when her leg had mended enough. She likened it to a spider, even though it didn't have eight legs. It might as well have. She didn't much care for spiders, either. It had sat in storage for years until recently. Things had gotten worse about six months ago, and when they didn't get better, she'd had Betty dig it out for her. She hadn't needed it a lot, but lately, it seemed she was wearing out. Kimo needed taking care of and that had further depleted her. She'd never been a physically strong person and the broken leg had made that worse. She made up for it in backbone, as her own mother would have said.

Her breathing returned to normal and she grabbed the cane. She was impatient. Too much to do to put up with this crap, she told herself. She started toward the atrium. Have a glass of tea, some toast and then finish those boring journals. She had to be sure nothing bad was in them. Damn Kimo and his stupid journals, his giant ego with his showboating and his vicious streak. This was all his fault.

Betty brought a tray with two glasses of tea and a plate of toast to the atrium. "Here you go. I'm going to get that fan from upstairs and bring it in here until the breeze decides to do what it's told."

"Betty," Mabel stopped her. "After you do that, can you bring the box of journals in here? We need to finish reading. Be sure they're safe."

"Of course. Be back in two shakes."

Mabel really didn't feel well. Must be the heat. She sipped her tea but even the fan didn't help. Her leg ached something awful today.

Betty noticed. "Are you all right? You look a little pale." She put down the box of journals in its customary place, between their two chairs. "Did you not sleep well?"

"I slept all right. I have a lot on my mind. My leg's aching some." Betty knew that was code *for hurting like a son of a bitch*, because Mabel never said anything about pain or not feeling well unless it was severe.

"No need to suffer. I'll get a pain pill. You eat some toast so it doesn't hit your empty stomach. Be right back."

"I don't want to be all muzzy-headed. We have to finish these today."

"We do? Why?"

"I just feel a need to get them off my To Do list. You know how it is."

"Well, you can't concentrate if you're hurting. You eat a whole piece of toast and you'll be fine. I'll help read, too. We're almost done, and we'll finish in no time."

This time Mabel didn't argue. The pain was really bad, and either way, she wouldn't be able to concentrate. Might as well not-concentrate with a Vicodin floating around and feeling no pain, as the kids say. She smiled grimly. The heat didn't help.

Betty returned with her pill. "This heat better break. Either it's gonna rain or the breeze will shift. You'll see."

Mabel swallowed her pill on top of the toast she'd consumed. The journal lay in her lap while she watched the unmoving plumeria outside.

Betty picked up a journal section and began to read. "I

204

know I've said it before, but I'm going to say it again. If this was Kimo's only legacy, you'd think he was the dullest man on Earth. This was a big day. He went fishing. He says he used new bait and caught a shark. That's the most exciting thing I've read in pages and—uh, oh."

"What?"

"I'm not sure. The next page after the fishing entry is a newspaper article. Oh, Jesus. You look. Tell me what you think." She handed the journal to Mabel. "I remember this story when it came out. Terrible."

Mabel read the journal silently and then read the article aloud. "Human Remains Recovered From Tiger Shark. Today a local man out fishing caught a twelve foot Tiger shark. When sliced open after weigh in, the shark had a human foot and shoulder section in its stomach as well as a hand with several fingers attached. One of the fingers still wore a distinctive green jade ring. It is suspected that the parts belong to Ellison Chang, the owner of Chang Pine, a local pineapple cannery, who has been missing since Sunday. He was last seen at his cannery office, working late. He was an avid fisherman himself, and it was not unusual for him to go night fishing. The investigation continues but it is presumed an accident."

Mabel studied the accompanying photo. "The picture is mostly of the shark. I guess that could be Kimo next to it, but it's so blurry it's hard to tell. The article doesn't name the fisherman who 'discovered' the body parts or caught the shark."

"That's certainly convenient. Why else would the article be in the journal? It's got to be a reference to Kimo. Didn't Chang Pine close after that? It's not around anymore, is it?"

"No. It's gone. I do remember Kimo being excited that Chang Pine was finally going to sell to him. I was busy with the children, so I don't remember all the details, but I remember the

205

discovery of that shark with the remains." She shivered. "Scary. I didn't go to the beach for a while after that." Mabel was lost in her memories. "When the kids were small, I guess I lost about a decade of local and world events."

"I know what you mean. When Margaret was little, before I met Tony, it seemed all I did was work and care for her. I don't think I even saw a movie that wasn't on TV and five years old."

Betty fussed with the journals. "Mabel, can I ask you something?" Betty's tone seemed strained.

"Sure." Mabel laid the journal and article in her lap. "What is it? What's wrong?"

"I've been thinking about something and I just need to ask you about it. We've been friends for so long, I just feel like we're more than employer and employee. Am I wrong?"

"Betty. Of course we're friends. I pay you because you provide me with a very important, in fact, crucial service. I need a skilled nurse. The fact that we get along so well is icing on the cake. What is it? Are you ill? Please, tell me."

Betty fidgeted. Mabel had never seen her so nervous. Maybe anxious was a better word. Even when Kimo had been at his worst, Betty was a rock.

Betty took a deep breath. "Remember when I told you Margaret was coming?" Mabel nodded. "And we had a big conversation about her mental illness and when she got here she said she was Kimo's daughter?"

Mabel nodded again.

"I've been thinking a lot about that. I've also been thinking about the night Margaret was conceived. *How* she was conceived. When she told us that he was her father, and she had found out she was a child of rape, you were so kind. To both of us. And since then, you haven't changed the way you've treated me. I don't know how you have managed that. I don't know if I could have been as gracious as you've been."

"I thought about it, too. But for a different reason" Mabel said.

"I wanted to thank you."

"Wait," Mabel stopped her. "I guess you need to hear my story, too. You know Kimo and I met in Texas when we were young, right? When he came home on leave? My family had moved from England and eventually settled in Texas where Kimo and I met. You know we married and were stationed in Hawai'i and just never left."

Betty nodded.

"The reason I believed you, and still do, and why we can always remain friends, is Kimo raped me, too."

Betty's mouth hung open.

"I know. I married him. I was young. I got pregnant. I didn't know what else to do. I had never had 'relations' with anyone. I thought that what Kimo did was how you did it." Mabel started to cry. "I was so young and naive. Even after I got pregnant, there were rumors about other girls. I was so scared."

"Why did he marry you? He was in the service; he could have just left all of that, all of you, behind. Why would he do that?"

"My family was wealthy. We had come over with money, invested well, diversified. My dad's company, White's Whitewalls, was rapidly going national. Kimo knew a good thing when he found it. At the time, I refused to believe the stories about the other girls. When I told Kimo I was pregnant, he said we should get married, just like that. He wanted it to seem legitimate. He went to my father with a big song and dance about loving me and wanting to serve his country. My father was a Royal Navy man and completely fell for it. My whole family did. I did."

"What happened?"

"I never told my family that I was pregnant before we married. We made like the rush was because he was being shipped out. We also said we wanted all the family to come who were able. Remember, I said I was an 'oops' baby—all my family was elderly, what there was of it. I was an only child, the darling of the White clan. I'm so glad my parents never found out the truth."

"What about Kimo's family? You don't really talk about them," Betty said.

"According to Kimo, they were a collective piece of work. I only met his parents one time, and they didn't come to the wedding. Kimo told me they are why he joined up so young. To get away from them."

"That's so sad."

"Yes. It explains a lot about Kimo. I've never told the kids about their grandparents on that side. We said Kimo's family was dead and left it at that. The one time I met them, his father was so abusive to his mother. They both drank some, and that only made it worse. I know Kimo hated to see his mother treated that way, but it seems that apple didn't fall far from the tree. I'm not excusing it you understand, but when that's all the role-modeling you have to go on. . ." Mabel trailed off. She sighed. "I didn't think Kimo would be this way. That way. After growing up in it, I thought, well, I thought he would be different."

"They say it's a cycle, you know." Betty patted her hand.

"I can see that now. His father was, what do they call it? A red-neck? A red-neck Texan who hated everyone who wasn't white. Nevermind that Texas used to belong to Mexico not long ago. . . he passed that onto Kimo, too, but I guess the war helped expand his hate to other races. I just don't know what makes people do what they do."

Mabel and Betty both dabbed at their eyes.

"Why didn't they come to the wedding? You're white. I

mean, your name is White after all?" Betty's little joke made Mabel smile a bit.

"Ah. I'm a foreigner. My father started a company that was becoming successful, so not only was he a foreigner, but he was 'taking good jobs from decent Americans.' Such nonsense. As Kimo got older, he became more like his father."

"I'm so sorry, Mabel," Betty said.

"Me, too. But the important thing is, the children can never know any of this. You are the only living person on Earth besides me, now that Kimo is dead, who knows."

"I would never--" Betty began.

"No, you have to swear."

"I do. I swear. We've been through so much; of course I will protect you. You know that."

"I do know. And I will protect you, too. Betty. We'll go down with the ship together, as my father used to say." Mabel reached out and Betty clasped her hand.

They heard Teresita's step on the tile hall coming toward them.

"Sounds like lunch to me," Betty said. They let go and wiped their faces as Teresita brought a tray in and set it on the wicker coffee table.

"More tea, ladies? You gon' float away, but it's so hot today," Teresita said.

"Yes please, more tea," Mabel said. "This looks delicious. Gazpacho and salad. My favorite. Thank you."

"You're welcome. I be back with the tea in a minute."

"All right. Back to the business at hand. What do we do with this?" Mabel indicated the article she still had in her lap. "It feels funny to keep something like this, but do we destroy it?"

Betty nodded. "Does it seem odd to you, that if what is implied in Kimo's journal, that this poor man was the new bait, that Kimo would then turn around and catch the same shark? Wouldn't it be suspicious? Wouldn't it be safer if the shark weren't caught?"

"I know what you mean. But remember, never underestimate Kimo's ego or power. He may not have dragged the man out to the boat himself, but he wasn't without help. A few times I saw him talking to people who looked, well, I don't know. Like gangsters."

"You never said!"

"What would be the point? I don't think he knew I saw. I might have gone on a late night fishing trip, too."

"Oh, Mabel, don't say that." Betty looked at the newspaper again. "At least it doesn't say who the fisherman was. Maybe the caption was cut off? And you really can't tell from the photo. Maybe it wasn't Kimo."

"He was always smart. He might have paid someone to pose as the fisherman. But don't forget, he kept that article all these years. It must mean something."

"I think we should remove the article. If you still want to try and salvage some of Kimo's reputation for the children, although I don't know why. They know who their father was."

"Should I save the article?"

"For a while. I guess. Put it with the other thing. We can decide what to do with it all when we're finished. Are you feeling any better?"

"Yes. I think the meds kicked in, thank you. And look!" She pointed out the glass doors. The plumeria was waving. "The breeze is back. Open 'er up."

Betty rose and did as she was bid.

They finished the journals and put them back in the boxes. Nothing else as suspicious or terrifying and turned up. They agreed that perhaps they should review them one more time, when this was all over. Just to be sure.

Chapter 19

Honolulu Star-Bulletin **Friday, September 29, 1995**
Kimo Lemon Memorial Today at Waikiki Shell
By Mick Kau'ula
 The public is invited to the Kimo Lemon Memorial today at noon at the Waikiki Shell. Parking is limited, so free shuttles are available from Ala Moana Center fronting Liberty House. The memorial is also free, but bring a low backed chair or blanket. The seated sections are reserved for company employees who must show company I.D.
 The event includes testimonials and entertainment by some of Kimo Lemon's protégés and favorite acts, including music, hula and stand-up comics, as well as a brief service in Hawai'ian and English. The service will be simulcast on KDEN radio and local TV station 19.
 Kimo Lemon, founder and CEO of such companies as Lemon Enterprises, O'ahu Cane & Pine and Lemon Tree, among others, died September 16 at his home of a heart attack. All the ramifications of his death have not been felt by the company, but

son and new CEO Roger Lemon seems to have it well in hand. The Lemon family has been very private and in seclusion for much of the time since the patriarch's death. A private service for the family was held Wednesday at Hawai'i Memorial Park.

*   *   *   *

Margaret sat on the edge of the guesthouse bed. She had kept a low profile since the meeting in the lawyer's office. She was shocked to find she'd been included in Kimo's will, but after learning it was a stopgap measure against a lawsuit, in spite of her anger, she felt a thread of admiration for him. Self-preservation to the end.

Unsure of her next move, she'd remained under the radar, refusing to attend the 'family' memorial and using the opportunity to search the house. The housekeeper had been a problem until she finally went shopping. Breaking into the main house would be easy; French doors and sliders particularly so. However, she didn't have to since the kitchen window had been left wide open. Although she appeared ratty, she was quite strong and had levered herself right through and onto an immaculate counter.

She found absolutely nothing helpful. Kimo's home office safe was wide open and empty. In fact his whole home office was peculiarly sterile. Nothing much in the desk drawers or closet. She presumed Roger had taken all company related material that Kimo kept at home. The desk held nothing personal at all. She wondered what Mabel would do with that room after the dust settled. It was designed as a 'man's room,' with dark paneling and heavy furniture that didn't really go with the rest of the home's decor. It was also a library of sorts, its walls lined with shelves full of books. Mostly history, and a lot of local history, biographies including Hitler, Stalin, Napoleon, Nero—*all the greats,* she'd thought.

She'd even spent an hour randomly pulling and shaking books in case there were letters or a code. Unsure of how much time she had until Teresita returned, she'd moved quickly and thoroughly, but turned up nothing. She had just decided to start on Mabel's rooms, or even her mother's when Teresita returned and she'd barely escaped in time to run into her near the kitchen and offer help with the groceries. It was declined.

She'd better check in. She got into the little car Betty had provided keys for and set off for Diamond Head Market, a convenience store and gas station on the slopes of Diamond Head where Monsarrat Avenue met Diamond Head Road. She parked on the street and glanced about, headed for the pay phone at the corner of the lot. It was a 'clean' line.

She dialed a memorized number and said, "Ghostrider" to the person who answered. She was transferred.

"Go ahead."

"No new evidence. The second office safe was all I was able to check. Documents, interesting but not valuable at this time. Nothing at the house."

"You are still intact?" Meaning, was her cover still in place?

"Yes."

"Stay put. Keep looking."

"Copy that."

"We have nothing new at this end. You're still the best option. Two days." The connection was broken. Of course she was the best option. She was born of Kimo Lemon and had been trained by the best. She was still young when Tony had married Betty, so he was the only real father she had known. When her mother continued to refuse to discuss her biological father, all the teen hormones came to a head and she left home. She was aimless

214

and literally lived on the street. After a brush with a kind Honolulu Police Officer who saw something in her—potential?--she didn't know, she chose to stay strong. As soon as she was 20, she joined HPD and graduated with honors at 21. She had been recruited immediately for covert work outside the department. Eventually, she was asked to work the Kimo Lemon investigation which spanned several countries. They knew she was Kimo Lemon's daughter—even if she didn't yet--and after rigorous interrogation to ensure she had no allegiance to him or her half-siblings, they helped her not only to stay hidden, both in person and career, but also she'd learned all the gory details of her birth father. She had told Betty the truth when she said she stayed away to protect her mother. She was shocked and angry to discover Kimo was her father and how that had come to be. Betty had never discussed it and Margaret realized what a sacrifice her mother had made.

The years of living undercover had taken a toll, but just when it seemed enough evidence against Kimo had been gathered at last to bring him in, he was dead. Part of her was thrilled. At his age, she doubted he would have served much time and that did not sit well with her. Dying at her hands would have been the best option. She had followed him as much as his goons had followed her. However, she had the best surveillance and back-up available, and it was never detected by Kimo. The hope was that although Kimo was old, possibly ill, he would flip on his contacts, many of whom were international. This in exchange for immunity and protection for his family. She had hoped to confront him at his arrest and let him see what he had, in part, created in her, but that obviously wasn't going to happen.

Initially, she was quite familiar with Roger's and Abigail's lives and monitored them along with the team for involvement in Kimo's schemes. It became clear that he was estranged from Abigail and thought Roger was an idiot and therefore would have told them nothing. Kimo's staff was the best bet for conspirators. They had been watching Yoshi Onizuki, a relatively high executive at OC&P, for a connection to the Yakuza. That didn't pan out and then he was fired. Further investigation found Onizuki to be innocent of criminal activity, so they had shifted the focus to others in the Lemon Enterprises hierarchy.

The frustrating thing was he didn't seem to keep records. Not like a normal business. Of course there would be two sets of books, but they had not been able to find the *other* set and they had not been able to find who handled the fine tuning of criminal acts. Kimo kept up his good ol' boy act right to the end. He'd had to know he was being watched. He had to have been laundering money, moving money all over the world. His company used computers and of course, that was the way to do it, but Kimo himself did not. Wire taps, when finally granted by a judge, revealed nothing. Even parabolic microphones and a few carefully placed employees at Lemon Tree garnered no tips.

The longer the investigation dragged on and the less they could prove, the angrier the team got. Margaret had been slated to reunite with her mother in order to jump start Kimo into action when he was found dead. She had done the reconnaissance on the house and the occupants as she'd told her mother. Just not for the real reason.

She hung up the phone, understanding she was to check back in two days. Since Kimo's death she'd been checking in more often, but living at the house as a supposed mental patient-homeless daughter reunited with family had made that more difficult. On the street she had her contacts and safe phones. Here, she could not use the phone and the house was far from phones that would be safe. Nestled in the heart of the rich and famous, the house was isolated by land and sea and gated from car entry, but the four foot wrought iron fence connecting the lava stone wall that surrounded three sides of the property did nothing for those wanting to climb over. As she well knew.

She'd had to get her mother to 'help' her get a Hawai'i drivers' license—that had been fun—and 're-teach' her to drive before she'd been granted the use of the spare car. Even her professional contacts had a hard time reaching her. An Oceanic cable truck just could not sit out on the street in Kahala for three days unnoticed, nor could 'salesmen' approach the house. She didn't live in the main house anyway, so it wasn't like she could run in and answer the door. The main house was Teresita's domain. Although she was polite, she guarded her territory which unfortunately, included Betty and Mabel. Teresita did not say two words to Margaret that were not household related. She had been there longer than Betty, so bribery was not an option. The gardening staff was another matter, but they only came monthly, and even if they instituted their own people, once a month would not help.

She had just gotten approval and the budget for bugging the house. Getting in unobserved would be interesting. Teresita didn't go out much. She lived upstairs and only grocery shopped about once a week, and not on a schedule. She was frustratingly organized and unpredictable. The recent grocery excursion had been a surprise, but not as helpful as Margaret would have wished, since she hadn't possession of the bugs yet. Yay government, budgets, and priorities. But gotta get those results.

Initially, Kimo's death was suspicious due to the timing of it, and that was why the body was held so long. An autopsy had in fact been performed as well as a much more in depth tox screen than Abigail had managed. Given Kimo's suspected contacts and activities, murder was not out of the question, but they had not been able to prove it. No obvious wounds and no poisons detected because either they had not been looked for, or they were

217

reabsorbed by the body, or they disguised themselves as something else. His official cause of death was heart failure.

Well, duh. Anything can cause heart failure and that told them nothing. If she were going to kill Kimo, she would never be caught. She had full access to the house now, if she could evade Teresita's watchful eye. Just pushing him down the stairs would have been easy. Head cracks like an eggshell at the bottom. Boom, done. And what she'd told Betty about the garden was also true. Half the plants in their garden were toxic in one form or another. Maybe she should rethink the gardener angle. They came once a month. Maybe someone else had figured that out, too, and gotten in that way. Kimo had been found dead, in his home office, windows wide open, at night. Who knew better than she how easy it was to get in that way?

Without meaning to, she had driven into Diamond Head Crater and finished her thinking on the case while she walked up the trail to the WWII bunkers that lined its rim. She found a bottle of warm Coke in the car and brought that along. Fortunately, her poor mental patient hand me down clothes included a pair of comfortable shoes. She always wanted to be able to run. Even undercover, although she hated running, she was quite capable of chasing someone, or running away, as suited the circumstances.

The day promised to be a warm one. She intended to be at the Shell memorial at noon. She didn't know what she'd see or hear, but she'd be there watching in case one of their suspects showed.

She reached the top after climbing through the darkened bunkers and up vertical metal ladders. She had no flashlight but all the other tourists had read the brochure and brought theirs so she had plenty of ambient light.

She turned left and went along the crater rim a quarter mile until the chattering of visitors was lost on the breeze. She sat on a concrete overlook, probably the top of another bunker, and let the air and view wash away the cloying sense of this case.

It was becoming more difficult not to come clean to her mother. The look in her eyes when she thought she was looking at her loser-crack head-daughter was unexpectedly painful. Margaret wanted to tell her she was one of the good guys, had always been, and was someone to be proud of. Maybe someday. Maybe never. She shook off the melancholy and made her way back to the car. She passed a pair of tiny Japanese tourists, both wearing little princess high heels on the steep, dirt trail. And giggling! *Good luck*, she thought. But it made her smile and she decided to go to Rainbow Drive-In for a chocolate shake before going to the Shell.

*   *   *   *

Roger was anxious and exhausted as he prepared to give his opening welcome to at least a thousand people at the Shell. Most of the permanent seating was filled with company employees, from Lemon Enterprises and its subsidiaries, and also from associated companies. Bright blankets and chairs packed the sloping lawn, a festive picnic air encouraged by a local Hawai'ian band that played upbeat music accompanied by hula dancers on some songs. The main musical attractions would be later in the program.

Roger sat in the green room, just off the stage entrance. Despite the air conditioning and his light, casual Aloha shirt and kukui nut lei, he sweated. Since his father's death he had gone from nearly invisible, to being the public face of Lemon Enterprises. Part of that was his doing, wanting to show the Board of Trustees that he, in fact, was capable of running the company and doing a better job than his father.

Well, a more honest job, as he was learning. Some odd things had occurred in recent days, not just the 'ten year clause,'

219

but also international contract negotiations he'd not heard of. The accounting department was all upset that he wanted a complete audit.

He had been going over documents and policies until he thought his head would explode. He had read each and every memo and saw that not only was his father not a nice person, but it seemed he was a criminal. Numbers didn't track; accounts petered off into nowhere, and now these phone calls. He hadn't slept a full night since his father died and although he was worried about the company, he was also worried about his mother. How she was handling this, and if in fact the company was in trouble, what that might mean for her future.

A cheer rose outside the closed door and a quick check of his watch said it was time. He was not ready for this, and public speaking was among his least favorite activities. At least his speech was written down and if he got too nervous, he could just read it. It would be interpreted as grief, he hoped.

The stage manager opened the door and said, "You're on, Mr. Lemon." He escorted Roger to the edge of the wing and Roger continued to the podium, miked and ready at the edge of the stage. This would allow the performances and the slide show to carry on with minimal transition time. That proximity reassured him since it seemed he could just run off if he got too nervous. He wouldn't, of course, but it was a comforting thought. The stage manager stood just a few feet away, headset on, to coordinate the program. He gave Roger the thumbs up and Roger began.

Margaret found a parking spot on Kapahulu, but so far from the Shell she might as well have stayed parked up at Rainbow Drive-In. She had changed into a more touristy look she'd found in a thrift store and left her other clothes in the car. Her objective was to watch who showed up and if anyone made contact with Roger. Because the memorial had been thrown together last minute, she hadn't had an ideal opportunity to set this up. She had to try. She couldn't get back stage, but other Shell security was undercover with them and had been apprised. She wasn't sure what she'd do if someone started shooting at Roger. Throw herself between him and the shooter? Not a great prospect. However, if the mob wanted Roger to take over for Kimo, then killing him wasn't their best option.

Sunglasses, hat, an Aloha shirt and shorts completed her disguise. She pulled her gray flecked hair into a sloppy bun and anchored it under the hat. She doubted anyone would recognize her as Margaret, or even 'Peg,' now. Peg rarely bathed and looked and smelled awful and she was pleased that incarnation was in the past.

She ducked into an ABC convenience store and bought a straw bag and $4.99 towel. Now she really looked the part. She chose a part of the lawn as close to the stage as she could without standing out. Although, really, with so many people, it'd be hard to find someone you knew here, much less someone you rarely saw. She spread her towel and sat. The band was pretty good. A humongous picture of Kimo Lemon hung behind them.

The song ended to thunderous applause and Roger came to the podium. *He wasn't so bad,* she thought. *So far, he seems to be completely ignorant of his father's doings which would save him from jail if that proved true.*

The speech was heartfelt and short. He seemed to lose his composure at one point, but she was so far away, it was hard to tell. Some boring testimonials, but she tried to pay attention in case someone surfaced. Nope. Just boring. More songs and some hula. That was nice. In the midday sun it was really toasty and most of the people not near the shade of the monkey pod trees ringing the lawn started to leave.

By 1:30 it was over and a huge waste of her time, she felt. She packed up her little towel and satchel and began the hike back to the car, cutting straight through the Shell gates in a more direct line. Head down, she almost ran into a man crossing her path. She sensed more than knew not to look up. Her peripheral vision saw it was Roger. Great. What were the odds? He apologized and she mumbled an acceptance and, heart pounding, continued over the acres of grass to the street.

She stopped to get an overpriced, but ice cold drink, which lasted less than one block. She wished it were vodka. What a day. She was looking forward to the guesthouse, its seclusion and quiet. And the cold shower she would take the second she got back.

*　　*　　*　　*

Roger was thrilled when it was over. Thank God he could leave and not do any of the packing up and the heartfelt good-byes. He had already told the staff that he would leave directly after, since it was such an emotional time for him. His car was in the VIP parking section directly adjacent to the Shell staff and performers exit. He grabbed a cold water and let the door bang behind him, leaving air conditioned comfort for heat that threatened to squash him into the grass before he ever made the parking lot. Head down, he staggered to the gate and nearly ran into a lady crossing his path.

"Excuse me, I'm so sorry. I wasn't looking where I was going," he said.

The lady mumbled that it was all right and kept going, veering away from him and farther into the park.

Something about her was familiar, but he didn't know what. If it was someone who knew him, she would say hello, wouldn't she? Maybe not if she'd come from the Shell and seen the memorial. Maybe trying to show respect. He found his car and turned on the A/C for a few minutes before getting in. From his

222

spot, he could still see the lady heading north across the park toward the businesses on Kapahulu Avenue. Something about the way she walked seemed familiar. He was so tired. *If it's important, I'll figure it out, or see her again.*

The interior was a few degrees cooler and the A/C had finally switched from blowing hot air to frigid. He turned the vents directly on him and drove back to the office. He would have loved to go home and sleep for a week, but there was too much to do for tomorrow. That was the big day and promised the potential of the stuff of nightmares. Roger had coordinated with security, but he still felt anxious. Every important businessman in the world, it seemed, would attend, along with too many celebrities. It was his job to make sure the whole thing went off without a hitch. No problem.

Chapter 20

Honolulu Star-Bulletin **Saturday, September 30, 1995**
Fiftieth Anniversary Gala Forging Ahead Despite Loss
By Mick Kau'ula

Preparations are in full swing for the Fiftieth Anniversary Gala of Lemon Enterprises despite the loss of its founder earlier this month. Yesterday was the public memorial service for Kimo Lemon at the Waikiki Shell. It was a success by all accounts. Both the reserved seating sections and the open lawn seating were packed and the event went smoothly. (See accompanying story on A9 "Shell Memorial—Aloha Kimo".)

Today begins the last of the big Alohas for Kimo Lemon, but the family and companies will be affected for months to come, according to son and new CEO Roger Lemon.

Activities begin at 10 AM today at the downtown offices as well as the plant locations. Business will be carried on as usual, but the priority is sharing Kimo and his legacy with the public.

In an earlier interview, Kimo said, "I just want it to be one big party. So many folks have helped get me where I am, I just want to say mahalo to everyone!"

Tours will be given on the hour and the downtown office will have continuous live music in the lobby until 4 PM. All events are free.

Since Kimo Lemon's death September 16, flowers have been dropped off daily at the head office. Today is expected to be emotional and flower-filled as well, and the public is asked to drop flowers and other tributes at a special area of the courtyard designated by his photo and ribbons that are tied to the parking garage boundary.

Tonight is the final event, originally designated as the Gala Anniversary dinner, but now part memorial as well. The star-studded evening is by invitation only, Kimo Lemon having hand-picked the guest list months ago. The Hyatt Regency ballroom preparation was in full swing when this reporter visited Thursday, and the menu and decor are flawless.

Cocktails begin at 7 PM and dinner and speeches at 8. The menu choices include tournedos of beef, mahi mahi with papaya salsa or eggplant remoulade with tomato coulis. The desserts will be buffet style; and trolleys will wheel around a variety of offerings to keep foot traffic down. Each course has its own wine pairing and mixed drinks are available, as is Lone Star beer, a nod to Kimo's original home state. Although he claimed Hawai'i as his home, he never lost his Texas twang.

Tributes to Lemon Enterprises will start at 9. Originally, Kimo was slated to relate the corporation's humble beginnings, but now his son and the new CEO, Roger Lemon, will fill those big shoes.

When interviewed earlier, department heads of Lemon's companies had nothing but good things to say. They paraphrased Kimo's wishes saying that this is to be a birthday party, a Gala, so the memorializing will be kept to a minimum. In Kimo's own words, 'one big party.'

*   *   *   *

Roger slept the sleep of the dead after the Waikiki Shell memorial yesterday. He had indeed gone back to the office and worked, but not as late as he had the last couple of weeks. Mrs. Marsden said she had things under control for the Gala, and since she had been right on and dependable when finalizing the Shell arrangements, he let that go and went home.

He woke fairly rested and the dark circles under his eyes had faded a shade or two. He felt ready to face a day of glad-handing and smiling, followed by an evening of more speeches, eating and drinking too much. He would be so relieved when this was over and he could drop the pretense and just get on with running the company.

As he knotted his tie, he thought over a couple unexpected phone messages. The Securities and Exchange Commission wanted a word with him, as did the IRS. He supposed it was all due to the change in leadership since Kimo's death, but it made him anxious. He'd been kept out of the corporate loop and was catching up as fast as he could, but there was still so much he didn't know. After the 'ten year clause' discovery, he wasn't willing to trust his 'advisors' blindly. He had found the memos, but the book manuscript still bothered him. He had no idea what to do about it, or where to keep looking.

He knew his father, and was learning even more about him, so semi-legal business practices would not be a big surprise. After reading the memos, he wondered about the wisdom of keeping them. If a search warrant were executed and those were found, would they reveal any illegal business practices? So much he didn't know. He did know, however, that his father's success was

226

built on the backs of workers and he wanted to protect their jobs. He had picked pineapples and cut cane as a teenager, his father insisting he learn all aspects of the company. He appreciated that now, although was still convinced it had been a way to keep him out of Kimo's hair while he 'trained' and eventually graduated from University of Hawai'i at Manoa with a degree in business. Even after that, Kimo had kept him at arms' length, never quite giving him the authority to run anything.

He poured a second cup of coffee into a driver-friendly mug with a lid while he mused. Was Kimo's operation largely illegal? Was he in bed with the mob, or the Yakuza or something Roger had never even heard of? Was that Kimo's peculiar way of protecting Roger? Keeping him far from the operation of the executive portion of the corporation; having him run pineapple canneries and sugar refineries and paper-pushing non-essential services until he wanted to kill Kimo himself?

How old was he when he finally realized he would never work side by side with his father? Would never be a partner in the business? He'd held onto that dream for years. He'd probably been in his early 40s when he'd finally let go. He felt himself grow bitter and hard inside at the memory. *Might as well have been running a lemonade stand on Kalakaua Avenue in Waikiki,* he thought, for all the good he'd done, or progress he'd made.

He shrugged into his suit coat and stopped. Wait. Not only was it Saturday, it was a party. And it was his company now. Or, he thought it was. He grimaced. Maybe it belonged to Uncle Sam or a Middle Eastern conglomerate for all he knew.

He threw off his coat and yanked down the tie. He pulled the wildest Hawai'ian shirt he had out of the closet. Okay, not that wild, he thought, looking at the subtle inside-out print fabric. It was of tropical fish amid a sea of surfboards and The Bus figures. Ha. That will show them.

He smiled at the figure he now cut. He grabbed his briefcase and travel mug and set out into the already warm day. He was ready to face, maybe not the IRS, but certainly the public.

*　　*　　*　　*

Mick again woke next to Abigail. This was becoming a delightful habit. They were in his bungalow in Manoa, not too far from the shopping center, but quiet. Just at the invisible rain line, where every afternoon at four it showered briefly; not as much as in the back of the valley, but enough to make it lovely.

Abigail had told him she was off today since she was expected to attend the Gala that evening. She would check on her patients, however, but would not officially be working. She had begged off the downtown celebrations saying she wasn't part of the company and no one knew or cared if she was there. Roger hadn't argued. Mick was pleased for her. She needed a break. She was so strong, but it was taking its toll. He was sure there were things she hadn't told him, and he couldn't argue with her unspoken logic. He was a reporter covering the biggest local news story in years which happened to be about her family, and their relationship was new. He wasn't sure where it was going, but looking at her face, still relaxed in sleep, he liked where it was.

Mick however, was not so lucky. This had been his story from the start, when the Gala was just a social event, albeit a big one. He was head reporter of the Entertainment section and also covered Local Business for the *Star-Bulletin*. When Kimo died, the editor allowed him to continue the coverage, with staff reporters covering only a few side stories. Now that it was turning into quite the 'do,' he was expected to cover every aspect possible. He would be downtown all day and then attend the Gala tonight. The press was already scheduled to be at the dinner, but he made sure he was the one to represent his paper.

He leaned over and kissed Abigail gently before rolling out of bed to start the coffee maker. He showered while it brewed. When he returned to the bedroom to dress, she had thrown one arm over her eyes. He moved slowly and quietly, pulling out clothes for the day.

"I'm awake," she mumbled.

"No, you're not. This is a dream. Relax and sleep," he said in a sing-song.

She rolled toward him. "You would make a terrible hypnotist. Can I have this?" She took his mug of coffee off the nightstand and drank. "Thanks. You saved me."

"Um, sure. Help yourself," he kidded. He sat on the edge of the bed and they shared the mug for a moment. "I have to get downtown and it's going to be a zoo. I need to go now and see if I can get a parking place within forty miles of the building." He took another sip of his coffee before she wrestled it away again. "It will be every bit as bad as a weekday. Worse around Lemon Head."

"True. Better you than me." She still sounded sleepy.

"Thanks. What do you have today?"

"Check some patients. My house is falling down around me. It's been pretty tough the last couple weeks."

"I know. I'm sorry." He stroked her hand, still warm from sleep.

"I'm going to do something for me."

"You deserve that. Good. What are you going to do then?"

"First, laundry. Then I'm going to clean my house and maybe some gardening." She scooted higher on the bed.

"That's 'something for you?' That's work!"

"When you don't get to spend any time in your own home, being domestic can be soothing."

229

"If you say so." He rose to refill his mug.

"Yes, I say so. Your house is clean and neat. You must know what I mean."

"I have to keep it organized or I can't find anything. I had a little dog once. I lost him in here and haven't seen him for years." He returned with a mug for her, too.

She smiled her gratitude and sat up to drink, arranging pillows to support her. "Funny." She sipped. "I'm going home to shower and change and then to the hospital. I can't be seen in the same thing I wore yesterday." She wiggled her eyebrows. "Think of the scandal."

"It's the opposite for me. If I change my shirt all the guys know someone's taking care of me."

She reached out to him and he sat once again, her hand in his.

He thumbed a light circle on the back of her hand. "I was thinking, just to save embarrassment you understand, that you could keep some things here. If you wanted." His eyes never left hers.

"I think, to save my reputation, that would be nice."

"I hoped you might say that." He leaned in and kissed her. "So much so, that in fact, I was neat and clean and you can have this drawer," he stood and opened the middle dresser drawer with a flourish, "and this part of the closet." He opened the tiny doors to reveal about a foot of open rail. "The bathroom real estate is still up for negotiation."

"I see. Where would I put my 'girl stuff?'"

"I was thinking of changing the pedestal sink to a cabinet style. What do you think?"

"I think you're pretty awesome."

"I have to go. Maybe next week we could go to City Mill and look at some styles together?" He felt suddenly shy asking

230

that. They had seen each other naked and in the most intimate of situations, and yet he felt weird about a home improvement store shopping trip. He shook his head at himself and leaned in for one more kiss.

"Sure. That sounds fun. Have a good day," Abigail said. "I will lend you my Parking Fairy for the day, since I won't need her. Don't wear her out."

Mick knew she meant she would share her good luck with parking and he appreciated the sentiment. "Will do. I'll be back here, maybe around five to get ready for the Gala."

"I've got to take off too. I won't see you until tonight, most likely. I'm there officially representing the family, so I may not be able to chat."

"I'm supposed to be working, so don't distract me by looking amazing. Wait, no, you can't help yourself."

Abigail's laugh followed him out the door. It would be a good day.

*   *   *   *

Mabel awoke a little later than usual to find the day was not already scorching. A good sign. She was not looking forward to the event tonight. As she'd gotten older, she disliked large crowds and avoided going into Waikiki. Roger had arranged a limo pick up, so at least she, well, poor Betty really, wouldn't have to battle traffic and parking. Even in the structure at the Hyatt it could be difficult. Her thrifty genes often denied her the expense and luxury of valet parking on principle. It was sweet of Roger to forestall all of that.

She knew it was her duty to attend the anniversary of the company, even though she was not feeling very sympathetic about

Kimo. But she adored her children and felt strongly about all the employees those companies supported. The last couple of weeks had just plain worn her out. Although she had given interviews to the *Star-Bulletin*, it had not stopped other papers, radio and TV stations from calling for more. She had declined.

Going through Kimo's journals had also taken its toll, and finding that newspaper article and the subsequent implications hadn't helped. She and Betty had agreed to go through them again, just in case. She really wanted to get rid of everything but hadn't made a final decision whether that was wise. The last thing she wanted was for her children to have concrete evidence of their father's lack of morals, scruples, good taste, well, *everything*. They probably knew anyway, but it was another thing to have evidence plopped right in front of them. She knew that from experience. She kept reminding herself they were adults, but it didn't work. They were her children and always would be. She would do anything to protect them.

Speaking of children, she hadn't seen Margaret around since the day she'd come to stay except at the lawyer's office. She hadn't joined them for meals and she hadn't seen Betty talking to her. Granted, the memorial and other arrangements had kept them pretty busy, but she hoped Margaret was attending her meetings, or whatever follow up care was needed. Perhaps she'd urge Betty to take some time to be with Margaret. Teresita was always willing to help out. Once when Betty'd had the flu, Teresita nursed them both.

Teresita was a kind spirit, and although not professionally trained, had raised three kids of her own. Her husband had died years ago, so she'd needed to work. By living at the house rent-free--Mabel refused any money--she was able to help her kids attend college. Mabel had also assisted behind the scenes to make sure the two daughters got the education they wanted, as opposed to only Teresita's son. It made Mabel smile to think that one daughter was an engineer with a firm working on the new freeway that would connect the Windward side and Pearl City. Imagine that! The second daughter was an architect and thinking of opening up her own company that would hire female employees to work with women clients who often are not heard when it came to making their wishes known. Too often they were written off as unable to comprehend the difficulties of design or construction, or even aesthetics. Although they were sometimes allowed to choose furniture. Teresita's son was a scientist, a botanist, at UH. All good.

Mabel laughed. Times had changed and Kimo sure hadn't changed with them. Well, that was over now.

Betty must have heard her moving around. A short knock on her bedroom door and Betty entered bearing a tray with a mug and a coffee carafe.

"How are you doing this morning? Did you sleep?" Betty opened the curtains and cracked the louvres to let in the first of the breeze.

"I did sleep a bit. I guess I was just so tired. I still am. And the emotion of it all. I suppose I didn't expect that."

"Well, you were married to the man for over fifty years."

"I know. Most of which were not terribly pleasant. I suppose his end was fitting, but all this hoopla is wearing me out."

"Only one more day. You can get through this dinner. As the widow, I don't think they expect much of you except to stand-- or sit--stoically and try not to cry."

"Right. I am not going to drape myself in widow's weeds and haunt the rooftop, so they can just drop that."

"Have some caffeine. That will help."

"If I do cry, it will be because I am so tired."

"Let them think what they like."

233

"What about you? Have you seen Margaret since she moved into the guest house? I was thinking of you two this morning and felt a little guilty. You should spend some time together."

"I really haven't seen much of her. She warned me she had her own things to do. I think some of that is meeting a social worker or something as well as her meetings. I don't know if it's Alcoholics Anonymous or the one for drugs, or what, but I see her drive off every day. She told me to stay out of the guest cottage. Teresita, too. When I asked her why, she said in the shelters and in the facility, she never had any privacy, so she really wanted some here."

"I can respect that," Mabel said. "We have to get in to clean once a week, though. I doubt if she's going to stoop to cleaning, do you?"

"Probably not. Should I ask Teresita?"

"Let's see how bad it is. When Margaret leaves today, let's take a peek. If Teresita doesn't see it, then we're not *really* invading her privacy, right?"

"You have no concept of privacy, do you?" Betty joked.

"Well, she has had a rough life. I am legally responsible for the property, however, so I'd feel better checking."

"I agree. She's my daughter and I want what's best for her."

"I just had that conversation with myself about Roger and Abigail. I owe it to them to get rid of the journals and everything else when this is over. They should not find out the truth about their father. More than they probably already have, at any rate."

"Breakfast first, then the cottage?"

"We'll have to keep an eye out for when she leaves. Have you picked out what you're wearing tonight?"

"Yes, all cleaned and ready. It was kind of Roger to arrange

234

a limo. I feel like a celebrity."

"He does have his moments. I'm starving. Let's see what Teresita has in mind for breakfast."

Betty linked arms with her and they shuffled to the kitchen.

As they finished their oatmeal with fresh and dried fruit, the phone rang. Teresita answered and handed the receiver to Mabel. "It's Roger."

"Hello, darling. How are you holding up?" Mabel asked.

"I'm doing very well this morning, Mother. I called to see how you're doing and if there's anything you need."

"I slept well, dear. Betty and I were just discussing you and tonight. How thoughtful it was of you to think of a limo for us. Are you getting one for Abigail, too?"

"Yes, I arranged one for her. She wasn't as excited, but she's practical and it will make it easier on her. She told me a taxi would be just fine, but we must keep up appearances, you know." He affected a terrible British accent and referred to one of Mabel's favorite British TV shows.

"I don't know why you keep trying to sound like that, Roger. My genes in the linguistics department have failed you miserably."

It was a family joke that when Mabel had been upset with them when they were children, her British accent and slang would spill out.

"Yes, well, one must keep a stiff upper lip and all that, what?" The accent got worse.

Mabel laughed and realized that was his goal: to cheer her a bit on this difficult day during this difficult time.

"Of course we must. I am doing well and thank you for checking on me. The limo is scheduled for 6:30. Isn't that awfully early? We're just over the hill." Mabel referred to Diamond Head crater, only a few miles from Waikiki and the Hyatt; Kahala being only a few minutes further from Diamond Head.

"Mom," Roger began. Mabel knew he was really trying if he called her Mom. "I know you don't get out much, but it's Saturday night in Waikiki. Try to think back a thousand years to when you were young. Now the traffic is even worse. What with dinosaurs being replaced with cars and all."

"Oh, you. Silly. I'll be ready. I love you, my sweet. Stay strong, this will be over soon."

"Love you, too. See you there."

"What was that?" Betty asked, having overheard Mabel's end.

"Roger, it seems, has developed a sense of humor along with his sense of compassion. Who knew?"

"That's wonderful. You did seem to enjoy it, whatever *it* was."

"I think I was bonding with my son. On some level other than the usual. My new life is turning out to be pretty good, so far." She smiled at Betty. "Should we dig out those stupid journals one more time?"

Betty nodded and they headed for the secret compartment in the office closet. The phone rang again and Teresita called down the hall, "It's Miss Abigail. You want it?"

"Yes, thank you. I'll pick up the office extension." Mabel settled behind Kimo's desk. An odd feeling; she didn't remember ever sitting here before. "Hello, dear. Roger just called. This is my lucky day."

"Sure, Mom. Lucky."

"You sound a little down. Are you all right?"

"Just tired Mom. Actually, things are going really well. I just called to see if you needed anything. Should I pick up your dress from the dry cleaners or anything?"

"No, I'm completely ready. Teresita and Betty have been

jewels. Really, I have all I need. I just maybe want to sleep for a week when this is over. It's been quite a strain. How are you doing?"

"I think I'm doing okay, too. Sounds weird, doesn't it? My father dies and I am doing okay. I know we weren't close, but should I be more concerned that I'm not more concerned?"

"No, I think you're all right. We all process things differently. Part of me said good-bye to your father a long time ago. This recent good-bye, although permanent, wasn't that big a leap I suppose. Is that terrible of me to say to you?"

"Not at all, Mom. I feel like that, a little, too. When I left for medical school, I sort of thought he would come around. That we'd make it up and be close. I guess that's why I tried so hard to be the best doctor I could. Nothing seemed to impress him, so I eventually gave up. It was like I lost my father years ago. I have some real empathy for Margaret. When Tony died, she lost the only father she'd known and he never came back."

"I understand Tony was nothing like your father," Mabel said. Betty stopped scanning journals when Tony's name was mentioned. Mabel smiled and nodded that it was okay.

"I know. But I still can't believe his pride or whatever kept us apart like that."

"I think when God was handing out parts he maybe forgot something in your father. I tried for years to believe he meant well, that providing for us all through his company was his way of showing love, but I don't think that anymore."

"I think you're right, Mom." A moment of silence. "I'm okay with it now, though. Or, I think I am."

"You sound more chipper, darling. Everything else going well?"

"Absolutely. Maybe I'll tell you about it later. Next week, when things calm down."

"What are you talking about?"

"Never mind, it's a surprise."

"Well, then I'll see you tonight."

"Yes. See you then."

They disconnected. "What about Tony?" Betty asked.

"Abigail just said that she felt for Margaret, losing her father, Tony. How distraught she must have been."

"Yes, that's true. But Kimo was nothing like Tony."

"Kimo was the only father Abigail had, and like most kids I suppose, she never stopped trying to please her father. I didn't know she felt that way. I know Roger did, because he spent all that time with Kimo, working in the company. I gleaned over the years from them both, that Roger was after his approval. But I really thought Abigail had written off that relationship during her time in medical school. It turns out she never had. She sounded more sad than angry, but there was plenty of anger there before. She and I used to talk a lot during her school years. I probably didn't help. I think I really believed that Kimo would come around and be proud of his daughter. He never did. It was like she was never born, it seemed. That had to hurt. I can't imagine that. I was born so late in my parents' lives, but they loved me to death and made sure I knew it. I did that with my children, but one parent can't fully substitute for two parents. I suppose the child always feels that something is missing, as indeed it is."

"I agree. I tried to be two parents to Margaret, and look what that got me. She hated me."

"I don't think she does now, though. She's here isn't she?"

"She did say something about staying away to protect me, but I'm not sure how true that is. I mean, she was using drugs, right?"

"If she *was* using drugs, if her perception was that she would endanger you, then it means she cared about you. Even if

238

that danger was from little green men or invisible international spies."

"I suppose you're right. I hadn't looked at it that way before."

"We would do anything to protect our children, right?"

"Of course."

"Maybe that means they would do anything to protect us."

"You have a unique mind, Mabel Lemon. And clearly underused. Come over here and let's go through these stupid things one more time. Then what? Should we shred them? Set fire to them? What?"

"Why not both? Let's be sure."

"We haven't used the fireplace in years. It might have a nest in it or something. It's probably not safe. I don't want to use the other one. In case it brings bad juju to our favorite room." Betty referred to the one in the atrium. That room was so well-used that a small Franklin stove had been added for the occasional cool nights.

"Oh, Betty, for Pete's sake. You make me laugh." Mabel thought. "And we can't ask Teresita to have it cleaned. Especially now, it's a million degrees. That's not suspicious." The women giggled like girls.

"I know. The barbeque!" Betty said. "We can shred them first, and then a little at a time, set fire to them."

"One small problem."

"What?"

"Okay, two. We never barbeque."

"Sure we do. All the time," Betty countered.

"No. Teresita does. *We,* do nothing. It will seem odd, won't it? And the other thing is the barbeque is gas. I can't imagine it will be safe to put a bunch of paper in a gas barbeque."

"You're probably right." Betty thought. "Oh! I know. The

239

gardener's trash barrel. They keep it behind the shed with all the garden tools. It's an old metal trash can they use to burn dry grass, twigs, branches and things like that. We can use it. I think we should only do a little at a time, though,"

"What do we say if someone catches us?"

"What do you mean by someone? Teresita or the gardeners?"

"I don't know. But what do we say?" Mabel asked.

They thought for a bit. "I know. It's not great, but we could take down some of Kimo's other things, not important or anything, so that if someone says something, we can say you're so distraught you just need not to have his things around. They make you too sad."

"I guess," Mabel said. "It sounds weak to me, but I can't think of anything better right now."

"It sounds weak to me, too, but we're two old ladies. And you're a new widow. And you're grieving. Who's going to suspect us?"

"All right. That's the plan for now. I guess the key is not to burn so much at once that the neighbor calls the fire department."

"I'll try to control myself." Betty smiled. "For now, let's just look at this stuff carefully in case there is any more incriminating, or even semi-incriminating stuff. That shark article really freaked me out."

Mabel raised her eyebrows in inquiry.

"I heard some kids say it and it certainly seems appropriate here."

"Yes, it does. I suppose I am freaked out as well. Mostly because I think he did it."

They continued until they heard Teresita leave for her shopping. They shuffled to the cottage and were astonished at what they saw. It looked absolutely sparkling. Neat as a pin. The bed was made; nothing remotely personal of Margaret's was anywhere in view. Even the bathroom was immaculate, towel refolded perfectly, if it had been used at all.

"Well," Mabel said, "I guess Margaret's doing her own housekeeping. I didn't expect her to be so tidy."

"Me neither."

"I supposed we don't need to clean in here, then."

"Well don't tell. The last thing I need is another reason for Margaret to be mad at me."

"We were never here," Mabel said. They locked up and left the guest house as they'd found it.

Chapter 21

Abigail's limo pulled up in front of the Hyatt Regency Hotel in Waikiki amid a long line of limos. She waited to get out until she was directly in front of the entrance. The Hyatt's staff leapt to open her door. She pitied the 'regular' people who might have accidentally wandered in for dinner, or who were staying there, for the services they might not receive due to the enormity of this event. She sighed. Leave it to her father to inconvenience everyone. She knew that wasn't quite fair, but it felt good to think it.

As she moved toward the entrance she saw the limo behind her disgorge her mother and Betty, so she waited. Her mother looked lovely in black crepe. Betty held her arm as usual, making sure she didn't misstep. Betty wore a dark plum gown, very understated. They both had their hair professionally coiffed. More than Abigail had done. She'd twisted hers into a bun with some loose tendrils that she'd curled with a curling iron. She had applied a little make up for the event, but other than making sure her one formal gown, in sea foam green, was clean, that was all the fancying up she'd done. She did like the dress. Inch-wide straps held the ruched fitted bodice and the skirt layers of filmy fabric rustled and moved like ocean waves when she walked. Very mermaid-y.

She kissed her mother and Betty hello. Betty was more like an auntie than an employee. She assumed Roger would already be inside, probably had been for hours. It was his event now, and being very hands-on anyway, she was sure he'd know it all down to the last detail.

She wondered where Mick was. At the ballroom entrance, they were escorted to the head table, and she begged off, reminding her mother that she had agreed to attend but not to sit there.

"Can I get you a drink? There's an open bar," Abigail asked.

"I think I'll wait with you," Mabel said. "No one's seated at the head table yet so Betty and I would look like we were waiting for a parade."

"Actually," Betty said as a waiter came by with a full tray of champagne flutes, "I think this will do me nicely."

"Me, too," Mabel added. Abigail took one as well. She'd work her way to the bar later. As people arrived, the first thing they did was detour to one of the bars along the sides and guests were three deep waiting.

Roger spied them and came over, kissing each in turn. "How are you doing?" he asked.

"I think a better question is, how are you doing?" Mabel replied.

"I am better than expected, I do believe." Abigail noted the twinkle was back in his eye. Something she hadn't seen in years and didn't realize until it returned.

Roger looked dashing in his tuxedo, tired, but revved for

his debut event. "Can I get you anything? Escort you to your tables?"

"No, we're just hanging out here, trying to pick up sailors," Mabel said.

That was so unexpected they all burst out laughing, drawing the attention of a few of the stuffier nearby patrons.

"Are you sure that's your first?" Roger indicated the champagne.

"Don't you worry about me. This is your night, dear. I'm proud of you," Mabel said.

"We're all proud of you," Betty added.

"Knock 'em dead," Abigail said.

Roger excused himself and Abigail began to look for Mick. Without looking like she was looking for someone. Fortunately, people had begun to notice the widow and come over to offer condolences and stories. Abigail was free to edge away and search more thoroughly, while Betty stayed propping up Mabel.

Abigail saw him before he saw her. He looked absolutely gorgeous in a tuxedo. He was conversing with an older pot-bellied gentleman, also in a tux, as were most of the men attending. Even the waiters wore formal black and white with black bow ties. The only difference was their jackets stopped at the hips. She watched Mick for a moment before making her way toward him. Yummy.

Other women had noticed him too. Besides Roger, there weren't too many men under the age of 100 here. Well, under 60. And most of the women were fairly transparent as well, held up by plastic surgery and tight gowns. Well *she* was getting catty.

A few women seemed closer to her own age. She guessed them to be Lemon Enterprises employees or perhaps trophy wives. She had no idea. She had spent zero time at her father's company once he had drawn his line in the sand.

Mick saw her as she approached and literally stopped

244

talking mid-sentence, but his mouth remained open. She smiled. He remembered himself and exited his conversation.

"Hello, Mr. Reporter," Abigail said.

"Hello beautiful total stranger," Mick said. "We are not supposed to know each other, right? Covert ops and all that?"

"Right now, I don't care. You look amazing."

"You look incredible. Let's leave right now."

Abigail laughed. "Love to. But duty calls. I want to be there for my mother and Roger, but I could give a hoot about Kimo."

"Give a hoot? Where did that come from?" Mick smiled.

"Well, we are all fancied up in a ballroom and these people look like butter wouldn't melt in their mouths. So, I'm cleaning up my act. Just for the evening, so don't get used to it."

He slowly eyed her up and down. "Oh, I could get used to it." He leaned in and kissed her cheek. "But later, that dress, as lovely as it is, has got to go," he whispered.

She felt her cheeks warm. "It's getting awfully hot in here. Not to change the subject, but where are you sitting?"

"Smoothly done. They have a press table in the back. You're at the head table, right?"

"No way. I gave my seat to Betty, my Mom's nurse and friend. She has to be on display, but I don't. They have me at a table near the dais, but off to the side."

"Your glass is empty. More champagne?" Mick offered.

"Sure. Why not?"

Mick got two flutes and they clinked glasses before taking a sip. "To endings," Abigail said.

"To beginnings," Mick said.

Roger could barely be heard over the din, but he urged people to take their seats for the dinner service. As people moved toward the tables, Roger's voice on the mike became easier to discern.

"I'd better get back to my table with the rest of the fourth estate," Mick said.

"Okay. I'd better find my seat, too. Meet you for dessert?"

"Literally or figuratively?" Mick's eyes sparkled.

"Oh, for Pete's sake." Abigail felt herself redden again.

"Pete this time, huh? We're going to have to work on your language." Mick pecked her cheek once more and moved toward the back of the room.

Abigail checked a seating chart posted on a stanchion and found her seat at a round table facing the head table. At least she wouldn't be turned around backwards the whole evening. Betty was helping Mabel up the two steps to the raised head table. Abigail saw the care Betty took of her mother and made a mental note to get her something. Flowers? She didn't know. She'd have to pay better attention to what Betty liked. She had always taken Betty's concern and dedication for granted, but since Kimo's death, she'd really come to see how much Betty did for her mother, and how much her mother appreciated it. They were like sisters.

Abigail's table filled with people she did not know. Oh, well, better jump in all at once rather than get wet an inch at a time. She turned to the gentleman on her right.

"Hello, I'm Abigail."

"Good evening. I'm Jerry and this is my wife, Moira." He indicated the woman to his right. She noticed his English accent immediately. They all shook hands.

"How do you know Kimo?" Abigail asked.

"Business you know. I'm in shipping. 'All Island Shipping,' that's us." He pointed to his wife, too. "Kimo's pineapples and sugar get all over the world with my help." He laughed—seemed like a nice enough man.

"All over the world? But it's 'All Island Shipping?'" Abigail sipped her water.

246

"England's an island too." He laughed heartily at his own joke and his wife looked as if she'd heard it a thousand times. She probably had. "Seriously, we ship everywhere, even places that grow pineapples and sugar, too." He seemed pleased by that.

Abigail wondered how the people in those economies appreciated his shipping expertise. And Kimo's finger in every pie. She sighed, brought back to Earth. Well, at least back to planet Kimo.

Roger was speaking again, so she was able *not* to converse with Jerry and Moira. For the time being, at any rate. Roger welcomed everyone and reminded them that tonight was a celebration, not a wake. "Because if it was a wake, there'd be more drinking." His joke was well received. He told them to enjoy dinner and a slide show would commence at 9 PM, along with a narrative of how everyone there had played a role in Lemon Enterprises. He mentioned that his father had written it before he died and it meant a great deal to him, Roger, to share some of Kimo's last words with the people who meant the most to him.

Abigail was served her salad and thought, *this may be the most boring evening in the history of the Universe. However,* she considered, *it can't last forever, and there was always Mick to look forward to afterward.*

Roger got up again at 9 and introduced the slide show. He also honored his mother as the stable base of Kimo and of Lemon Enterprises. Abigail wasn't sure that was in Kimo's original script, but Mabel had sure done her share of the work. It was thoughtful of Roger to recognize her, and even more thoughtful not to make her stand or speak.

She allowed herself to take a luscious slice of chocolate cake from the trolley as it made its way around the room, and also noted a dessert buffet set up on the far wall. That was more like it.

The history of the company was actually interesting.

247

Abigail had never allowed herself to participate in it, other than living with Kimo, and she found the old photos fascinating. Unfortunately, most of them had Kimo in them, but she admired the hard working pineapple and cane cutters, arms slung about each other's shoulders, clearly exhausted and filthy from their difficult jobs but still able to mug for the camera. From the plantation shots, the focus shifted to the various refineries and the cannery, the photos of higher quality, and Kimo's attire distinctly upgrading as the years passed. Eventually, the building that now housed Lemon Enterprises became the centerpiece and Abigail hoped the evening was finally coming to a close.

She glanced back to look for Mick's table but there were too many heads in the way. She noticed several large men in black suits had moved to the sides of the room. Body guards? For whom? She snuck off to the side and looked for Mick on her way to the ladies' room. He noticed her leave and met her in the hall outside the ballroom.

"It's almost over," she said. "Thank God."

"Your place or mine?" His gaze was intense.

"Yours is closer," she said. She felt his body heat from a foot away.

"An hour. Spare key under the frog if you get there first." He kissed her fast and hard and returned to the ballroom.

A little breathless, she continued to the ladies' room. "Frog? What the hell?"

*   *   *   *

Mabel leaned over to Betty during the slide show and history presentation. "How soon can we blow this pop stand?"

"What?" Betty had been watching intently, having been unaware of the Lemon Empire prior to her employment. Those seated on the dais had been moved to the sides so they could watch the screen at the front. "What are you talking about?"

"I'm ready to go. How about you? I lived through this, and I'm not sure I want to see it again from the jolly old elf side of things."

"How much champagne have you had?"

"Not nearly enough. I am tired though. It's way past my bedtime."

Betty glanced at her watch. Going on 10:30. "Oh, my yes. I'm tired too, now that you mention it. The early days were just so fascinating. I didn't know any of this."

"Yes, but remember that article on the shark, and how things have been; things we've discovered. All this 'success' and home spun wisdom cost a lot of people quite a bit, and some their lives."

"True. I guess I've had my fill."

They rose and made their way surreptitiously to the exit. They didn't see Abigail or Roger to say good-bye. Alone at the elevators, Mabel said, "I had my fill years ago, but I stayed for the children when they were small, and then I broke my leg. I had to stay then. Maybe it's the champagne talking, but I wondered at the timing of it all. The night before my accident, Kimo and I'd had another fight. He was spending all his time with the business, with his boys, not his kids. The kids were in college, but they still needed a father. And after he abandoned Abigail I'd just had enough. I was still young enough to work. He would have had to cough up alimony for sure. Hawai'i's not a community property state, but I could have gotten a lawyer to argue that we built the business together during the marriage, that he didn't come to the marriage with the millions he has now, that I helped him earn. I still have family money socked away. More than Kimo knew about, that's for sure. I was dumb in some things, but not in

249

finance. My father taught me that. Some little voice told me to hold back. . ."

The elevator arrived.

"Somebody did her homework," Betty said. "I'm impressed. You should have been a lawyer. No, really. The world could use a few more like you."

"Married to Kimo? I don't think so. My plan, such as it was, fell apart anyway when I broke my leg. You know better than anyone it was shattered to pieces. I couldn't have felt safe leaving at that point. Besides, if I had, I'd never have met you."

"True. And we all know I'm the best nurse, best friend, best Auntie, well, best everything in the whole wide world." They worked through the crowded lobby to the valet podium and asked for the limo.

"I don't have to worry about any of that anymore," Mabel said.

"Nope. Problem solved," Betty agreed. "Here we go," she said as their limo pulled up.

"We'll congratulate Roger tomorrow," Mabel said. "And we have one last piece of business of our own to finish."

"Are you sure?"

"Absolutely."

They rode home in comfortable silence.

*   *   *   *

Roger glad-handed; made sure everyone had a great time, attended to the celebrities' and businessmen's wants and drinks. But his mind never stopped wandering to his father's potential underhanded business partners. The Texas oil tycoon who claimed they knew each other as kids in Black Bluff, Texas and reconnected through business contacts? The Japanese-American

Business Alliance, who claimed to foster better business relations between Japan and the US, encouraging American products imports like pineapple and sugar? The shipping magnate wanting to continue to ship more than Hawai'ian agriculture? The thought made him sweat. He was able to forget a little during the speech and slide show, and he did enjoy looking back at his family's history. But as soon as that was over he knew his brain would fill right up again.

What would happen Monday morning? Since Kimo had treated him like an idiot, would his father's underworld partners know he had been kept out of the loop? If they in fact existed? Would someone call, or knock on his door late at night? Or worse, just stab him in the parking garage, the victim of an apparent mugging? Someone was helping Kimo or the company, even after death by hiding that manuscript, which meant that person was *not* helping Roger.

He planned to evaluate and increase security immediately. He would handle it himself, since he wasn't sure who to trust. He needed to seriously clean house. Was his family in danger, too? This just got better and better. What if Kimo had been murdered? Christ. Probably not. Those guys like to make an example, and Kimo had clearly died of a heart attack. They would have shot him in the back of the head, or sliced of his head with a Samurai sword, or left a horse head in his bed. Right? He had no idea.

He was exhausted and probably not processing this in the best way. The only tangible thing he had to validate his suspicions was the manuscript he could not find. That was the link, the weight that might sink him and the company. He'd looked everywhere he could think of. All he could do was wait for 'them' to contact him. Kimo's business contacts could just be that, a little shady, but not unusual. They didn't have to be assassins. So why couldn't he find the manuscript; the tell-all book that would sink the USS Lemon and presumably all the men and companies he'd screwed or blackmailed over the years?

Time would tell whether he'd be blackmailed for the book or for his continued cooperation in whatever Kimo had going.

As the slide show neared its end, he noted his mother and Betty making a discreet exit. He also noted several men in dark suits had moved to the sides of the room. He didn't recognize them as his celebrity guests but perhaps they were members of their staffs? He had beefed up security, so they had to be invited, didn't they?

A sudden undercurrent circled the room and before he could close the slide show, a number of things happened in the semi-dark. The timed slide show stopped on the last slide but the room lights did not come on.

A voice yelled, "Everyone freeze. FBI. Hands where we can see them."

Roger had no idea how 'they' would see anyone's hands in the glow from the projector. He froze and remained at the podium where he had been narrating into a microphone. He briefly wondered if he made a good target and if he should duck.

The lights came on and as that switch was flipped, it seemed to galvanize people in the audience. Roger saw a few guests and waiters with guns out and the black suited men hustling for the exits, escorting or kidnapping (Roger couldn't tell) other men, also dressed in evening wear. Wait, waiters and guests with guns?

Roger saw the woman from the park, he thought, in a subdued black dress holding a gun and a badge. She shouted that she was the FBI again, and for everyone to stay where they were. Most listened but those running for the exits were pursued by . . . waiters?

Roger had a great view of the action from the raised dais.

He hoped the podium was bullet proof.

He had a brief moment of gratitude that his mother had already left the room and hoped his sister had as well. He didn't see her, but since a lot of people were cowering under the tables, he might not. He felt strangely dissociated from the event, the shouting and chaos--was that a gunshot--were coming from a foggy place in his brain. He knew he was in danger, but beyond crouching behind the podium, he didn't do anything to protect himself.

He recognized some of the suits now, his father's business contacts in Japan and other parts of Asia, as well as a few from the Mainland that appeared to be, well, connected, for lack of a better word. Those men and their muscle were quickly cuffed and separated from the crowd.

"Roger? Are you all right?" asked the woman from the park, gun dangling from her hand.

"Yes." He looked closely. "Margaret?"

"That's me. Only, I go by Maggie at work. Well, *this* work."

Roger's brain scrambled to catch up. "You're an FBI agent? What are you doing here? What's going on?"

"A sting we've been working on for months. I've been working on it much longer than that. Your father, well, our father, was dirty up to his eyebrows. This isn't how we really planned to get these guys, but after Kimo died, we thought this might be our only shot."

"Get them? What do you mean?"

"One at a time, quietly. We had actually planned to arrest them after this event. We didn't want to endanger the guests, but they were moving in. It appeared you were a target as well as your family. The factions your father cultivated and worked with wanted to ensure your continued participation after his death. Wire

253

taps led us to believe a kidnapping might be in the works to encourage your cooperation."

"My mother and sister were in danger?"

"We've had security on them, too, but word came down that you were a target tonight. We had to move quickly. You don't look too good. Why don't you sit." Maggie helped him to a chair.

Roger exhaled loudly. "What's next?" Roger surveyed the room: overturned chairs, shaken guests, the band standing in the doorway. The band!

Maggie sat next to him. "We have to interview everyone before they can leave. We've rounded up the knowns, but we need to get contact information and double check."

Roger's organizational skills kicked in. "Can I let the band set up? Maybe some music will help calm everyone. Can they eat and drink? How can I help?"

Maggie thought. "That should be okay, but let me tell my people. Have the band set up. At least that will be a distraction. I'll interview you first."

"Right now? It can't wait?"

"This whole thing was to get you on board to continue the old plan under the new regime. You being the new regime. You probably know things that will help us. Be right back. Get your band going."

Roger waved the musicians over and gave them a brief, watered down version of events. He was pretty sure Maggie didn't want the whole thing revealed. She nodded at him to go ahead and he made an announcement.

"Everyone, can I have your attention? I'm sorry about what happened. The authorities need our help for just a bit longer, but we will have some music soon. Please help yourselves to more food and drinks. We'll have some fresh goodies unless *all* the waiters are undercover agents." His attempt at humor got a few weak chuckles. "Please be seated and you'll be on your way momentarily."

Roger's interview was brief and unremarkable. He answered Maggie's questions as thoroughly as he could. His mind was on the criminals the FBI uncovered and the nature of the business his father ran. His stomach was upset, but he circulated and gave hugs to the ladies and handshakes to the men. He hoped this wouldn't impact the whole corporation. Maggie and her agents efficiently took guests out for interviews and a number of them opted to return to the party. Never under estimate the power of free drinks.

His mind couldn't quite reconcile Margaret and Maggie. He knew she was truly his half-sister, but he had just begun to deal with that when he discovered she's undercover FBI and part of a sting. He shoved that to the back of his brain for the time being.

The evening wound down more pleasantly than Roger could have hoped. By the time the FBI was finished, it was almost like a regular party.

Maggie saluted him with two fingers. "We'll be in touch. You'll be asked to testify but we can go over all that another time. Thank you for your cooperation."

Roger felt she was thanking him for more than just tonight. He smiled. "You're welcome."

He ushered out the last of the party-goers. The Hyatt staff had been quietly and efficiently keeping all the guests content for hours. He asked them all to come to the ballroom. The band was still breaking down its equipment, the poor drummer always the last.

Roger thanked everyone for their hard work. He asked if they were all there, or if anyone had needed to go home early.

"Malia's daughter got sick. She's only three, so Malia left a coupla hours ago, as soon as they released people. But don't get her in trouble please, she needs this job," a young woman dressed as a food prepper said.

"I wasn't even thinking of it. I just want to make sure I thank everyone properly. I couldn't have done this without all of your help and dedication." He turned to the young woman who'd spoken. "Are you a friend of Malia's?"

She nodded. "We usually ride the bus to work together."

"Then please make sure she gets this." Roger began passing out generous cash tips. The staff was so stunned that he was half way down the line before anyone spoke up. Then there was a chorus of "Thank yous" and "Mahalos" as he finished. He moved onto the band.

As he shook the drummer's hand, he passed him an extra twenty. "I know it's a pain, brah, so thank you for hauling all that in here."

Absolutely beat, Roger went downstairs to his own limo. Waikiki was far from quiet this Saturday night. Roger felt like he'd been run over by a bus, but the lights, people, action of party central was in full swing, and would be for several hours. Roger remembered being young and when the bars closed at 2 AM, he and his friends would wander down to a 'cabaret' which stayed open until 4 AM. Then they would stagger into Uncle John's restaurant for 99 cent breakfast, because by then, that was about all they had left in their pockets.

Good memories. He flopped into the limo and rolled all the back windows down, letting the fresh air wash across him as they turned away from the ocean and toward his condo downtown.

Chapter 22

Sunday morning and bright sunshine filled the atrium. Mabel and Betty had their coffee and read the paper; an article on last night's event.

Mabel exclaimed. "You won't believe what happened after we left! A bust!"

"What? Let me see." Betty took the paper. "I can't believe it! We missed all the excitement."

"Just as well. It sounds like it went late."

"FBI sting, multiple arrests, wow." Betty continued to scan.

"We might have been asked some uncomfortable questions, too." Mabel sipped her coffee.

"It says here that the company was under investigation for months and that Kimo was about to be arrested when he died. Ha. Serves him right."

"I thought something funny was going on. Didn't really want to know, I guess. I'm not sure if I should have done something about it. I didn't want the children to get hurt."

Teresita poked her head in. "You two okay for a while? I going to Times, do a little grocery shopping for dis week. Want anyt'ing special?"

"Mango juice," Mabel said.

"Not that I can think of," Betty said.

They put down the newspaper and listened for Teresita's car leaving.

"I think I'm ready. You?" Mabel asked.

"Yes. Shall we go?"

They both rose stiffly and went to Kimo's home office. Betty crouched in the closet and opened the secret cubby. She pulled out several hundred pages of manuscript entitled *Kimo Lemon Tells it Like It Is*.

"Do you want to read it all?" Betty asked.

"No, what we read when we found it was plenty. That's what started this whole thing. Grab the shredder, would you?"

"Do you want to shred the journal entries, too?"

"Yes, but later. Except that shark thing. Find that if you can. We'll start with that. That's the only weird entry."

Betty pulled the box out and they located the section with the shark and began feeding it to the shredder.

"What's going on?" Roger stood at the doorway to the office. "Mom, what are you doing?" He stepped forward and saw the open closet with the cubby revealed, the box of journal entries, and the manuscript lying on the desk.

"Oh, hello, dear. We didn't hear you come in." Mabel tried to cover the manuscript, but it was too late. Roger picked it up.

"Where did you get this? Do you know what this is?"

"Yes, dear, I know what it is. That's why we're getting rid of it. No one should see that."

"Did you know about this all along?"

"No. Of course not. I would have solved the problem a long

258

time ago. I think it's terrible and so many people would get hurt if it came out."

"Have you read it?" Roger asked.

"Enough to know it's bad news for all of us, and for anyone who ever worked for your father."

"Is there a publisher?"

"I don't think so. I haven't found anything to indicate that. Have you? How did you find out about it?"

"I found a flier among Dad's things about it. I haven't been able to find this, though. You don't suppose there's another copy, do you?"

"I haven't seen any sign of one."

Betty still hunched over the shredder with a sheaf manuscript pages. She stood and moved next to Mabel. "We were wondering about a computer. Do you suppose he has a copy on a computer somewhere?"

"I've never seen my father use a computer, so I don't think so."

"Well, Roger," Mabel said, "are you going to stop us? We were going to shred this and then burn the shreds in the garden barrel. I want no trace of this left."

"I think that's a great idea. I can help."

"No, I don't think so. Right now, you are the head of Lemon Enterprises and your hands are clean. I think it's better if we do this. Besides, this is a small shredder." She smiled at her son. "I think your father may have left you enough problems with the business. At least now you can claim ignorance if this ever comes to light."

Roger thought about the phone calls from the SEC and IRS, last night's bust and the tangents his thoughts took from there. And maybe variables he had no knowledge of. He sighed.

"Okay. I suppose you're right. I'll go now. The reason I

stopped by was to see how you're doing. I guess you're doing fine."

"Relatively so, dear. You're not going into work today, are you?"

"No. I got a call to go back to the FBI for a follow-up. You saw the paper this morning, right?"

"Yes, we did. Quite remarkable," Mabel said.

"You were gone by the time the FBI got there, right?"

"Yes."

"Then you don't know."

"What, Roger?" Mabel said.

"Margaret." He pointed at Betty. "Your daughter is the FBI agent in charge of the sting."

Betty's mouth fell open. She sat weakly on the arm of the sofa. "My Margaret? FBI?"

Mabel hurried to comfort her. "Well, what do you know?" She patted Betty's arm. "That's certainly something to think about. Roger, we have a lot to do. And now a lot to process. You should get going. Don't want to keep your sister, the FBI agent, waiting." Mabel's eyes twinkled.

"You're gonna get a lot of mileage out of this, I can tell," Roger said.

"Really, though, Roger. We'll talk later. We'll do this like just about everything else. Like a family."

Roger kissed her cheek and patted Betty's arm. "Can I at least start the fire in the barrel for you?"

"No, you can't. You need to stay out of it now. Go." She hugged her son tightly.

Roger turned and walked out. They heard the front door close. "Do you think he suspects what we've done?" Mabel asked.

"No. I think he's full of company things now." Betty sighed. "I'll think about all of this later, but now I'll start the fire.

We're almost ready here." The small shredder was nearly full. Betty went to the garden while Mabel finished filling the shredder receptacle.

Betty returned and they continued shredding almost 300 pages of Kimo's book.

"It didn't take as long as I thought it would," Betty said.

"We just have to keep the fire going until it's all really gone." They each took a bin of shreds out to the garden and tossed them in small batches onto the fire. "Not too much at a time, we don't want to smother it," Mabel cautioned.

"How long before he starts putting things together?" Betty asked.

"I don't think he will." Mabel sprinkled a bit more on the flames.

"I hope not. It was a long road to here, wasn't it Mabel?"

"It surely was, Betty. It surely was." Mabel looked up at the beautiful coral tree with its deadly cargo. "Remember when we decided Kimo had to um. . . go?"

"About the time we found this manuscript, wouldn't you say, Mabel?"

"He never should have endangered the children. I would do anything for my children. You know that, Betty."

"I do, Mabel."

The two old ladies smiled together, shook the last bits out of their bins, and watched as the flames consumed them.

They linked arms as they so often did and returned to the house just as they heard Teresita's car return.

Author's Note:
Many of you familiar with Hawai'i's native plants will know that poisons or thorns of any kind are rare. However, those of us researchers also know that just about anything can be made more toxic and even deadly. Particularly for characters who are older with weak hearts, but I wanted to emphasize that the information of my sources was accurate. I just got creative. Enjoy.

Victoria Heckman is the author of six novels, many short stories and articles and the editor-compiler of a number anthologies. She divides her time between California and Hawai'i. Visit her website at www.victoriaheckman.com

Lightning Source UK Ltd.
Milton Keynes UK
UKHW010928060223
416537UK00002B/679